# SUNSHINE ON
# SCOTLAND STREET

Center Point
Large Print

Also by Alexander McCall Smith
and available from Center Point Large Print:

The Corduroy Mansions Series
  *The Dog Who Came in from the Cold*
  *A Conspiracy of Friends*

The 44 Scotland Street Series
  *The Importance of Being Seven*
  *Bertie Plays the Blues*

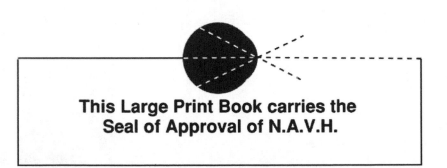

**This Large Print Book carries the
Seal of Approval of N.A.V.H.**

# SUNSHINE ON SCOTLAND STREET

*A 44 Scotland Street Novel*

## ALEXANDER McCALL SMITH

CENTER POINT LARGE PRINT
THORNDIKE, MAINE

This Center Point Large Print edition is published
in the year 2015 by arrangement with Anchor Books,
an imprint of The Knopf Doubleday Publishing Group,
a division of Random House LLC.

This book is excerpted from a series that
originally appeared in *The Scotsman* newspaper.

The text of this Large Print edition is unabridged. In other
aspects, this book may vary from the original edition.
Printed in the United States of America on permanent paper.
Set in 16-point Times New Roman type.

ISBN: 978-1-62899-402-5

Library of Congress Cataloging-in-Publication Data

McCall Smith, Alexander, 1948–
 Sunshine on Scotland Street : a 44 Scotland Street novel / Alexander
McCall Smith. — Center Point Large Print edition.
 pages cm
 Summary: "Scotland Street witnesses the wedding of the century of
Angus Lordie to Domenica Macdonald, but as the newlyweds depart on
their honeymoon, Edinburgh is in disarray. However, the residents of
Scotland Street rally, and order is restored by the combined effects of
understanding, kindness, and, most of all, friendship"—Provided by
publisher.
 ISBN 978-1-62899-402-5 (library binding : alk. paper)
 1. Families—Scotland—Fiction.  2. Edinburgh (Scotland)—Fiction.
  3. Large type books.  I. Title.
 PR6063.C326S88 2015
 823′.914—dc23
                                                          2014037666

This book is for Barbara Fleischman

# 1. Omertà, and Fascinators

Even if she had not been an anthropologist, Domenica Macdonald would have understood the very particular significance of weddings. Anthropologists—and sociologists too, perhaps even more so—often tell us what we already know, or what we expect to hear, or perhaps what we are not surprised to learn. And so we all know, as did Domenica, that weddings are far more than marriage ceremonies; we know that they are occasions for family stock-taking and catharsis; that they furnish opportunities for naked displays of emotion and unscheduled tears; that they are a stage for sartorial and social ostentation; that they are far from the simple public exchange of vows they appear to be.

These insights had been impressed upon Domenica decades earlier by a visiting professor, one Salvatore Santaluca of the Istituto-Antropologico-Sociologico-Culturale of the University of Palermo. Santaluca's study of the traditional marriage practices of the hill villages of Sicily was something of an anthropological classic, considered by some to be the equal of Margaret Mead's *Coming of Age in Samoa*, exposing the labyrinthine negotiations and discussions that preceded such weddings. Unfortunately, the publication of these details was viewed in some circles in Sicily as a breach of omertà, and the professor had some months later been shot in a restaurant in Messina, a crime that had yet to be solved, largely because those who were charged with investigating it were precisely the people who had committed it. Things had changed since then, of course, and the Italian state had tackled the criminal culture that had for so long blighted its southern regions; too late, though, for Santaluca and the various courageous Italian magistrates and policemen who had taken on the secretive bullies holding an entire state to ransom.

It rather surprised Domenica that she should suddenly think of poor Professor Santaluca after all these years. But it was quite understandable, really, that she should be contemplating the institution of marriage and its customs, given that she was herself about to get married—to Angus Lordie—and was now sitting in her flat in Scotland Street, attended by her friend, Big Lou, preparing for the moment—only three hours away—when she would walk through the door of St. Mary's Cathedral in Palmerston Place. Her entry would be to the accompaniment of "Sheep May Safely Graze" by Johann Sebastian Bach, this piece having been selected by Angus, who had a soft spot for Bach. Domenica had acceded to this provided that it would be her choice of music to be played as they left. That was Charles Marie

Widor's Toccata, from his Symphony No. 5, a triumphant piece of music if ever there was one.

"People will love it," she said. "It's such a statement."

"Of what?" Angus had asked.

"Of the fact that the marriage has definitely taken place," said Domenica. "It's not a piece of music that admits of any . . . how should I put it? . . . uncertainty."

"Maybe," said Angus. "It's the opposite of peelie-wersh, I suppose."

Domenica was interested. As with many Scots expressions, the meaning of peelie-wersh was obvious, even to those who had never encountered the term before. "And which composers would be peelie-wersh?"

"Some of the minimalists. The ones who use two or three notes. The ones you have to strain to hear. Thin music. Widor is thickly textured."

They had moved on to discuss the hymns. Domenica felt vaguely uncomfortable when it came to hymns. She understood why people sang them—they performed a vital bonding function and undoubtedly buoyed the spirits—but she felt that the words rarely bore close examination, mostly being rather sentimental and somewhat repetitive. There were exceptions, of course: the words of "For Those in Peril on the Sea" were cogent and to the point. It was entirely reasonable, she felt, particularly in an age of global warming and rising sea levels, to express the desire that "the mighty ocean deep / Its own appointed limits keep." But could one sing that at a wedding? One might at a mariner's nuptials, perhaps, but neither she nor Angus were sailors. And then there was "Fight the Good Fight" which again had a perfectly clear message, but was clearly inappropriate for a wedding service, unless, of course, it was that of a pugilist, in which case the words would be taken as referring to professional rather than marital conflicts. "Jerusalem" was inspirational but referred to England, rather than to Scotland, and would seem quite out of place in a Scottish wedding. "Jerusalem" was inappropriate, too, Domenica felt, because right at its opening it asked a question to which the answer was almost certainly no. Its first line, stirring and dramatic though it may be, "And did those feet in ancient times . . ." invited the firm answer No, they certainly did not, words which could perhaps be set to music to be sung as a descant by the choir.

Angus had not been particularly helpful in his suggestions. He had himself composed the words of a hymn some time ago when he had offered to the hymn revision committee of the Church of Scotland a composition called "God Looks Down on Belgium." The opening words of this hymn, however, proved to be not quite what the committee wanted: "God's never heard of Belgium /

But loves it just the same / For God is kind and doesn't mind / He's not impressed with fame." The second verse was even more unsuitable, making reference to Captain Haddock and Tintin, both of whom, it was felt, had no place in a modern, or any, hymn book.

"You do remember that I wrote a hymn called 'God Looks Down on Belgium'?" said Angus.

Domenica gave him a warning glance. "I do indeed, Angus, and we are certainly not having that."

"Pity. I always rather liked it."

Now, sitting at her dressing table, while Big Lou attempted to fix on the fascinator she had acquired at great expense from a milliner in Fife—"One hundred and eighty pounds for four feathers!" Big Lou had exclaimed—Domenica remembered her first wedding. That had been so different. It had taken place in India, in Kerala, where she had married the eldest son of a Cochin mercantile family and had become for a brief time Mrs. Varghese.

That wedding, like many Indian weddings, had lasted for days, with legions of relatives and friends coming from all over India and beyond. It had not been a particularly happy marriage and was very brief, her husband being electrocuted in the small electricity factory owned by his family. She regretted him, but, if she was honest with herself, she did not miss him unduly; nor did she miss her former mother-in-law. Angus came with no family baggage of that sort—except for his dog Cyril.

Domenica knew that she was taking on Cyril, but felt that given a choice—between an impossible mother-in-law or a dog—many might choose the latter . . . discreetly, of course.

## 2. Late Climbers

"Does it really matter what I wear?" asked Domenica. "This obsession with the bride's outfit is understandable when the bride is twenty-something, but in my case . . ."

"Everybody will be just as interested," said Big Lou, still struggling with the fascinator she was attempting to pin into Domenica's hair. "It doesn't matter how old the bride is . . . not that you're all that old, Domenica."

She was not quite sure how old Domenica was. Forty-five? A bit more? Or less, perhaps? And Angus was difficult to date too: in some lights he looked as if he was barely into his forties; in others, he looked considerably older. He was one of those people who could have been anything.

"I suppose age adds character," said Domenica. "Or so we can console ourselves." She looked in the mirror. It would have been ridiculous to wear a conventional bridal dress. It would have been mutton dressed up as lamb, she thought—a metaphor that would mean less and less as people forgot about the distinction. Where could one buy mutton these days? It seemed more or less to have disappeared; everything, it seemed, was lamb because lambs presumably did not have the chance to reach muttonhood. So the expression would go, and the language would be further impoverished. Tell that not in Gath. That had gone completely by now, as had the habit of piling Pelion upon Ossa. Or making it to the altar. To the what? a contemporary teenager might be expected to ask. Down the aisle. Down the what?

"Yes," said Big Lou through lips pursed to hold two hairpins. "I can't be doing with those smooth faces that you see on film stars. You know the sort? All smooth—no lines. Nothing that shows us where the face has been."

"A few lines," agreed Domenica. "But one would hardly like to look too much like a prune."

She paused. The fascinator was not going to hold; she was sure of it. "Or like W. H. Auden."

"The loon with the wrinkly face?"

"Yes. His face was described as looking like a wedding cake left out in the rain."

Big Lou laughed. "It was a good face."

"Yes. He referred to it as a geological catastrophe. And of course he smoked, which must have made it worse. The kippering effect." She paused again. "You know something, Lou? I feel slightly embarrassed about all this."

"About getting married?"

"Yes. I just don't know . . ."

Big Lou laid a hand on her shoulder. "Haud your wheesht! It's fine getting married at your age, for goodness' sake. You're still a spring chicken compared with some."

Spring chicken, thought Domenica: another meat metaphor. So much of our language is still based on the things we used to do—like knowing where food came from. It was good of Big Lou, of course, but the fact remained: this was a late wedding.

"Everything's changed when it comes to age," Big Lou went on reassuringly. "Remember how people used to give up early? Remember how our parents' generation behaved? They put on carpet slippers when they were in their fifties. They did, you know."

"I was going to agree," said Domenica. "I was

14

thinking of my father. He retired from the Bank of Scotland when he was fifty-six and he stopped driving at the same time. He said he was too old. Whereas today . . ."

"People run marathons at seventy."

Domenica nodded, inadvertently loosening the fascinator. "Exactly."

"Keep your head still," muttered Big Lou. "I'm going to have to do it again."

"And they climb Everest, or try to, in their seventies."

"That's going too far," said Big Lou. "But you can certainly take fifteen years off everything these days." She paused. "But you can't take height off a mountain."

"So forty is the new . . ."

"Twenty-five. And fifty is the new thirty-five. It's all a question of attitude."

Domenica smiled. "So I shouldn't feel embarrassed about getting married at . . . at the age I am?"

Big Lou finished with the fascinator. "No. And that bunnet, if you can call it that—that wee bawbee's worth of over-priced feathers isn't going to move now."

Domenica felt at the delicate construction: it seemed firmly embedded. "Thank you, Lou. And thank you for being my bridesmaid."

"Two auld hens together," said Big Lou.

Domenica stood up and allowed Lou to smooth

out her dress. She had chosen silver-grey Thai silk that had been made into a strikingly smart suit. Grey T-bar high-heel shoes completed the picture of elegance.

She looked at Lou. "Do you think I'm doing the right thing?"

"Marrying Angus? Of course I do. I wouldn't have agreed to be bridesmaid if I didn't."

"I suppose not," mused Domenica. "Can you imagine a bridesmaid who fundamentally disapproved of the groom? She'd have to stand there and shake her head ominously as the service went ahead. And perhaps the occasional glance at the congregation to say, Not my doing, any of this."

Big Lou smiled. "Well, I have no reservations in this case. Except maybe . . ." She stopped herself, but it was too late.

Domenica looked at her anxiously. "Except what, Lou?"

Lou shook her head. "Nothing."

"Come on, Lou, you can't say 'except that' and then leave it at that."

Big Lou looked down at the floor. "Well, it's just that . . . well, about a year or so ago when Angus was in the coffee bar, he left his briefcase behind. You know that leather thing he carries . . . Well, he left it and I took it behind the counter to look after it for him and an envelope fell out." She stared at Domenica. "There was a typed name and address on it and I couldn't help but notice it as I picked it up."

Domenica held her breath. "Go on."

Big Lou lowered her voice. "The envelope was addressed to Mrs. A. Lordie. That's what it said. Mrs. A. Lordie, and it had his address on it. Drummond Place."

Domenica stood quite still. She said nothing.

"So I thought: is Angus already married?"

Domenica sat down heavily. The fascinator fell off; the feathers came into their own and it floated gently to the floor, where it lay, a small insubstantial thing, a vanity.

"Of course," Big Lou went on quickly, "it's very unlikely, isn't it? So I never mentioned it to you, and I'm sorry I did now. Really sorry."

## 3. Buildings, Bridges, Whisky

Drummond Place, where Angus Lordie lived, and where, like Domenica, he was now dressing for his wedding, was at the top of Scotland Street. The flat that Angus occupied also served as his studio, and was on the opposite side of the square from the Scotland Street entrance; not that Drummond Place was really a square—parts of it looked as if they belonged to a square, while others were semicircular. It was, he thought, a circle that had run out of architectural room, and had been obliged to draw in its skirts and become a sort of U-topped semi-rectangle; either that, or it had

17

been the work of two architects, one starting at one end in the belief that they were to build a square, and another starting at the other end under the firm impression Drummond Place was to be a circle, or circus. If that is what happened—and of course that was just a fantasy—then Angus imagined the moment of the meeting of the two sides, a moment of trigonometrical tension, no doubt.

Of course buildings can be made to join together without too much difficulty—a bit more stone here and there and one has the necessary coming together; how much more difficult it must be for those builders of bridges who start on opposite banks simultaneously. These must meet in the middle, and meet exactly: even a few inches can be a problem, and to miss by yards would be disastrous: no bridge should have a traffic circle or junction in the middle. And as for tunnels: how fortunate it was that the builders of the Channel Tunnel got it right and met, as planned, in the middle.

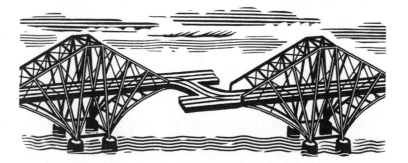

The studio in Drummond Place occupied the top two floors of a section of the handsome Georgian sweep. Its position was important: no artist likes to live and work in a basement, or even on the ground floor; such as are obliged through circumstance to do that find their paintings are starved of light and become gloomy: they paint a world of shadows and dim, overcast skies. By contrast, those, such as Angus, who occupy the natural realm of artists, further up, in garrets—the traditional abode of artists—have studios, and paintings, flooded with light. And his light, too, was of exactly the right quality: he faced north, looking out over the rooftops towards distant Trinity and beyond that the Firth of Forth and the hills of Fife—that strange kingdom beyond the Forth, as Angus sometimes called it. This northern light was clearer than the light to be had on the other side of the flat: southern light, Angus felt, seemed buttery by comparison; an impasto light, thick, greasy, torpid.

Facing north meant, too, that he could look across the gardens in the middle of Drummond Place to what he called the literary side, where two houses boasted commemorative plaques: one to mark the house of the poet Sydney Goodsir Smith, and the other to remind the passerby that this was the house of Sir Compton Mackenzie, novelist, former spy, president of the UK Siamese Cat Association, and founder of the *Gramophone* magazine. Commemorative plaques are helpful but often commit an unintended solecism: they say something to the effect that So-and-So, author, or painter or composer (or whatever) lived here, and that is it. But did they live there alone? Usually not. What about their spouse, the mute inglorious husband or wife who might not have been a distinguished practitioner of the arts, might not have invented something or stolen somebody else's territory, or done anything of that nature, and moreover is ignored? Such spouses or partners may not be of great public interest, but surely should not be viewed as if they never existed.

So, in the case of Compton Mackenzie, there was Faith, his first wife, and then his loyal housekeeper, Chrissie McSween from the island of Barra, whom he married, and, after her death, her sister Lillian, whom he also married. They all lived there, and perhaps should be remembered too in wording such as *Compton Mackenzie, author, lived here with his three wives*. That could be misunderstood, of course, but it would seem pedantic to provide further explanation by inserting additional wording at the end, possibly such as *one after the other of course* or *seriatim*. The last word, being Latin, might cause further confusion although not, obviously, to Edinburgh people, whose command of Latin is usually quite adequate for everyday purposes such as reading plaques, translating Cicero, and so on.

Compton Mackenzie, of course, was the author of that rollicking tale, *Whisky Galore*. Angus had read this book as a boy but did not remember much about it other than that it was about islanders in the Hebrides who discover a cargo of whisky washed up on their shores: a Scotsman's liquid dream, so to speak. Walking past Compton Mackenzie's house one day had given him an idea: the finding of a cargo of whisky was, in a sense, like the finding by the Israelites of manna in the wilderness. And that brought to mind Poussin's painting of that exact subject in the Louvre, and that . . . Yes, yes! The subject he had been looking for for some time: the discovery by a group of early Scots (much earlier than Compton Mackenzie's islanders) of a cargo of whisky washed up on the shores of Ardnamurchan. It would be a large-scale painting—as large as the Titians in the National Gallery of Scotland—and every bit as powerful, as emotionally arresting, but painted with the same cool palate as Poussin used in his later works. It would be the great Scottish painting, perhaps—dare one even imagine such a thing?—as great a painting as produced by any Scottish artist before him; as haunting as Cowie's *Portrait Group*, as whimsical as Raeburn's *The Reverend Robert Walker Skating on Duddingston Loch*, as geographically rooted as any view of Mull from Iona, or indeed Iona from Mull, by Peploe or Cadell.

He thought of this as he stood at the top of the stairs and waited for Matthew, his best man. Matthew was late, but they still had plenty of time to get ready, although there was a rather awkward issue to be addressed—and that was the large hole that Angus had discovered in the kilt he was proposing to wear. It had not been there the last time he had worn it, but it was there now, the result of the attention of moths. Matthew might have an idea what to do—or might not; but the point about having a best man was that he would be available to deal with crises, of which this undoubtedly was one.

## 4. How We See the World, and Scotland

"Angus," panted Matthew, "I'm so sorry I'm late. It was the boys, you see. Tobermory had been sick over Rognvald and Elspeth was just at her wits' end. You know that stuff you give children, that Calpol stuff, it's pink, and you give it to them when their temperature goes up; that stuff, well we couldn't find it and so I had to run down to the chemist in Stockbridge and buy some and it was only when I was standing in the queue in the chemist's that I realised that Tobermory had been sick over me too . . ."

Angus, opening the door to his best man,

laughed reassuringly. "We've got plenty of time—plenty. Look, it's three hours at least before we have to be there."

Matthew glanced at his watch. "I know, but still, it's going to take us twenty minutes to walk over to Palmerston Place and you have to speak to the minister and so on."

"The Provost," said Angus. "It's a Piskie cathedral."

"Well you have to speak to him," said Angus.

Angus ushered Matthew into the flat, placing an arm around his shoulder to calm him down. "There's nothing to worry about. We've got hours."

They went into the drawing room, a shabby, faded room furnished with ancient, chintzy chairs, a cocktail cabinet of obscure provenance, and a writing bureau stuffed with letters. Angus had inherited this bureau from an uncle in Broughty Ferry, and the correspondence had nothing to do with him, but related to the affairs of an earlier generation: personal letters postmarked 1952; bills from long-departed traders for sums that seemed so tiny now (three pounds for a new central heating radiator, for instance; one pound ten shillings for a jacket from Forsyth's); an invitation to attend a Highland Ball in Inverness, and so on. They should all have been thrown away, and Angus had occasionally steeled himself to do just that, but had cavilled at the idea every time: to throw all this away seemed to him to be

23

throwing away the memory of a life. Nobody could be interested in these minutiae of his uncle's existence, but they were the physical remnants of a life, and somehow they bound Angus to one who had been fond of him, and who had proved generous.

Matthew, having regained his breath from running up the stairs, moved over to the window and looked out at the sky. "It's a great day for a wedding, Angus," he said. "Look at that sky. Not a cloud in sight. Not one. Blue, all the way up."

Angus joined him at the window. "Good," he said. "Domenica will be so pleased."

Matthew turned to him. "That's a very significant thing you said, you know."

Angus looked puzzled. "What?"

Matthew explained. "You said that Domenica would like this weather. That shows that you're looking at the world from her perspective. And that's a good omen for the marriage."

Angus was embarrassed. "Oh really . . ."

"No," Matthew went on. "I mean it. I haven't been married all that long . . ."

Long enough, thought Angus, to become a family of five.

"I haven't been married all that long," Matthew went on, "but one thing I've learned is this: you have to look at things from your spouse's point of view. You have to get used to seeing the world through four eyes rather than two."

Angus frowned. "A peculiar sort of vision, surely."

"You may scoff, Angus, but it's true. What I really mean to say is that if your first thought is for her—and you've just shown that by thinking of how Domenica will feel about the weather— then that shows that you're already thinking in the way I said you should."

Angus looked at his friend. Dear Matthew; so serious at times, so . . . so vulnerable, standing there in his Macgregor kilt with that curious buttonhole in his jacket—white heather? *The White Heather Club*: his aunt—the wife of the uncle in Broughty Ferry—had gone on about that when as a small boy Angus had visited them for weekends. It was all tied up with Andy Stewart and country dancing and shortbread and all those . . . all those Broughty Ferry things, as he thought of them. He smiled at the memory. And yet, that was what Scotland— or a bit of it—was all about. It was about that mawkish sentimentalism just as much as it was about the hard life of bleak high-rises or dank tenements; "Grey over Riddrie the clouds piled up"—that haunting line of Edwin Morgan's that somehow summed up the hard-faced countenance of Scottish deprivation and defeat, that landscape of blighted and disappointed lives that we had to do something about but that we inevitably failed to heal.

He mused on this, and would have liked to talk to Matthew about it. He would have liked to say to him, "What can we do, Matthew? It seems that everything we try in this country fails. We know what we want Scotland to be, don't we? We know that we want it to be a place where there's justice and freedom from want. We know that we want people to be . . . well, we want them to be warm, don't we? We want them to have decent health. We want them to feel that . . ." But he could not speak to Matthew about all this now, as they stood at his window, only hours from his marriage.

He looked at Matthew. How often, he wondered, do we look at our friends, really look at them; because to look at somebody, to stare at them intently, makes one aware of their humanity, their being—exactly that thing that he, as a portrait painter, tried to capture; their life, really; their vitality, their essence.

Matthew looked back at him. "Is there anything wrong?" he asked.

Angus nodded.

Matthew's alarm showed on his face. "Oh no," he groaned. "You're not going to tell me you've changed your mind. It's that, isn't it?"

Angus shook his head. "No, no. I still want to get married, and I want it to be this afternoon, but it's just that . . . well, you see my kilt . . ."

He pointed across the room, to where the kilt was draped over the back of a chair.

Matthew's gaze moved to the kilt, and he gave a start. "My God, Angus. You're a Campbell."

# 5. *The Misunderstanding of Glencoe*

Angus was surprised by Matthew's observation on the identity of the tartan—his mind had been fixed firmly on the problem of the hole in the kilt rather than its pattern of dark green squares.

"Well, yes, I am," he said. "The Lordies have always worn the Campbell tartan; I think they are a sept of the Campbells. And my mother was a Campbell too: that was her surname. So I've got a double dose of Campbell blood."

Matthew was smiling. "And you're marrying a Macdonald. Not that these things count for anything, but that's why I was surprised to see the kilt."

"I see no reason for anybody to pass comment on that," said Angus, slightly huffily.

"No, of course not," agreed Matthew. "It's ancient business. The Massacre of Glencoe was an awful long time ago."

"1692, to be precise," said Angus. "And if I may correct you, Matthew, it was not a massacre—or rather, that's not the word we should use any longer to refer to it. The correct term nowadays is the Misunderstanding of Glencoe."

"The Misunderstanding of Glencoe!" exclaimed Matthew. "That's rich, it really is! Let me remind you, Angus, what actually happened. There was . . ."

He did not finish. "No," interjected Angus. "Let me remind you. William and Mary were the legitimate monarchs. James was ousted and should have accepted it. The Highland chieftains were given plenty of time, Matthew, to take the oath of allegiance." He looked at Matthew balefully, as if he, Matthew, was somehow condoning Jacobite insurrection, positively encouraging people not to take oaths of allegiance.

"And certain Macdonalds," Angus continued, "certain assorted Macdonalds who had earlier stolen cattle—Campbell cattle, remember . . ." And here Angus looked reproachful, as if Matthew, and any other Macdonald apologist, could not be trusted with cattle. "These Macdonalds dragged their feet in reporting to take their oath and can hardly complain if they came to be treated as outlaws."

Matthew listened to this . . . this nonsense (in his view) with growing incredulity, only momentarily distracted by Angus's mention of Campbell cattle—a term that made him picture cattle whose natural coats were of characteristic green tartan. "Angus," he said at last, "I'm somewhat surprised by your view of all this. I would have thought that the proper thing for a Campbell to do about all this is to hang his head in shame, and a whole lot of other matters, including the persecution of Macgregors. After all, what actually happened? All those Campbells went to stay with those poor

Macdonalds, as their guests." He paused, allowing the word guests to hang heavily in the air. "They stayed with them and enjoyed their hospitality and then turned round and massacred them. That, I believe, is not in accordance with traditional Highland notions of hospitality—nor of traditional Scottish notions of hospitality, I might add. One simply doesn't fall upon the people who have put you up. If that sort of thing were allowed, then just imagine how perilous it would be running a B and B up in the Highlands. Imagine."

Angus laughed. "Oh really, Matthew, stop havering. All this happened when the whole country was pretty dangerous, especially up in the Highlands. They were all as bad as each other—plotting and scheming, raiding one another, left, right, and centre. Stealing cattle. Ignoring every health and safety consideration in the book."

They both laughed.

"History," mused Angus. "History doesn't bear much thinking about."

"We have to stand back from it," said Matthew, remembering a teacher at the Academy who had made that point to him. "I remember being taught that it shouldn't be used politically. It shouldn't be used to make other people feel guilty about the past." Or should it? he wondered. Should one not remember certain things in order to prevent their recurrence?: that was a familiar point, and one with much to recommend it. If we did not remember wrongs, then wrongs could so easily be committed again. Perhaps it was a question of not laying those wrongs at the door of those descended from the wrongdoers: that could be unjust in the extreme, and dangerous too. The world was full of historical hatreds that still had power, now and then, to complicate and poison relationships between people.

Angus moved across the room to retrieve his kilt. "A bit of a disaster, I'm afraid. I've discovered this large hole, right here in the front. There have been all these moths, you see."

Matthew joined him to inspect the damage. It was extensive—a hole about the size of an extended hand had appeared in the cloth; rather too big for a moth, he thought, but the aetiology of the damage was not the point: the point was that this kilt could hardly be worn in its current state.

"You can't wear this," he said. "You'll have to wear a suit. What about that grey suit of yours? The one with the chalk stripes?"

Angus shook his head. "Out of the question," he said. "I must get married in the kilt."

Matthew said that he understood that, but it clearly could not be that kilt. He wondered whether Angus could borrow a kilt from somebody. Was there a neighbour, perhaps?

"No," said Angus. "I can't think of anybody who can lend me a kilt. Not round here, anyway."

They stood in silence. Matthew was aware that

this was a situation that any book on wedding etiquette would unambiguously declare to be the responsibility of the best man. It was without question the best man's role to get the groom to the church, in his wedding outfit, and in possession of the ring. That was not much to ask, really, and yet here he was, as best man to Angus, floundering at the first little hitch, even if this hitch was, to be fair, not all that little.

"We should fix it," he said decisively.

Angus looked at him with interest. "How?"

Matthew frowned. What did one do with holes in cloth? The answer came to him immediately.

"We need a patch," he said. "If we cut the edges of the hole—carefully—to make it regular, then we could get a patch and sew it on."

"A Campbell tartan patch?"

"Yes," said Matthew. "Have you got anything else in your tartan? A rug, maybe? A scarf?"

Angus shook his head. "I don't drape myself in Campbelliana. Credit me with some taste, Matthew."

Matthew looked thoughtful. He remembered when he had had his new kilt made up there had been a book of cloth samples—one of those floppy volumes that tailors have of which the generously sized pages are swatches of fabric.

"I think I have the solution," he said.

He sounded so calm, so decisive—just as a best man should.

# 6. Subjects and Symbols in Art

Matthew managed to persuade Angus to don his chalk-stripe suit for what he called emergency cover. "I know you don't want to wear it for the actual wedding," he said, holding up a hand to forestall Angus's incipient protest. "I know that, and, as I've said, I have a plan. But you need to be dressed accordingly in case my plan doesn't work." He paused, giving Angus the sort of warning look that he imagined a best man should give to a potentially recalcitrant groom. "And anyway, as everybody knows, nobody in the church will be looking at you. The groom plays a very minor part in a wedding. All eyes are on the bride. Fact."

Angus nodded. What Matthew said was true, he thought, and now, as he cast his mind back to the last wedding he had attended—the wedding of an Arts Club friend's daughter—he found that he could hardly even remember what the groom looked like, let alone what he wore; nor his name, for that matter. "I don't think that weddings are for men," he said. "I'm not sure if they actually enjoy them."

Matthew was clear that they did not. "No man likes a wedding," he said. "They pretend to, for the sake of women, but if you look at their faces you'll see they have fixed grins. They look vaguely uncomfortable. Whereas the women guests . . . that's quite another matter. The hats. The outfits. That's what weddings are all about. And romance too, I suppose."

"Which men don't go in for?"

Matthew thought for a moment. "I'm not sure. Some men might, but generally they don't. Men tend to be more . . . more prosaic."

Angus retreated into his bedroom to find the chalk-stripe suit, but continued the conversation through the open door. "Of course, these are all very sweeping generalisations," he called out. "Men can be every bit as feeling as women, every bit as sensitive . . . if they allow themselves."

"But that's the whole point," replied Matthew. "If they allow themselves. And we don't, do we? Especially in Scotland."

Angus mumbled something from the bedroom that Matthew did not quite catch.

"So," Matthew went on, "I know it's the usual spiel—we're all bound up in our masculinity, all afraid to cry, all trying to be strong, when we aren't really. We're every bit as weak as women. In fact, they're actually rather stronger than we are. They don't go round pretending to be strong, as we do, but all the time they're tough as nails."

"Yes," shouted out Angus. "But what sort of tie should I wear?"

"Wear the tie you're going to wear with your kilt."

"That's green."

"That's fine. But take another tie that will go with the suit. So if you need to wear the suit after all, then you can put that tie on."

There was silence from within the bedroom. Matthew walked over to the window and looked out. The sky was still clear, although he could see that there was a breeze moving the tops of the trees in the Drummond Place Gardens. He thought about the conversation he had just had with Angus. Were there many best men who spoke to their friends about that sort of thing while they prepared for the wedding? Were there any men in Scotland who spoke to their friends about expectations of masculinity? Was that in itself the problem?

Angus emerged from the bedroom. The chalk-stripe suit was a bit crumpled but at least his white shirt seemed clean and the tie, although Matthew would not have worn it himself, was relatively inoffensive.

"All right," said Matthew, as breezily as he could (his best-man's voice again, he thought). "All right: now I need the ring."

Angus looked at him blankly. "What ring?"

Matthew gasped. "You're getting married in . . ." he glanced at his watch, "in just over two and a half hours and . . . The wedding ring, Angus. The wedding ring."

Angus grimaced. "You know, I've been so busy

34

with all this . . . all this wedding stuff. I hadn't really addressed the issue of a wedding ring. I suppose it's important?"

Matthew sighed. "Of course it's important, Angus. You have to put a ring on her finger and she has to put one on yours. It's symbolic."

Angus frowned. "Symbolism's very interesting, isn't it? I remember when we were at the Art College we had a marvellous talk from Robin Philipson, I think it was, about symbols. I rushed out and bought a secondhand copy of Hall's *Dictionary of Subjects and Symbols in Art*. Do you know it, Matthew? It's a wonderful book."

Matthew stared at Angus mutely. He had seen a book entitled *A Guide for the Modern Best Man*, although he had not bothered to buy it. He wondered now whether there was a chapter that dealt with a situation where the best man had to ask himself whether the groom was sufficiently grounded in reality to get married.

"If you look at early paintings," Angus continued, "you'll be astonished at the extent to which symbol and allegory are at work. Take a picture of a garden, for example. You may think it's just a garden, but it's doing much more work that that. It represents the taming of nature—the process of civilising. Or unicorns. If there's a unicorn in a picture, then the artist clearly intends to say something about purity and chastity. And so on. Symbols were very important before there was widespread literacy. People might not have been able to read, but they could see all right . . ."

Matthew moved forward and seized the lapels of Angus's jacket. The suit smelled dusty, he thought, and suddenly he found that he was remembering the smell of dusty cloth. But this was no time for a Proustian moment, and he steeled himself for the firm attitude that was now very clearly required. Angus was going on about symbolism in art because he was panicking—that was now obvious to Matthew. "Angus," he hissed. "Get a grip! You say there's no ring? Is that correct?"

Angus nodded miserably. "I feel really foolish. I should have thought about it." But then he brightened. "Couldn't we use some other sort of symbol?"

## 7. Matthew Is Sorely Tested

Matthew counted to ten, not overtly, not so that Angus could hear him, but mentally, in that inner region of contrived calm we create when we want to assert control over some emotion—anger, perhaps, or worse. It was an ancient trick he had been taught by his mother, that calm, collected woman who in the face of provocation never manifested any reaction beyond the mildest irritation. "Count to ten, Matthew," she had said.

"Count to ten and the world will look slightly different." It was folk wisdom of the sort that mothers tend to espouse, and it was exactly the sort of thing that we reject out of hand when we are young (what self-respecting young person says, "You know something? My mother's dead right"?). And yet with the passage of the years we realise, much to our growing chagrin, that mother was indeed right. And for that very small and privileged number of people who grow up in a household in which there is a nanny (a tiny number now), there is the additional necessity of recognising that not only was mother right, but so was nanny! And some people, *mirabile dictu*, would go so far as to say Mrs. Thatcher too! (Not that many concede that the last was right, on anything, even if subsequent prime ministers, of every stripe, appeared to have a sneaking admiration for their predecessor.)

But not in Scotland. No politician operating within a purely Scottish context could bring himself to make such an admission publicly, although it is widely said, sotto voce, that several Catholic politicians in Scotland have confessed as much to their priests, relying on the secrecy of the confessional box to unburden themselves of that fact. I must confess, Father, that I have reached the conclusion that some of the things Mrs. Thatcher did were in the best interests of the country. Silence. How often have you had these thoughts, my son? Slight hesitation. Once or twice a week, Father. Silence. My son, you must understand that these thoughts are impure and you must try to put them out of your mind if they occur to you. Imagine what your family, your friends, your political colleagues would think if they knew that this was what you were thinking. Flood of guilt; and the priest continues: Make an act of contrition and . . .

Matthew had, of course, laughed at his mother's advice, but had secretly followed it, and discovered that it worked. Not only that, but he had extended its ambit to include counting up to fifteen before pressing the send button on an e-mail. That, he discovered, had been an invaluable way of preventing oneself from saying things that on reflection one would not really wish to say. Like all of us he had written e-mails that he regretted, and on one or two occasions had sent immediate countermanding messages. This second message, though, would inevitably be too late to limit the damage done by the first. Indeed, he had decided that if one sent an e-mail one regretted sending, it was probably better not to do anything at all, as there was always the chance that the recipient would simply ignore the first one, or perhaps read it in a hurry and not take the full insulting meaning from it. After all, not everybody opened every single e-mail they received, and not everybody paid much attention to those that did arrive. Unwise remarks, then, might simply fade into the general electronic noise that today surrounds the lives of most of us—a noise not unlike the screeching of cicadas in the forest, omnipresent, unremitting, and ultimately forgettable.

That morning, faced with Angus Lordie's remarkable lack of preparation for his own wedding, Matthew reached ten rather more quickly than he had anticipated. He decided to continue to fifteen, in order to give himself more time to calm down. It was not the end of the world, he now told himself. There must have been other bridegrooms who had forgotten to buy a ring; there must have been other bridegrooms, now safely married, who had discovered at the last moment that there was a large hole in their kilt. These were small things, really, and like all small things could be remedied.

"Fifteen," he muttered.

Angus looked at him in puzzlement. "Fifteen what?"

"I've just counted to fifteen," he said. "I find it helps in moments of stress."

Puzzlement was replaced by concern. "Are you feeling stressed by being best man?" Angus asked. Perhaps he should not have assumed that Matthew would find the role easy. Perhaps Matthew was one of those people who became acutely anxious if required to say anything in public; for such people being a best man could well be an excruciating experience.

But Matthew was not anxious—or certainly did not appear to be. "Let's get going," he said briskly. "We can walk up to Queen Street and then head west. There's that pawnbroker on the edge of Frederick Street."

Angus frowned. "What's that got to do with it?"

"Rings, Angus. What do you see in the windows of these places? Rings. Wedding rings."

Angus looked pained. "I see. Well, yes, of course. I should have bought one. I'm very sorry. It was a bit of an oversight."

Matthew began to hustle him out of the flat. "We'll be fine," he said reassuringly. "Let's just enjoy this. No need to worry about anything: it's just a social ritual, after all."

Angus smiled. "I'm not worried. I'm perfectly sanguine about all this."

"Good," said Matthew as they moved towards the door. "Now who's going to look after Cyril?"

"Look after him? He's coming."

Matthew stopped in his tracks. "To the wedding? To the actual church?"

Angus had now fixed Cyril's lead to his collar and was busy tying a small paisley scarf round the dog's neck. Cyril, who appeared to enjoy being dressed in this way, looked up at his master appreciatively.

"But who's going to hold him during the ceremony?"

Angus shrugged, as if the question was too

obvious to require answering. "I thought the best man normally does that."

This was too much for Matthew. He closed his eyes and began to count. Twenty? Twenty-five? Thirty?

# 8. *Au Contraire*

There were other people in Edinburgh getting ready for the wedding, although none of them in quite the same fraught atmosphere as the groom himself. One of these was Bertie Pollock (6), the son of Irene Pollock and her husband, Stuart, a statistician employed by the Scottish government to assemble figures and—although this part of the job was never explicitly referred to—to advise on how to portray these figures in the best possible light. Unemployment figures of, say, 10 per cent could always be described as employment figures of 90 per cent, and a 15 per cent increase in knife crime in the central belt of Scotland could always be disguised by making much of the complete lack of knife crime on, say, the island of St. Kilda. In this way, Dr. Pangloss's famous precept might not only be put about as the truth but might also be believed because it was, in a strict sense, true.

Bertie had first become aware of the impending wedding when Irene had opened the invitation at the breakfast table. With one hand she was feeding

Bertie's younger brother, Ulysses, with mashed boiled egg, while with the other hand she was opening the envelope that had dropped through their door that morning.

"Hah!" she said as she read the printed white card the envelope had contained. "So that Macdonald woman has snared Angus Lordie at last. She'll be rubbing her hands." She paused, and passed the invitation over to Stuart. "See? And we're invited, including you, Bertie."

Bertie watched as his father read the invitation. "And what about Ulysses, Mummy? Will he be allowed to come?"

"Of course," said Irene. "They haven't put his name there because I'm not sure that they know he exists. But you can take babies anywhere you like, Bertie." She glanced at Stuart. "See the wording?"

Stuart shrugged. "Seems all right to me. Gives the time and place. You don't need much else, do you?"

Irene reached for the invitation. "It's twee, Stuart. Terribly twee. You are invited to share our wedding. How twee can you get?"

"I don't know," said Stuart. "Maybe that's better than requesting the pleasure of your company. That's always struck me as being somewhat cold—almost as if their company won't be all that pleasurable."

Irene was looking at the invitation again. "And did you see the embossed hearts up at the top?"

Stuart shrugged again. "If that's what they want . . ."

"Oh, they can have whatever sort of invitation they want," said Irene, generously. "Embossed livers, if one has to be anatomical. It's just that there's this awful, cloying sentimentality about weddings."

Bertie listened intently. He had observed that his mother was dismissive about things like weddings and birthday parties, and yet she had herself had a wedding—Bertie had seen the pictures—and she always enjoyed celebrating her birthday. Perhaps she just felt that about other people's weddings and birthdays and not about her own . . .

Bertie was looking forward to this wedding. He had seen his own name written at the top of the invitation and had felt profoundly boosted by this. It was his name—his—and they wanted him there. It said up at the top Stuart, Irene, and Master

Bertie Pollock. He gazed at the wording. Master! That was him!

"We must get them a present," said Stuart. "And that'll be a bit difficult when they've both got households already. They'll have all the necessary junk." And with that he gestured to the contents of the Pollock kitchen—necessary junk.

"We'll think of something," said Irene, scraping the last of Ulysses' boiled egg from the plate. "At least we won't be getting them a decanter."

Stuart looked thoughtful. "A decanter? They might find that useful . . . although I imagine they've got one already, or Angus will, I'm sure, with his fondness for wine. Should we ask . . ."

Irene cut him short. "Oh really, Stuart! Do you seriously imagine they'd like a decanter? A decanter is a complete cliché. No person of any . . . any discernment would give anybody a decanter—not anymore." She looked at her husband witheringly, and sighed. "Don't you know about the ur-decanter? The decanter that's been doing the rounds in Edinburgh for the last forty years? People get given it as a wedding present and then wrap it up and pass it on the next time they're invited to a wedding. I've heard that it changes hands every three months—as a recycled present."

Stuart was not sure whether to take this seriously. He had heard of a legendary box of After Eights that had done the rounds of Edinburgh dinner parties, being taken as a present for the host and then passed on, unbroached, by the recipient. By now the chocolates were said to be in an advanced state of decomposition—not that anybody would ever find out, as nobody ever opened them. They were, in a way, rather like the Flying Dutchman, doomed to circulate forever and never find a home.

"Bourgeois Edinburgh," Irene continued, shaking her head. "It's a most extraordinary place. I'm so glad we're not part of it."

Stuart looked at her with surprise. "But you . . ." He stopped. Irene did not like to be reminded that she had started life in Moray Place. Of course that was haut-bourgeois, if anything, but he knew better than to raise that point.

It was as if she had not heard him. "Yes," she went on. "There is so much to be thankful for. For our freedom from all that; from the chains of respectability; from the sheer clutter of middle-class existence. We're very lucky."

But what are we? Stuart asked himself. If they were not middle-class, then what were they? Did these labels matter, anyway, or were they all part of a political and social battlefield that had long since been abandoned?

He looked at the invitation. "I knew about this already," he said.

"About this wedding? Who told you?"

He had no alternative now but to confess.

"Angus did, actually. He told me and then he asked me."

"Asked you what?"

"Whether we could look after Cyril when they went on honeymoon."

Irene stared at him. "And?"

"I said yes, of course."

Bertie's face broke into an immediate and delighted grin. He was fairly indifferent to weddings, but dogs—well, they were another matter altogether.

Irene gasped. "Have you taken leave of your senses, Stuart?" she hissed. "Have you?"

Stuart closed his eyes.

"No," he said. *Au contraire.*" It was strong language for the Edinburgh New Town, but he had to say it.

"Don't *au contraire* me," said Irene.

But it was too late. He had.


## 9. *A Room at the Gritti Palace*

Bertie could barely control his excitement when he learned that Cyril was to board with the Pollock family while Angus and Domenica were away on their honeymoon. He had only the sketchiest idea of what a honeymoon was, having been told by Tofu, with whom he had raised the subject, that it was a form of compulsory holiday, taken immediately after the wedding, in which children were acquired. Some people, Tofu revealed, went off on honeymoon and came back several weeks later with three or four children. This was unusual, he said, but had been known to happen. "Most of the time, they just come back with one baby," he said. "That's the way things work, Bertie."

Olive, who had overheard this conversation, was quick to pour scorn on Tofu's theory. "Shows how much you know, Tofu," she said scornfully. "Honeymoons are all about getting away from other people. If you've just married somebody, then it's nice to get away from other people so that you can get to know the person you've married. It's very romantic, not that you'd know anything about that, Tofu."

Tofu started to remonstrate that he knew a great deal about these subjects and that his uncle had just got married and had come back from his honeymoon with two small babies; Olive could come and look at them if she didn't believe him. The uncle in question lived in Balerno and all that Olive would have to do would be to catch a bus.

Olive was scathing. "I don't care where your uncle lives, Tofu," she retorted. "And I certainly don't want to see those babies of his, who are bound to be really horrid, since they're related to you and have your yucky genes." She paused. "No, I'd prefer to think about the honeymoon that

Bertie and I are planning to take after we get married. When we're twenty, that is."

Bertie began to protest. "I didn't ever say I would, Olive. I really didn't."

Olive was not listening. "We're going to go to Venice," she said. "That's a place in Italy where they have lots of canals and restaurants. Bags of people go there to do their honeymoon. We're going to stay in a hotel called the Gritti Palace— I've seen photographs of it and have made a booking already."

Bertie drew in his breath sharply. "You've already booked?"

"Yes," said Olive, somewhat smugly. "I've sent them an e-mail asking them to keep a room for us for when we're twenty."

Bertie's voice was small. Olive really should have asked him about this. It was bad enough to try to force him to marry her, but to book a honeymoon too was, he felt, taking matters too far. "And?"

"They haven't been in touch," said Olive. "But they've got my booking. We don't need to worry."

"But I never said that I wanted to marry you, Olive . . ."

She cut him short. "Yes you did, Bertie. And I've got it in writing, remember? I've got a piece of paper that has your signature on it. It says that you agree to marry me—those are the exact words, Bertie, and you can't deny them."

"But . . ."

"No buts, Bertie. If you don't keep your promise then you'll get into serious trouble. Big time. You could go to prison, and then what? And there's God too. God watches these things and if he sees you breaking promises he can really get you. He does it all the time."

At this point, Tofu decided to intervene on Bertie's behalf. Walking up behind her, he leaned forward suddenly and spat down the back of her neck. "You can have that in writing too," he said. "I promise to spit at Olive once a day for the next five years. Official. Signed: Tofu. Hah!"

It had ended in tears and recrimination, as it always did. But now, wearing his best clothes for the wedding—a smart white shirt, a pair of black trousers his mother had bought from a charity shop in Stockbridge (a couple of sizes too big but very rarely worn by the previous owner, and, blessedly, not crushed strawberry), and his best lace-up shoes—Bertie closed his eyes and imagined what it would be like to have Cyril staying in the house. It was the most delicious of thoughts: a dog in the house, always there at his feet, ready to go out for a walk, to run after a ball, to fetch sticks, to bark at cats . . . And at night, Cyril would sleep on a mat beside him, or even creep onto the end of the bed. One of the boys at school had a dog that did that, he claimed; and another had two dogs that he said actually slept under the blankets with him. That must be almost unimaginable bliss, thought Bertie.

Icy in defeat, Irene had made no further mention of Cyril's impending arrival, leaving all arrangements for the arrival of what she described as "our uninvited guest" to Stuart. Bertie had suggested that they should get supplies of food for Cyril from Valvona & Crolla, but Stuart had explained that delicatessens usually did not stock dog food and that they would need to go to a pet shop. That trip, undertaken with his father, had thrilled Bertie to the core, admitting him to an Aladdin's cave of caged birds, scurrying hamsters, mewing kittens, and a litter of tiny Highland terrier puppies.

They had purchased a whole case of tinned dog meat, a bag of dry food called Super Dog, and a large carton of dog biscuits called Good Boy Treats. Bertie had gazed in fascination at the box of biscuits and marvelled at the name. Somebody should make something like that for real boys, he thought—not just for dogs. Boys deserved treats, especially if they were good, and Bertie felt that he did his level best to be good. But the world, it seemed to him, was not like that. You could do your best to be good but would get precious little credit for it. All that would happen would be that you would be told to do even better. It was very hard, very unfair.

They took the dog food supplies back to the

flat, where they were stacked behind the door of Bertie's room, ready for Cyril's arrival.

"I can't wait!" Bertie whispered to his father.

Stuart looked at his son and smiled. "I know," he whispered back.

And he reached out and ruffled his son's hair, leaving his hand there where it lay, in a gesture that was one of both complicity and love.

## 10. Irregular Marriages in Scots Law

Matthew at last managed to get Angus out of the flat and into the street. He was more aware of the time now, as they had at least two important tasks to perform on their way to Palmerston Place; not for them, then, the leisurely few hours that most grooms spent before their appointment at the altar—a time of quiet reflection on the significance of the ceremony to come. One's last few hours as anything were always very important, thought Matthew: those moments one spends thinking, This is the last day of my working life, or This is my last morning at school, or This is the last time I pilot a jumbo jet. He had read somewhere about how an American president—it was President Clinton, he thought—had spent his last night in office awake and thinking; and what thoughts those must have been. These are my last few hours of power. What could a person do in such circumstances? Grant pardons, it seemed, was one thing he could do, and indeed did. How much better that was than a last-minute, rash decision to press a red button before the codes are taken away from one.

And so a bachelor might think, These are my last hours as a single man, my last hours of freedom. That, of course, thought Matthew, cast a pejorative light on marriage—a boyish, immature vision of what marriage amounted to. Matthew did not feel unfree being married to Elspeth Harmony. Quite the contrary, in fact. He had found that marriage had relieved him of anxiety, and that was a freeing, a removal of a psychological shackle. He no longer had to worry about whether he would find somebody who liked him: he had found her. He no longer had to worry about how he looked and whether his distressed-oatmeal sweater would be the subject of scorn; married men could wear distressed oatmeal if that was what they wished to do. No, marriage was not a diminution of freedom, Matthew thought; it was its enhancement.

Did Angus think that? he wondered. Looking at Angus now as they walked up Dublin Street towards York Place and Queen Street, he was not at all sure what Angus thought. Angus had failed to make the most elementary preparations for the wedding, failing to check his kilt and forgetting altogether to buy a ring. Matthew was not sure whether that amounted to a lack of organisation that went with the artistic personality, or whether it was symptomatic of a lack of enthusiasm for his wedding. It was too late, though, to enquire: his responsibility now as best man was to ensure that he got Angus to the right place at the right time and with the necessary ring. If Angus had any reservations, then it was simply too late. Matthew now had a responsibility to Domenica to ensure that she was not embarrassed in any way, and he would discharge that to the best of his ability.

Angus was largely silent as they walked up Dublin Street. At the top of the street, though, and when they began to make their way along the pavement opposite the Scottish National Portrait Gallery, he began to talk again. "It's a pity weddings can't be a little bit more low-key," he said. "All this dressing up—all this fuss. It should be simpler."

"It can be," said Matthew. "Some people have very simple weddings."

"That used to be the case in Scotland," mused Angus. "I think these fancy weddings are a result of us trying to imitate the English."

"Really?" asked Matthew. "I thought Scottish weddings were always rather more enjoyable affairs. Big parties and lots to eat. I've always been under the impression that English weddings are much less lavish—a few canapés and so on, not a sit-down meal."

"I was thinking of the actual ceremony," said Angus. "We had these things called irregular marriages in Scotland until our political masters decided that they didn't like them. It's the old story of the state wanting to regulate everything."

"You mean Gretna Green and all that?"

"Yes," said Angus. "Gretna Green was all about parental consent not being needed in Scotland. Young lovers from England could hop over the border and get married in Scotland in the face of their parents' disapproval. And good for them. But it was all about informality as well. You could simply declare yourself married in Scotland—you didn't need a minister to do the necessary, as long as you had witnesses. And there was also a wonderful system called marriage by habit and repute."

"By habit?"

Angus nodded. "And by repute. It meant that if you let everybody think that you were married—called yourself Mr. and Mrs. Macgregor or what-ever—then the courts could hold that you were in fact married. It helped with things like pensions and wills and so on."

"How nice," said Matthew. "Pension funds do that sometimes with dependants, don't they? People who live together and rely upon one another might be looked after."

"I believe they do," said Angus. "It's always struck me as rather cruel that people who are to all intents and purposes married to somebody can't enjoy the benefits that those who are formally married get."

"I agree," said Matthew.

They both became silent and this silence continued until Angus broke it. "I cannot understand it," he said. "There are people who seem to take pleasure in belittling others, in denying them their small chance of happiness. Why? What pleasure do such people get out of making others feel bad, or somehow inferior? What possible pleasure?"

Matthew shook his head. "I don't know. Perhaps they feel it builds them up. Perhaps they think they'll feel bigger inside if they make somebody else feel smaller."

Angus thought about this. "Perhaps." He paused. "Cyril, you know, disapproves of nobody. Look at him. He's happy to lick anybody who comes his way."

Cyril, who was trotting at his master's feet, now looked up at him and gave him a lopsided canine grin—all pink tongue and saliva, and of course his single, flashing gold tooth. Then he looked down from gazing at his master to the contemplation of Matthew's ankles. Cyril had been tempted by Matthew's ankles ever since he had first seen them under the table at Big Lou's coffee house. He had wanted to bite them more than anything else he wanted to do. They were delicious— uniquely and overwhelmingly delicious. And yet he knew that he could not do this, and especially not today, as something was definitely in the air and he had an impression that something momentous, something life-changing from both the human and the canine point of view, was about to occur.

## 11. *The Campbell Kilt Is Repaired*

As they approached Frederick Street, Matthew pointed to a corner shop with an elaborate panelled frontage. "In there," he said, taking Angus's arm and propelling him through the doorway.

Angus knew immediately what Matthew had in mind. "I feel extremely embarrassed," he mumbled. "To buy one's wedding ring in a pawnshop . . ."

"It's the thought that counts," Matthew retorted. "Rather than the foresight."

An assistant came up to them. "A wedding ring for a bride," Matthew announced.

The assistant smiled. She had seen the kilt draped over Angus's arm and the jacket on its hanger carried by Matthew.

"This afternoon?" she asked.

Matthew nodded. "Imminent," he said.

The assistant slid a tray out of a display case. "I imagine that we don't have the bride's finger size, do we? No, I thought not."

"She has very nice hands," said Angus, trying to

salvage what dignity was left to him. "Not too large and not too small. Ideal size."

The assistant nodded. "It might be better to err on the side of caution," she said. "It's awful when the groom can't get the ring on the bride's finger." She pointed to a line of wedding rings all neatly placed in velvet slots. "One of these perhaps?"

Matthew bent down to peer at the rings and then turned to look at Angus. Angus met his gaze dolefully. "I'm terribly sorry," he said. "And now we're taking somebody else's ring. Just think of the story behind each of these. The desperation."

"Not necessarily," said the assistant cheerfully. "People pawn their jewellery for all sorts of reasons. Sometimes they can't wait to get the wedding ring off their finger. Sometimes they're marrying again and the new husband is giving them something better. You never know." She hesitated. "Or they've died, of course."

Matthew looked at his watch. "Just choose, Angus."

Angus pointed to a plain gold band. "That one, I think."

"A very good choice," said the assistant. "Plain. Can't go wrong—and it's average size."

"Good," said Matthew. "Now just pay for it and let's go."

Angus padded the side of his chalk-stripe suit. "I'm terribly sorry, Matthew, but I don't seem to have my wallet. You couldn't possibly . . ."

Matthew pursed his lips. "Yes, I can." He reached into his inner pocket and extracted a credit card.

The transaction completed, they left the shop and continued along Queen Street. "I'll give you a cheque tomorrow," said Angus. "Before we go off on our honeymoon."

Matthew assured him that that would be all right. "Where are you going, by the way? I don't think you told me." He had read that one of the best man's duties was to ensure that the newly married couple's departure went smoothly.

"Actually, I hadn't really thought very much about it," Angus said.

Matthew stopped in his tracks. "You hadn't thought about where to go? Are you serious?"

"Yes. I mean, no, I haven't quite fixed it up yet."

Matthew's tone was incredulous. "So what did you say to Domenica?"

"I said that it would be a surprise. I told her that all she would need would be her passport." He paused. "I suppose I can see what's available tomorrow, flight-wise. You can get to quite a few places from Edinburgh Airport these days."

Matthew opened his mouth to say something, but thought better of it. "All right," he said, trying to sound as businesslike as possible. "The important thing is to get you married. So let's carry on."

It was only a block or so to their next stop, the outfitter Stewart Christie. Matthew was a regular customer there and knew the proprietor well. If anybody could help them deal with the kilt emergency it was Mr. Lowe.

"Here we are," said Matthew, again propelling Angus through the door.

Mr. Lowe was fetched from upstairs by one of his assistants and had the nature of the crisis explained to him.

"I know you have those books of tartan swatches," Matthew said. "I was wondering if you could cut one of them up and use it as . . ."

"As a patch?" prompted Mr. Lowe. "Why not? We've done that before, you know."

"Really?" asked Angus.

"Yes," said Mr. Lowe as he led them into the back of the shop. "We've helped a number of people who've discovered holes in their clothes at the wrong time. Some years ago, for instance, we had the Moderator of the Kirk in here. His breeches had developed a hole just before he was due to meet a delegation to Scotland of the Coptic Church, and we fixed him up with a patch from an old set of tails. And David Steel's yellow waistcoat developed a hole when he was Lord Commissioner at the Assembly and we found an old duster that matched it perfectly. Nobody could tell. We've saved the day on numerous occasions."

He extracted a thick book of swatches from under the counter. There was something reassuring about the heavy covers of the book and the satisfying way in which it flipped open to reveal an astonishing range of tartans, all arranged alphabetically.

"Burns," muttered Mr. Lowe, paging through the samples. "Caledonia, Cameron, and . . . yes, here we are, Campbell."

The familiar dark green tartan was an exact match of the kilt. Now taking the holed fabric in his hands, Mr. Lowe squared up the swatch so that the lines of the pattern met. Then, reaching for a large pair of tailor's scissors, he cut into the swatch, producing a patch slightly larger than the hole in the kilt. "A few stitches with some strong green thread and we'll be right as rain," he said.

Angus leaned forward and put a hand on the outfitter's shoulder. "I'm very grateful," he said. "I really am."

"We try to be as helpful as possible," said Mr. Lowe. And then, discreetly, "Your suit, by the way, would you like us to . . . help you in that department?"

"Indeed I would," said Angus. "When I return from honeymoon, I shall bring it in for . . ."

"For adjustment," supplied Mr. Lowe. "By all means."

The kilt was soon ready and Angus changed into it in the changing room.

"I feel much more confident now," he said. He stopped. Cyril was looking up at him, his mouth in a wide smile. The paisley scarf round his neck had been changed for a striking piece of Campbell tartan.

"I think that's more suitable," said Mr. Lowe, with a smile. "He is after all a Campbell too."

"Exactly," said Angus.

"A Campbell dog," muttered Matthew.

"What was that you said?" asked Angus.

He suspected it was another tiresome reference to the Misunderstanding of Glencoe, but this, he thought, was no time for a misunderstanding with one's best man.

## 12. Dearly Beloved

It could have been a disaster, but it was not. The proposition that the best laid plans of mice and men gang aft agley has, presumably, its converse: that badly laid plans rather than ganging aft agley can actually gang aft rather weel. Anybody who had witnessed Matthew's experiences from the time he arrived at Angus Lordie's front door that day would have imagined a steadily deteriorating situation; would have steeled himself, perhaps, for further disasters flowing from the almost complete lack of planning on the groom's part; would have foreseen embarrassment after embarrassment as things got steadily worse. But none of this happened, and when Matthew looked back that evening on the day's events he was able to reflect that just as weather reports can occasionally threaten and not deliver, so too can weddings that seem to be headed for disaster turn out to be successful and even enjoyable.

With this verdict Big Lou would also have wholeheartedly agreed. The bridal camp had also had to contend with its own crisis, one that was nothing to do with bad planning but that flowed entirely from Big Lou's chance remark that Angus might already be married. A bridesmaid should not say that sort of thing, since if there is one piece of news that a bride does not wish to hear on her wedding day, it must be that. And the effect was, indeed, dramatic.

"I think that we should perhaps call the whole thing off," Domenica said. "I can't face that possibility. I'm sorry, I just can't."

Big Lou, immediately regretting her comment, sought to undo the damage. "I'm sure he wouldn't do a thing like that," she said. "And it was only one letter addressed to Mrs. A. Lordie. That's hardly evidence of anything."

They stared at one another glumly. Big Lou, however, was not one to be defeated. Having been raised on a farm, she could cope with most challenges: a difficult lambing, a nest of rats in a byre, a broken-down tractor—and these skills had been further developed in her years working in the Granite Nursing Home in Aberdeen, where the small emergencies of such a place regularly tested the staff.

"I'm going to phone Matthew," she announced. "I'm going to get him to tackle Angus about it."

She gave Domenica no time to raise any objections, getting through to Matthew on his mobile phone shortly after he and Angus had left the outfitters. Matthew was now in good spirits, having resolved the immediate crises of the ring and the kilt. Big Lou's question, however, could hardly do anything but bring a frown to his face.

"I'll ask him directly," he said after Lou had finished what she had to say. "Hold the line."

They were now in Ainslie Place. Turning to Angus, he fixed him with an accusing stare. "Angus," he said. "Big Lou tells me she saw a letter addressed to Mrs. A. Lordie. Tell me right now: does Mrs. A. Lordie exist? Are you already married?"

It would not have surprised Matthew had Angus suddenly hit his forehead with the flat of his palm and said, "Oh, how silly of me to forget!" But he did not. For a few moments he stared at Matthew in incomprehension, and then he smiled.

"Of course not," he said. "Those letters are from the electricity people. They have me down as Mrs. A. Lordie for some reason. I've tried to inform them, but I get on to a call centre in Timbuktu and they never seem to pass on the message. I don't mind too much. I'm secure enough in my identity, you know."

Matthew resumed his conversation with Big Lou, passing on the explanation. It seemed convincing enough and, for all his occasional vagueness and lack of organisation, he knew that Angus was strictly truthful. And that, it transpired, was the last hitch in the proceedings. They reached the Cathedral in good time and sat calmly through an inspiring and calming organ recital by Peter Backhouse before Domenica arrived.

The ceremony itself was conducted according to the liturgy of the Scottish Episcopal Church. Eschewing the arid simplicities of the modern service, with its language deprived of all poetry, they had opted for the form of words used in the Book of Common Prayer and related prayer books. This brought them back to the language of the time of James VI, Jamie Saxt, that extraordinary king who left Scotland for the greater prize of England, but did the most profound service to the English language with his espousal of the King James Bible.

"Dearly beloved," began Dr. Forbes, the Provost of the Cathedral. "We are gathered together here in the sight of God, and in the face of this congregation, to join together this Man and this Woman in holy Matrimony; which is an honourable estate, instituted of God in the time of man's innocency . . ."

Dearly beloved, thought Angus; how right that we should speak to our fellows in such terms, for that is how we should see them; not as my friends or anything like that, but beloved and dearly so. And then we are gathered in the face of this congregation, which expresses exactly the full solemnity of making the promises that we are about to make before these people; this is something we are doing in the face of the congregation, not among them or before them, but in the face of this group of people, of those who are dearly beloved. And in the time of man's innocency: what a marvellous echoing phrase, what a magnificent way of referring to what is very old, to a better time.

For there was a better time, thought Angus; there was a time of our innocency. There was a time when the world was fresher, less used, less polluted. There was a time when we really did think that humanity had a future and that our tiny human lives, our tiny human concerns, meant something, and that we were not just the brief tenants of an insignificant planet in a great and incomprehensible emptiness.

He brought himself back to where he was: at the altar, at his own wedding. Dr. Forbes had moved on and had now reached the point at which the collective breath of the congregation is briefly held: "Therefore if any man can shew any just cause, why they may not lawfully be joined together, let him now speak, or else hereafter for ever hold his peace."

There was a brief silence, and then, from within the congregation there came a voice.

## 13. Bruce Visits Crieff

That morning, Bruce Anderson, surveyor and rugby player, stalwart of the Watsonians Rugby Club—and briefly secretary of the social sub-committee—was driving down from Crieff to Edinburgh. The morning sun was sufficiently warm to allow the hood of his Japanese two-seater sports car to be wound back, or half back, rather, as the mechanism had never been entirely reliable and tended to stick. This did not affect the performance of the car or the comfort of the driver and Bruce was very much enjoying this drive. He knew exactly where the speed cameras were and on which stretches of road he could take the car up to eighty-five. Bruce said that he did not believe in going much faster than that, which was convenient, as he had bought the car cheaply and that was its maximum speed. "It's irresponsible," Bruce opined in the rugby club bar at Myreside, "to go more than eighty-five. Speed limits are there for a purpose, you know."

There had been nods of agreement from Gerry, Martin, Bill, and Fergus. "Yeah, sure," said Martin. "Except sometimes. The other day I did a hundred and five on the A68 on that stretch just before Lauder, you know? You know where the turn-off to that hotel is? Just after that there's a straight bit and you can really motor. A hundred and five, and I still had a bit in reserve. I reckon my car's capable of a hundred and fifteen in the right conditions."

"Great, but you shouldn't," said Bruce. "Eighty-five max."

Now, with the needle on the speedometer nudging up towards that critical figure, Bruce sat back in the driver's seat and felt the wind on his brow. Perfection! Behind him lay the gently rising Perthshire hills that marked the beginning of the Highlands; behind him lay Crieff and the parental villa in which he had spent the last two nights;

ahead of him lay Edinburgh and a new phase in his life. Bruce was still in his twenties, and even if he was now closer to thirty than to twenty—three years away, in fact—that melancholy milestone seemed sufficiently distant not to worry him unduly. Certainly, one had to be aware of the fact that the thirties existed—one had to be, as there came a day, and that day had recently come for Bruce, when one received one's first invitation to a thirtieth birthday party.

"She can't be thirty!" Bruce had muttered when he had opened the invitation in question. She was still attractive, and he had even considered her himself as a prospect, and now here she was planning to hold a thirtieth birthday party (no presents please). Thirty! It had been a sobering thought, and the party itself had been a rather dull affair, almost like a wake, Bruce thought. If that was what it was like, then he certainly had no intention of being thirty himself.

The last couple of days in Crieff had been a bit of a strain. Bruce had gone up to stay with his parents because his father was celebrating his sixtieth birthday. There had been no party—his parents were not that type—and the birthday itself had been marked with no more than a family dinner at which Bruce's uncle and aunt from Fort William had joined them. Bruce had spent the rest of the visit watching a Danish crime thriller, punctuating Copenhagen with sporadic and rather drifting conversations with his parents. Bruce was fond of his parents and considered himself a dutiful enough son—he just did not want to become like them. In that respect, of course, he was not unlike most of us. How often does one meet people whose ambition it is to become just like their parents? Parents, by definition, are less fashionable than their children; have worse dress sense and less understanding of the world; are so completely and irretrievably uncool. Of course there is always the problem of the camera—that notoriously mendacious instrument—that may suddenly reveal in a photograph a striking similarity between the generations: a way of holding the head, for instance, the angle of the nose, even something as fleeting and subjective as a look in the eye. But those are just externals! What counts is the way we are inside, and let there be no doubt about it; we are utterly different from our parents—of course we are!

Bruce contemplated his parents and wondered how it was that people like that could produce somebody like him. And here was the same father going on and on about the need to take stock where one was in one's career. "You have to make progress, Bruce. You should be able to look back every two years and say: Two years ago I was there, and now I'm here." Bruce's father demonstrated with his hands the difference in the two positions: one hand was low and the other was a good foot higher.

Bruce thought: one foot in two years—not very much.

"Are you listening, Bruce?"

"Yes, Dad. I'm listening."

"Good, so in your case you need to think about getting a job where there are partnership prospects." His father paused. "Are there any in the firm you're with now?"

"Probably not," said Bruce. "I'll find something."

There was a brief silence. Then: "So you're interested in moving?"

"Always am, Dad."

Bruce's father smiled. "In that case, I think I might have just the opportunity you're looking for."

Bruce froze. "Well, I wasn't thinking . . ."

His father cut him short. "There's a job right here. Just outside Crieff. You know the Easter Cairn estate? The one off the Comrie Road? I know the factor there, Jock Blain, and he's planning to retire this year. Jock and I play bowls together and I know him pretty well."

Bruce said nothing.

"Jock says that if you're interested he could suggest to the estate that they take you on as factor. You've got all the qualifications—your RICS and so on. It's not a very big place, as you know, but they've got plans for some new holiday cottages and a wind farm if they get planning permission. There'd be a lot for you to get your teeth into. It's ideal, Bruce, and you could use it as a stepping stone. You could get into one of the Perth firms where it'll be far easier to get a partnership than in Edinburgh."

Bruce looked down at the floor.

"Come home, Bruce," said his mother, who had been listening to this conversation from the kitchen door. "Come home, darling."


## 14. Bruce Meets Two Sporting Girls

That had been a narrow escape, thought Bruce, as he approached the Forth Road Bridge. Of course there had never been any possibility that he would agree to his father's proposal, but it had not been easy to explain to the olds, as Bruce referred to his parents, that he had no intention of returning to Crieff. His father had not given up easily, urging Bruce at least to have a word with Jock Blain, at least to look at the place. Meeting resistance, he had let drop the fact that the owner of the estate had a daughter and no son. This daughter, it seemed, was a few years younger than Bruce and could be, his father tactfully suggested, a possible friend for Bruce. "She's very keen on horses, you see, and that's why she hasn't flown the nest, so to speak. Of course she'll take over the estate, I suppose, in the fullness of time . . ."

Bruce had paused at that, but only briefly,

suddenly remembering that he had seen pictures of this daughter in *Perthshire Life* and, well, she may be a perfectly decent girl, and she may eventually be in possession of four thousand acres, but he had certain standards and . . .

"Sorry, Dad. No deal. I've got too much to do in Edinburgh. Big plans. And, as you know, I've just bought a flat. Sorry."

His father had acknowledged defeat. "It would have been nice to have you back, but you must do what you want to do, Bruce."

And now filial duty had been done—a full two days had been spent in Crieff—and Bruce was free again, crossing the Forth Road Bridge with the Pentlands now in sight, and only half an hour or so away from the new flat of which he was to take possession that morning. Although it was a Saturday, he would be able to collect the keys from McKay Norwell, where somebody would be coming in specially to hand them over to him. He would go straight round to the flat and open it up for the delivery of the few items of furniture he had ordered: a bed, some chairs, and a table. The cooker and fridge had been left in place by the seller, alongside the curtains and the lightbulbs. Of course it would have been extremely mean to take the lightbulbs, although Bruce had heard of its being done. In Aberdeen, he believed, it was standard practice, and there were even cases there of floorboards being removed too, and glass from the windows. That was hard to credit, but they were certainly canny in that part of the world and one never knew . . .

The traffic into town was light and in a very short time Bruce found himself in Rutland Square and parking in front of the McKay Norwell offices. The lawyers' assistant handed over the keys with a smile and Bruce drove off again. His new flat was in Albany Street, just off Broughton Street—a part of town that Bruce knew from his time, some years ago, in a flat in Scotland Street. It was a step up from Scotland Street, he thought—a bit more room and slightly closer to the really prestigious addresses of the Edinburgh New Town. After all, Albany Street became Abercromby Place and Abercromby Place in turn became Heriot Row. And Heriot Row was probably the very smartest address in town, smarter even than Moray Place.

This suited Bruce, who fancied the idea of moving in a slightly more elevated social set than was currently his lot. Bruce was not quite sure exactly who these people were, but he suspected they existed. They were people who went skiing regularly in France and Switzerland and did not stay in cheap hotels. They stayed in rented chalets, or, better still, owned them. Bruce could ski, and it was only a matter of time, he felt, before he received invitations to ski with people like that. And when they weren't skiing in France or

Switzerland, they went on weekend parties in East Lothian or Perthshire, where they had houses. In summer, they went to the British Virgin Islands, where they had yachts, and they also went to the Skye Ball, where they danced all sorts of complicated reels until the early hours and then came back to Edinburgh, quite danced-out. These people existed—Bruce was sure of it—and he felt that that was where he belonged. He did not belong to the world of his parents—to the world of Crieff and the Crieff Hydro and everything that went with that. Oh no, Bruce was a cut above all that.

He drove through Charlotte Square and turned into Queen Street. Halfway along Queen Street, he stopped at a traffic light, in a rather long queue of traffic. The top of his car was still down and a car drew up beside him, also held up by the red light. Bruce became conscious that he was being observed, and he looked over to the neighbouring vehicle. Two young women, a few years his junior, looked over at him and exchanged comments that Bruce did not hear.

Bruce smiled, and the young woman in the passenger seat smiled back.

"Hallo, gorgeous!"

This was followed by laughter from the driver.

Bruce smiled back. "Any time, *bella*!"

This led to delighted shrieks.

Bruce made up his mind quickly. Leaning over,

he shouted out his new address, adding, "Give me an hour to get everything ready."

The girls laughed, and the light changed. Bruce put his foot down on the accelerator and the sports car shot forward impressively, and in his rear view mirror he was able to make out the smiles on the faces of the two young women. You never know, he said to himself. You never know.

He reached Albany Street and parked the car. As he got out, a man walking along the pavement slowed down. Bruce noticed the look—half concealed, half overt. It was a look of frank admiration.

Bruce smiled, remembering the proximity of Albany Street to Broughton Street, Edinburgh's gay headquarters. He was used to admiring glances from all and he did not in the least mind their source. He gave equal visual pleasure to women and to men. Why not? It was a calling, a noble vocation, and he accepted it as his lot.

He caught a glimpse of his reflection in the highly polished bonnet of the car. Perfection, he thought. Adonis. Utter perfection.

# 15. Bruce Meets Mike Snazz at Watsonians Rugby Club

Bruce manhandled his suitcase up the common stair of his flat in Albany Street. It was heavier than he had imagined, and seemed to become weightier with every floor. It was not the clothes that weighed it down, rather it was the personal grooming products—the bottles of shampoo, of hair conditioner, hair gel, pre-shaving balm, post-shaving restorative, aftershave lotion, eyebrow conditioner, heavy-duty hand moisturiser, light facial moisturiser (for masculine skin), skin toner, eyeliner (manliner), neck and shoulder conditioner, leg and groin conditioner. These were essentials, of course, and had to be moved in with Bruce, along with his iMac, iPod, iPad, and iPhone, together with their appropriate i-chargers, i-supports, and i-keyboards. Once all that was in the flat, along with his Nespresso coffee machine and his Nespresso coffee-pod dispenser, Bruce felt fully at home and ready to begin this new phase of his life.

He looked at his watch. That brief encounter with the two girls in Queen Street had taken place about twenty minutes previously. That gave him forty minutes to have a necessary cup of coffee, unpack his clothes and products, and have a quick shower before the girls arrived—if they arrived. They had laughed when he had shouted out the invitation, but it had been, he thought, a laugh of delight rather than a dismissive laugh. And putting himself in their shoes, Bruce thought it highly likely that they would at least be tempted to come. After all, he said to himself, how often do you get somebody who looks like me inviting you to drop by?

The previous owners had thoughtfully left the electrical appliances switched on and ready for him. The fridge was running and spotlessly clean, the stove responded when he tried the switches, and, most important of all, the hot water system disgorged a good flow of piping hot water when Bruce turned on a tap; all of which buoyed Bruce as he walked about his new flat, savouring the sheer pleasure of ownership.

Of course, there is ownership and ownership. While Bruce was the person whose name was on the deeds that gave title to all three bedrooms, living room, kitchen, and bathroom, the reality of the situation was that this ownership was qualified by an 80 per cent standard security that entitled the bank, in the event of non-repayment of mortgage payments, to move in and deprive Bruce of his home. He understood that, as do all those who live with a mortgage, but he saw no reason to think that this eventuality would ever arise. His current salary was good enough—even if partnership prospects were distant—and Bruce had, as he put it, a "serious iron in the fire." Property development beckoned: it was a good time to get property cheaply, as long as one could lay one's money, and by the time the development was ready the market would have almost certainly picked up. And Edinburgh was ripe, Bruce thought, for some really imaginative schemes. It was full of old buildings, most of which had long since served their purpose. These could be replaced with imaginative, high-rent developments—luxury apartments, office suites, perhaps a spa or two, and, of course, any number of hotels and bars. Of course there were those fuddy-duddy conservationists—those gloomy killjoys who wanted nothing to change—but there were ways round them, thought Bruce. Look at what was going to be done behind Waverley Station. What vision! What understanding of what made this city important! That's what this city lacks, Bruce said to himself: commercial vision, a sense of economic possibility, a bit of can-do spirit.

And it was not just pipe dreams. Bruce had met a man in the rugby club who had big plans for doing something with Princes Street Gardens. They had been sharing a beer after watching a game between Watsonians and a Kelso club (66–3 to Kelso). ("There's no shame in losing to a Borders side," said Bruce. "It's in their blood down there.") The man, Mike Snazz, had asked Bruce what he did for a living and was interested to hear that he was a surveyor. When Bruce then went on to give an account of his various spells of employment with a number of Edinburgh property companies, Snazz's interest had increased.

"As it happens, I'm in property myself," he said. "I do a bit of development. It's a company called Forward Looking Developments."

Bruce had heard of them. "You did that rather nice shopping centre down in Leith, didn't you?"

"That was us," said Snazz proudly. "We were pretty pleased with that. And we've got this plan to build twenty-five storeys just behind Charlotte Square."

"Great," said Bruce.

Snazz looked at him. "We're expanding," he said. "Everybody else is contracting, but we're expanding. Stands to reason somebody can expand—it's like breathing: in, out, in, out. One person inflates while the other deflates."

"Absolutely," agreed Bruce. "You just need to seize the moment. Have the courage to get in there."

Snazz leaned forward. Nobody was listening, but he was always careful when it came to discussing sensitive plans.

"You know Princes Street?" he asked.

"Of course."

"You know those gardens?"

Everybody knew Princes Street Gardens. Everyone knew the Ross Pavilion; the floral clock; the lawns on which people sprawled during the long Scottish summer (July 18th to 25th) and gazed up at the Castle, that great towering edifice, the symbol of Scottish resilience and solidity.

"Yes, I know the gardens."

Snazz dropped his voice even lower. "We can get them," he whispered.

Now, standing beneath the steaming shower in his still somewhat uninhabited bathroom, Bruce remembered this conversation with a frisson of excitement. Most businessmen talk about the single golden opportunity that comes one's way in life—the single real chance—and this, Bruce thought, was his. He had arranged to meet Snazz again next week to talk about a job. "You'll be in on the ground floor," said Snazz. "But I expect one hundred and ten per cent commitment. You on for that?"

Bruce was.

He lathered himself with shower gel—sandalwood, ideal—and gazed at his reflection in the glass panel along the side of the shower. Drop-dead gorgeous, he thought. You fortunate, fortunate girls!

And was that the bell? Yes, it was. He reached for a towel and wrapped it round his waist. Perfect. Superb.

# 16. At Prestonfield House Hotel

"Well, Bertie," said Stuart Pollock as he stood with his son in the entrance hall of Prestonfield House Hotel. "Your first wedding."

Bertie politely corrected his father. "No, Daddy, not quite. My second wedding. We went to Miss Harmony's wedding to Matthew, remember? It was at that church at the end of King's Stables Road, the one under the Castle, and then we went to that tent in Moray Place Gardens where everybody had so much to eat and Tofu was sick all over Olive. Remember?"

Stuart remembered. "Of course, Bertie. I was forgetting that you were an old hand at weddings."

"This one's been a nice one," mused Bertie. "And I don't think that anybody minded when Ulysses shouted out like that."

Stuart smiled. "I don't think they did, Bertie. Poor little chap. It was just rather unfortunate timing—right after the minister had asked whether anybody knew of any reason why Angus and Domenica shouldn't get married."

"It was because of Mummy," said Bertie solemnly. "Have you noticed how Ulysses screams whenever she looks at him? Or he's sick? Have you noticed that, Daddy?"

"I don't think there can be a connection, Bertie,"

said Stuart, looking nervously over his shoulder. "Babies are rather inclined to cry—and to be sick. Even you were sick from time to time, Bertie, even you."

"I think I know what he shouted," said Bertie. "It had nothing to do with the wedding."

Stuart looked at his son with amusement. "And what do you think it was, Bertie?"

"I think he shouted Help! Either that or Hell!"

"I don't think so, Bertie! Why would Ulysses shout Help, do you think, or Hell for that matter?"

Bertie began to explain. "It's because of Mummy. I think that Ulysses feels . . ."

He was unable to finish his explanation. Irene, who had retreated into the ladies' room on arrival at the hotel, had now reappeared, carrying Ulysses, who had been changed. The infant, whose expression had been grim, now beamed broadly when he saw his brother and waved his hands about with wild enthusiasm.

"Much fresher," said Irene, handing Ulysses to Stuart. "Now then, do you think our hosts' generosity runs to a drink?"

"I'm sure it does," said Stuart. "I think I see a seating plan over there."

"My goodness," said Irene. "They're going to feed us too. The miracle of the five loaves and two fishes will no doubt be repeated."

They moved through the crowd of other guests in the direction of the large room where tables had been set out for the wedding meal. Waiters, young men in dark kilts, moved from guest to guest offering glasses of champagne, orange juice, or whisky. In one corner of the room, surrounded by a press of guests, stood Angus and Domenica; Irene and Stuart made their way over to the bride and groom, leaving Bertie sitting on a chair with Ulysses on his lap. Bertie was feeding Ulysses small pieces of a sausage roll that he had found on a plate, a treat that his young brother was receiving with undisguised pleasure.

Bertie looked about him. He recognised some of the guests, if not all. There was Big Lou, of course, whom he had spoken to on a number of occasions, and liked a great deal; and that friend of Domenica's, James Holloway, who came for tea with her from time to time, and was also a friend of Mr. Lordie's; and Mr. Linklater, who lived in Drummond Place, and was always kind to Cyril if he met him in the street; and his wife, who was kind too; and Mr. Backhouse who played the organ and people said knew more about old railways than anybody else in Scotland; and Mr. Dalyell, too, whom Bertie had met in the Valvona & Crolla coffee room quite a long time ago and who had told him the answer to the West Lothian Question when Bertie had gone up to his table and asked him politely. All these people were there, and they seemed to be enjoying themselves rather a lot judging by the level of noise, which was getting higher and higher. Grown-ups were like that, Bertie observed: they were always telling you to keep quiet and yet they themselves made such a terrible noise when they had the chance, as they now did.

Bertie suddenly became aware that Matthew and Elspeth were standing in front of him, looking down at Ulysses.

"And is that your new baby brother, Bertie?" asked Elspeth.

Bertie beamed at Elspeth, who had, until the unfortunate incident with Olive, been Bertie's teacher. They still loved her, and missed her, and he was pleased that she was here.

"Yes," he said. "He's called Ulysses. Do you want to have a shot with him, Miss Harmony?"

"Of course, Bertie," said Elspeth, picking up Ulysses. "What a lovely little baby he is, Bertie! He looks so sweet!"

"He looks just like Dr. Fairbairn," said Bertie.

Matthew and Elspeth exchanged a quick glance. "Oh well," said Elspeth.

"How are your babies, Miss Harmony?" asked Bertie. "Are they here?"

Elspeth laughed. "No, it would be a bit much to bring three small babies to a wedding, Bertie. We have a very helpful Danish girl who's staying with us. She helps with the boys and is looking after them for us right now."

Bertie nodded. He looked at Matthew. "Where's Cyril?"

"I tied him up outside," said Matthew. "I don't think they wanted dogs inside."

Bertie frowned. "Is he all by himself?"

"He'll be fine," said Matthew. "I left him a few dog biscuits and Angus said I should take him out some champagne in a bowl a little bit later on. He's fine, Bertie."

Bertie looked uncomfortable. "Do you think I could go and see him?" he asked. "Could I leave Ulysses with you? I think he likes you, Miss Harmony."

Elspeth nodded. "Of course you can, Bertie." She turned to Matthew. "He can go outside and play with Cyril, can't he?"

"I don't see why not," said Matthew. "I'll tell Stuart that's where he is."

Bertie did not wait. Turning on his heels, he darted out of the room and ran down the stairs to the main door of the hotel. Matthew had said that

Cyril was round the side of the house that faced Arthur's Seat, and it was in that direction that he now made his way. He stopped. Something was wrong. Something was terribly wrong. He felt it at first, and then he saw it.

## 17. Lament for a Bird

One of the great charms of Prestonfield House Hotel—apart from its rich history—is the open parkland in which the house sits. *Rus in urbe*—the countryside in the city—would be as appropriate a motto as any for the place chosen by Domenica for her wedding reception and enthusiastically agreed to by her new husband, Angus Lordie. For Domenica, the choice was an obvious one, as she claimed descent, although by a distant and convoluted route, from the Lady Cunyngham who lived in the house at the time the Jacobite army camped within sight during the 1745 uprising. Her son, Alexander, had met and befriended Charles Edward Stuart, the Bonnie Prince himself, in Italy, and she had been generous to the prince when he eventually arrived in Edinburgh from his Highland triumphs sorely in need of financial support, a change of clothing, and midge repellent.

This parkland is used to dramatic effect: at night, burning brands are placed at intervals along the drive that leads from the gates to the house itself, providing a sense of imminent occasion that electricity alone would never achieve. And in the grounds, with all the assurance (and quarrelsomeness) of their breed, peafowl strut and call their strident bugle calls. It was one of these, a distinguished and well-ornamented peacock, that was now seen by Bertie as he rounded the corner of the house on his way to comfort Cyril in durance vile.

Bertie stopped in his tracks as he took in the terrible scene. It was obvious to him that Cyril had slipped free of the leash that had secured him to a garden tap beside a flower bed. That leash now lay abandoned on the ground, with Cyril's collar at its end, while the dog himself stood, some yards away, the long tail of a decorative peacock firmly clasped in his jaws, the bird itself collapsed before him.

Bertie ran forward, crying out as he did so. Cyril, surprised by the shouts, half turned, glanced at Bertie, and then once again busied himself with worrying the elaborate display of feathers.

"Cyril!" screamed Bertie as he reached the scene of the crime. "Drop it, Cyril! Let go, you bad dog!"

Cyril, who was obedient to a fault, reluctantly opened his jaws and let go of the peacock's tail. Too late, though, for the poor bird. It took a couple of staggering steps, let out a strangled cry, a final wail, and then fell forward. It had been too much for the tiny peafowl heart; the bird was dead.

Bertie held the bird's neck in his hands. An eye looked up at him, but it was lifeless, unseeing. In it he noticed the sky—a tiny patch of blue, the last thing the poor bird had seen.

Bertie turned and stared at Cyril. "Look what you've done, Cyril," he said. "Just look."

Cyril stared back at Bertie. He was not sure why the bird was still. He had been having fun with it; it was the most natural thing in the world for a dog to seize a bird and shake it. What was wrong with that? That was what happened. And yet here was Bertie clearly cross with him, and Cyril felt stung by his displeasure. He lowered his snout and whined apologetically. Then, for good measure, he rolled over on his back and adopted a sub-missive position. He closed his eyes.

Bertie stood up, suddenly aware that he was no longer alone. One of the young men in kilts who had been directing the guests as they arrived was now beside him.

"Oh my goodness," said the young man. "Oh jings!"

Bertie looked up. "I don't think he really meant it," he said. "He was just pulling the tail."

The young man bent forward and kneeled beside the bird. "Oh no," he muttered. He stood up again. "Is this your dog?"

Bertie shook his head. "No. He belongs to Mr.

Lordie. He was tied up over there but he slipped out of his collar."

The young man glanced in the direction of the leash. "I don't think Mr. Thomson will be pleased," he said.

Bertie looked down at the ground. "Will they shoot Cyril?" he asked. "I hope they don't. He's a good dog, really. I promise you: he's a good dog."

The young man shook his head. "Don't worry, of course they won't shoot him . . . what's your name, by the way?"

Bertie gave his name and the young man introduced himself as Alastair.

"What shall we do?" asked Bertie.

Alastair stroked his chin. "I think we should bury it," he said. "Bury the evidence, so to speak. After all, Cyril was just doing what dogs do. And I'm sure you're right—he didn't mean it."

He suggested to Bertie that he stay where he was while he fetched a spade. Within a few minutes he was back, carrying a large green spade and a rectangular black box. Then he and Bertie lifted up the inert body of the peacock and carried it over towards a stand of large elms. At the foot of one of these trees, Alastair dug a hole, not a very deep one, as roots were in the way, but large enough to take the body of the peacock.

"All right, Bertie," he said. "We can say good-bye now to this poor bird."

They placed the bird in the grave and Alastair then shovelled the earth back over it. All that showed now was a small mound; the grave of a bird is not a large thing.

Alastair now opened the box and extracted a set of pipes. "Even a bird deserves a send-off, don't you think, Bertie?"

Bertie nodded gravely.

Alastair prepared the pipes and took the chanter into his mouth. " 'Flowers of the Forest,' " he mumbled. "It's a sad tune, Bertie, but it's the one for this sort of thing."

Bertie stood to attention, his small hands stiff by the sides of his trousers, trying to be as brave as he could be, trying not to cry. But as the notes of the lament rose from the pipes, his eyes filled with tears.

Alastair put the pipes away. He put a hand on Bertie's shoulder, and left it there for a few moments before the two of them walked back towards the house.

## 18. Cyril in Exile

Matthew's concern over the failure of Angus Lordie to make any honeymoon arrangements was understandable, but, as it happened, unnecessary. Not only had Domenica organised—and paid for—the reception, but she had also wisely assumed that Angus would have done nothing about bookings, or even decided where they might go. Acting on this well-founded suspicion, she had contacted a cousin who owned a house in Jamaica and had in the past offered to lend it to her. If husbands could make surprise arrangements for honeymoons without consulting their future wives, then future wives could certainly do the same, and, in this case, did.

The cousin was generous. "It's yours," she said. "A wedding present from me. It's near Port Antonio. It's a very creaky place, but it's on top of a hill and it gets wonderful breezes. You'll like it, I think, and there's plenty for Angus to paint."

Domenica had never been to the Caribbean, and was intrigued. A house on a hill outside Port Antonio sounded very romantic to her, even if she

91

understood that it was likely to be a far cry from the villas frequented by the likes of Noël Coward and Ian Fleming, who did not, she imagined, inhabit creaky houses. Port Antonio was close, she read, to a place called the Blue Lagoon, and that, in her mind, was the clinching attraction. If one was going to have a honeymoon, and if one was in the fortunate position of being able to afford to fly all the way to Kingston and back—as Domenica and Angus were—then what could be more attractive than the prospect of swimming in the Blue Lagoon and then sitting in the shade of one of the surrounding sea-grape trees—and any piece of water called the Blue Lagoon was bound to be ringed by sea-grape trees—reading, perhaps, *A High Wind in Jamaica* or *Wide Sargasso Sea*, or something of that sort, and counting the slowly moving hours until it was time for a sundowner of rum punch, followed by an evening meal of Jamaican Thirteen-Bean Soup and spicy stew with ackee, all to be rounded off with flambé bananas and a cup of pungent Blue Mountain coffee?

And that was the destination for which Angus and Domenica left the next morning, leaving behind them, for three weeks, their Edinburgh lives, their Edinburgh flats, and, of course, their Edinburgh dog. Cyril, of course, was now in the care of Bertie and his family, who had welcomed him with enthusiasm, except for Irene, who remained coldly hostile.

"You got us into this," she said to Stuart. "That wretched dog is nothing to do with me." She fixed her husband with a warning stare. "You're in charge of everything, remember—everything. Food, watering, walking—all the things, whatever they are, that dogs require."

Stuart nodded. "No problem," he assured her.

"And please don't say that to me," Irene snapped. "No problem! No probs! I can't stand those expressions."

"No p—" began Stuart, and then quickly changed to "pifficulty."

"Pifficulty?"

"I said difficulty. No difficulty."

Irene looked at him. "And I don't want him anywhere near the kitchen. Dogs are walking reservoirs of every sort of infection you'd care to name. Ulysses likes to crawl on the floor there and I don't want him picking up anything."

The creation of an exclusion zone—rigorously enforced—was one of the hardest things for Cyril to understand once he moved into his new home. In Angus's studio in Drummond Place, he had enjoyed the free run of every room, and had never been forbidden to sit on any chair or sleep on any bed. Not only that, but he had been trained by Angus to open the fridge door with his nose and to help himself, within reason, to anything he found inside—a piece of bacon, perhaps, a cold sausage, the occasional lamb chop. Angus minded none of this: Cyril, after all, lived there, just as he did, and he saw no reason to impose burdensome restrictions on a flatmate, even if that flatmate happened to be a dog.

How different it was in Scotland Street. Not only was the kitchen a no-go area, but so were all chairs, all beds, and, most difficult of all, every carpet in the house. That last interdiction meant that Cyril had to negotiate his way around the Pollock flat staying as close as possible to the walls. At one or two points, where the positioning of rugs was particularly tricky, he had to jump for several feet if he were not to infringe the rules about not walking on carpets. He was an intelligent dog, and quite prepared to abide by a few necessary rules (such as not sinking his teeth into ankles), but he found this new set of proscriptions utterly opaque and quite beyond canine mastery.

The effect of this regime soon caused Bertie more than a little distress. He had been so looking forward to having Cyril to stay with him and now he found that all the time he could have spent playing with the dog was occupied in enforcing his mother's rules in order to avoid direct conflict between the two of them.

"I'm sorry, Cyril," he whispered. "I didn't make the rules."

It was a protest that any child might voice: no child made the rules. The world, as seen by children, was one regulated by rules not of their making. Rules were like the weather or the facts of physical geography—they were just there, imposed by adults, to be complied with by children . . . and dogs. And no amount of explanation as to why rules existed made them easier to understand or to bear in their arbitrariness.

Cyril looked at Bertie with that curious melting, liquid look that dogs have. He liked Bertie, and he sensed that this new life of his—one beset with all these strange prohibitions—was not of his creation. But where was Angus? Why had he abandoned him? Was this how the rest of life would be?

## 19. Cyril in Disgrace

The conditions now imposed on Cyril by Irene soon began to tell on the dog's general demeanour. Whereas his normal mood had been one of jaunty cheerfulness, the dog gradually became withdrawn, almost to the point of being furtive. On Bertie's departure to school each morning, he would sit in a corner of his young guardian's room, gazing wistfully out of the window at a sky that represented the freedom that he once knew but that he now so clearly lacked. And had he been thinking about anything in particular, it must have been about how he would get through the next six hours or so before Bertie came back.

Bertie was aware that something was wrong, and understood.

"She doesn't really mean it," he tried to explain to the dog one afternoon. "She's just not used to dogs."

Cyril gazed at Bertie longingly. He knew that Bertie was fun on his own; the difficulty was that whenever they went out, Irene contrived to accompany them, and Ulysses too, whom Cyril was yet to fathom. He thought that Ulysses was probably a human, but was not quite sure yet; no doubt it would become clear in time. But the effect of these other presences was to destroy any chance of a good game—of a session of chasing sticks in Drummond Place Gardens, of going for a good long walk along Queen Street, or even of being allowed to run free of the leash in the old marshalling yards at the end of Scotland Street. All the things a dog might like were now firmly out of reach.

The sense of resentment brewing in Cyril eventually began to show itself. There was the occasional growl, sotto voce, of course, and usually directed against Irene. There were episodes of irrational barking and chasing of the tail. There was a general sneaking about the house, eyeing the doors, as might a prisoner test the bounds of his incarceration.

"There's something wrong with that dog," Irene observed to Stuart. "Very odd."

"He's just taking time to settle in," said Stuart. "I'm sure he'll be all right."

But Cyril was far from being all right, as was to become apparent a day or two later when Irene took Bertie and Ulysses to Valvona & Crolla to replenish supplies of pasta and sun-dried tomatoes. Initially she had forbidden Bertie to bring Cyril with them, as he would have to be tied up outside the shop and she therefore saw no point in his accompanying them. Bertie, however, had begged her to allow Cyril to come, and she had eventually, and somewhat uncharacteristically, weakened.

Now, striding up Broughton Street, a few yards ahead of his mother and Ulysses, Bertie felt considerable pride at being in charge of Cyril in public. Passersby, he imagined, would think that Cyril was his dog, and it was perfectly possible that they might then ignore the crushed-strawberry dungarees and the T-shirt with the name *Melanie Klein* printed across the front. That T-shirt had been an idea of his mother's, and a particularly bad idea at that; she had ordered it, on impulse, to mark the anniversary of the celebrated psychoanalyst's birth, along with a matching T-shirt for herself. Bertie had been covered with embarrassment, and had taken to telling friends who enquired what the words meant that Melanie Klein was, in fact, a fashion designer and that the T-shirt was the latest thing in designer-wear. To his surprise, this story had been readily accepted. Olive, for instance, had claimed to know all about her and to possess already a pair of Melanie Klein jeans as well as a T-shirt that was very similar, even if of a different colour. "Not that I wear them any more, Bertie," she had said. "They're very last year, you know. Ed Miliband's the new designer. I've seen him in the papers. That's what everybody's wearing."

"Ed Miliband's rubbish," said Tofu. "Nobody wears him any more, Olive. You're the one who's last year. You're the one who's really tragic."

When they reached Valvona & Crolla, Irene instructed Bertie to tie Cyril's lead to a lamp-post.

"He'll be fine," she said. "Dogs are used to waiting."

Cyril looked at her with venom. It was not his usual expression, but since moving to Scotland Street his brow had become quite furrowed with anger.

"We won't be long, Cyril boy," Bertie whispered as he secured the leash. "And I'll ask if we can buy you a treat."

Cyril licked Bertie generously, to show that if there was ill-feeling it was certainly not directed towards him.

The delicatessen was busy when they went in. Irene spent some time considering her choice of pasta and was diverted by a sampling of various olive oils that was being conducted at the end of one of the aisles. For his part, Bertie detached himself from his mother and Ulysses and went to gaze at the selection of panforte di Siena and amaretti di Saronno. He looked carefully at the prices on the small boxes of panforte and worked out how many weeks of pocket money would be required to purchase one of them. It was a depressing calculation. How wonderful, he thought, it must be to be a boy growing up in Siena, where presumably people had panforte for breakfast. And garlic sausage. And pizza. And where they didn't have psychotherapy and yoga but rode around, instead, on noisy little scooters and waved to their friends all the time . . .

Suddenly there was a cry and the sound of tins and jars crashing to the ground. Bertie looked up from the display of panforte to see one of the assistants emerge from behind the counter in pursuit of the scurrying form of Cyril.

"Salami!" shouted the assistant. "He's got a salami!"

His heart hammering within him—he understood immediately that Cyril had once again slipped his leash—Bertie set off in pursuit of the miscreant dog. And Cyril, hampered as too-successful thieves sometimes are by the sheer size of their booty, was soon apprehended on the pavement outside and a large Milanese salami prised from his jaws.

Bertie handed the stolen salami back to the assistant.

"He's a good dog," he pleaded. "He normally doesn't . . ."

The assistant was examining the tooth marks in the skin of the sausage.

"Nobody will notice," said Bertie. "Nobody will see the tooth marks. Honest."

## 20. Dog Therapy

"So," said Dr. St. Clair, leaning back in his chair. "So, tell me, how are things going with our young friend through there?"

Irene, who had left Bertie and Ulysses in the waiting room where Bertie was reading, and Ulysses was eating, a copy of *Scottish Field*, had a lot to tell him. "He's fine," she began. "But unfortunately we have a major issue in the household. I thought I might tell you about it, if I may."

Dr. St. Clair nodded. "That's why I'm here," he said. "Household issues are very much individual issues. The dynamic, you see . . ."

"Yes, yes," said Irene briskly. Sometimes she wondered whether Dr. St. Clair was aware of just how much she knew about psychodynamics. Hugo had certainly known, and appreciated her insights, but Hugo, for reasons she had never been able to fathom, had taken it upon himself to go off to Aberdeen. "The domestic issue concerns a dog."

"Ah," said Dr. St. Clair. "That is something on which I happen to have views. People often forget, you know, just how much pets enter into the equations of family psychopathology."

"Exactly," said Irene.

"It's actually an interest of mine," continued Dr. St. Clair.

Irene looked at him keenly. "Really?"

"Yes," continued the psychotherapist. "I took an interest in the subject when I was working on my PhD in Melbourne. We had somebody in the department at Monash who had quite a thriving practice in dog psychotherapy. He knew all the big names in the field—Mugford, and people like that—and he had written quite a lot himself; some very interesting papers. When I was there he was just about to publish a paper that became quite influential—'Barking as a Cry for Help.' It was something of a classic, actually."

"Fascinating," said Irene. "And did you do any work in the field yourself?"

Dr. St. Clair nodded. "A bit. I sat in on a number of his consultations. Fascinating stuff." He paused. "Have you read James Serpell's book?"

"Not yet," said Irene. "But . . ."

"It's very instructive," continued Dr. St. Clair. "*The Domestic Dog: its evolution, behaviour and interactions with people*. It's a collection of first-rate chapters on a whole range of subjects. It has some very good strategies for dealing with disturbed behaviour in dogs. And they can be very disturbed, you know."

Irene had become increasingly interested. She was now sitting on the edge of her seat, listening to Dr. St. Clair. "You mentioned sitting in on consultations," she said. "Would the dog be present?"

Dr. St. Clair shook his head. "Usually not in the first instance. We took a history from the dog's owners to begin with. That gave us a good enough idea of the problem. Of course, quite a number of them came to us feeling guilty. They blamed themselves, you see."

"For the dog's behaviour? They blamed themselves for that?"

"Yes," said Dr. St. Clair. "Some years back there was a rather well-known dog trainer called Barbara Woodhouse. She expressed the view that there was no such thing as a bad dog—it was really a case of a bad owner. So this encouraged people to think that if their dog behaved badly, then it was because they were at fault."

"And they aren't?"

"Sometimes they may be, but often the dog misbehaves because of some quite other factor. He may misinterpret what's going on, or may interpret things correctly but get confused in relation to what's expected of him. The aetiology of canine behavioural issues is pretty broad—and complex too."

"Fascinating," said Irene.

"Yes," agreed Dr. St. Clair. "It's truly extraordinary how our lives intertwine with these creatures."

Irene said that she was of the same view. But how odd it was, she went on to say, that dogs should have chosen to throw in their lot with us.

"Oh, but they didn't," said Dr. St. Clair. "It was the other way round. We chose dogs, or, rather, we chose their ancestors—wolves."

Irene waited for him to expand upon this.

"You see," Dr. St. Clair went on, "dogs are descended from wolves. About ten thousand years ago they didn't exist as a separate species at all—there were just wolves. And then some ancestor of ours got chummy with a wolf cub, tamed him, and discovered that he made quite a good hunting companion. Result? The domestic dog—after a number of years, of course."

Irene gazed at him with admiration. Dr. St. Clair was so much more interesting than Stuart, as had been Dr. Fairbairn. Did Stuart even know that dogs were descended from wolves? If he did, he had never told Irene about it and one might assume that he had no ideas on the subject at all. Yet here was a man—and a rather good-looking man too—who could talk with complete ease and confidence on the lupine ancestry of dogs.

"I remember back in Melbourne," he reminisced, "we had a very wolf-like dog brought in by its owner. The dog had a number of problems that were making life rather difficult for his owners and, frankly, he was on his last chance. That always ups the stakes a bit. One never has that with human clients—nobody's threatening to put them down if they don't respond to treatment!"

Irene laughed politely. "Of course not." She was trying to keep her mind on the subject under discussion, but she was finding it difficult. The conversation might have been about dogs, and their problems, but she could not help thinking about Dr. St. Clair, whom she was now envisaging standing on an Australian beach wearing one of those very fetching swimming costumes of the kind that Australian lifeguards wear with such distinction—a tiny slip of a costume that seemed to suit them so well and surely would suit Dr. St. Clair too. Not Stuart, though. Stuart needed to go to the gym and get rid of that waist of his, so that he could one day aspire to an Australian swimming costume.

She stopped herself. I am a married woman, she said to herself. I have a husband and two sons. I should not be thinking of Australian swimming costumes. But what else was there to think about?

"Would you be prepared to undertake some

therapy on this wretched dog we're looking after?" she asked.

"Delighted," said Dr. St. Clair. "Just make an appointment."


## 21. *Wonderful, Wonderful Copenhagen*

Matthew and Elspeth were able to enjoy the wedding reception at Prestonfield House without thought to their triplets thanks to their extraordinarily competent Danish au pair, Anna. This young woman, who had come to live with them shortly after the birth of the three boys, Tobermory, Rognvald, and Fergus, had provided a lifeline for both Matthew and Elspeth, in whom the symptoms of chronic sleep deprivation had been manifest soon after their return from the Royal Infirmary's maternity ward.

"I am come from Copenhagen to help you," Anna had said, using the powerful and poetic construction I am come. It would undoubtedly have sounded more prosaic had she said I have come; how much more portentous was I am come, a construction that one might expect to be used by Fra Angelico's annunciatory angel, perhaps, or some other great and welcome messenger—an Automobile Association mechanic, for instance. I am come implies purpose and solution all rolled into one: I am come to help you is as reassuring to one awaiting great news for mankind as it is to one awaiting rescue at the side of the road. And so it proved with Anna, who immediately and without a murmur took over the running of the triplets, allowing Elspeth to recover her strength after the birth, and Matthew to return to something resembling a normal sleep pattern.

Anna's presence also enabled Matthew and Elspeth to accept social invitations once more and even to go out for the occasional restaurant meal or trip to the Filmhouse on Lothian Road.

"It's such an amazing feeling," said Elspeth. "Going out and not worrying about the boys. I can hardly believe it."

"We have many things to be thankful for," said Matthew. "And one of those things is Anna. Thank God for the Danes! Do you think we're still producing girls like that in Scotland?"

Elspeth pondered this for a moment. "Probably not. We're having great difficulty finding nurses, aren't we? Wasn't there something about that in the paper recently?"

"There was," said Matthew. "There was some big report to the effect that nobody wanted actually to nurse anybody any more. Nurses are too busy filling out forms, they said."

"So nobody's prepared to give people bed-baths and mop their brows? Or even just hold their hands?"

"Apparently not. The report said that nurses

were far too grand for that now. They leave that to ward assistants—their menials."

"Are you sure?" asked Elspeth. "I've met some very sympathetic nurses."

Matthew shrugged. "It's what the report said." He paused. "But back to Anna: frankly, I just don't see many people like her wandering around. She's so competent. So warm. So helpful."

These qualities of helpfulness were to be tested to the utmost fairly shortly after Anna's arrival when Matthew and Elspeth moved out of their ground floor flat in Moray Place back to India Street. The move to Moray Place had been a mistake. Although the flat was spacious, and although there was a useful strip of lawn running down to the top of Lord Moray's Pleasure Gardens, both Matthew and Elspeth secretly pined for India Street, with its far more pleasing proportions. Fortunately Matthew was in a position to buy the flat back from Bruce, who had acquired it from him only a couple of months earlier. The price was high: Bruce had realised how desperate Matthew was for a deal to be made and had extracted every last penny his superior bargaining power could secure. Matthew bit his lip and paid. He hoped that Bruce would come unstuck one day, but did not imagine that this day of reckoning would come early, if at all. People like Bruce had a nasty habit of getting away with things.

The arrangements for the move were demanding. Everything so recently unpacked had to be packed up again and made ready for the removers. Arrangements had to be made to ensure that gas and electricity flowed without interruption during the handover and, at the same time, Moray Place had to be shown to prospective purchasers. Estate agents will tell you that there are various things you can do to prompt viewers of a property to form a favourable impression. The old trick of baking bread is well enough known, as is the expedient of placing large bunches of flowers in just the right places (in front of any known defects). It is also wise for the sellers to drop the occasional remark about how sad they are to be leaving, and if this leads to the direct challenge "Then why are you moving?" the seller must be ready to activate his cell phone in his pocket, making it necessary for him to excuse himself to take the call.

But what no estate agent or conveyancing solicitor will say is that the presence of triplets in the house will help the process. Anna, however, had risen to the challenge and not only had she kept the boys' nursery extremely tidy, but she had also taken them out for a walk in their triple buggy whenever a prospective purchaser was due to arrive.

"What tidy babies you have!" remarked one woman, as she popped her head round the nursery door.

"Yes, they are," said Elspeth.

"Just what one expects in Edinburgh," the woman continued.

"Indeed," said Elspeth. "And now, may I show you the dining room?"

But Anna also organised the packing of the flat's contents, wrapping the china and crockery in old copies of *The Scotsman* and placing them securely in the crates provided by the movers. And when it came to the day of the move, she took command of the situation as a skilled general will move men and equipment from camp to camp. Matthew and Elspeth found that they had very little to do as Anna, standing in the hall with a clipboard in her hand, ticked off items and gave orders to the four powerfully built mesomorphs from the removal company. These men complied with her every command, recognising authority when they saw it, even going so far as to mistake her for a German.

"How lucky we are with her," said Matthew, as he and Elspeth sat in their reclaimed kitchen in India Street.

Elspeth looked at him with affection. "Yes," she said. And she thought: does Anna have any flaws? Any?

## 22. The Reel of the 51st

Matthew and Elspeth did not return from the reception at Prestonfield House until shortly after midnight. Both were exhausted: Matthew from all the anxiety of being best man to Angus, and Elspeth from the sheer amount of dancing she had done at the evening ceilidh. In that respect she had been more energetic than Matthew, who would dance only the Gay Gordons, the Dashing White Sergeant and, if pressed, an eightsome reel. Elspeth, by contrast, had briefly served on the committee of the Royal Scottish Country Dance Society and had learned—and remembered— many of the more obscure dances. Speed the Plough (frequently danced in Inverness and the Laigh of Moray) held no terrors for her, nor did the Wind on Loch Fyne (a popular dance with those inclined to flatulence), or even the Reel of the 51st Division and the De'il among the Tailors. Matthew admired the intricacy of these dances, but did not have a good memory for the steps, and preferred to sit them out and watch Elspeth undertake them with confidence and style. He was so proud of her—as a wife, a mother of triplets, and now as a dancer. I am very blessed, he thought; I do not deserve the good fortune that has come my way, but at least I'm aware of it.

In the taxi on the way home, he said to Elspeth, "I loved watching you dance. You looked so . . . so . . ." He paused. "So beautiful."

She smiled at him, taking his hand briefly in hers and pressing it gently.

"Well, now they're married," she said. "For better or for worse. And I hope they'll be as happy as we are."

Matthew hoped so too. He was concerned, though, at how Angus would make the adjustment. "He's not very well organised," he said. "You know that we bought the ring on the way to the church? And his kilt had this muckle great hole in it."

Elspeth laughed. "They'll be all right. He wants mother—that's all."

He wondered what she meant.

"Most men do," Elspeth continued. "When they're boys, they have their mothers, and then when they're men, they have their wives."

Matthew frowned. Could that be true? "Are you sure?"

"Of course," said Elspeth lightly. "Angus wants somebody who will take care of him. He wants somebody who'll make him meals, run the household, and generally take care of him. Comfort—that's what we search for in life, you know. Comfort. It's as simple as that."

"And women?" asked Matthew. "What do they want?"

"Oh, that's simple enough," said Elspeth. "They want to do exactly what men want them to do. They want to nurture. They want to be maternal."

"Not everybody wants that," said Matthew.

Elspeth agreed. But most did, she said. "Look at the way that little girls play," she said. "Look at the way they fuss over their dolls—pretending to feed them, put them to bed, and so on. Look at poor wee Bertie. Look at the way he yearns to do boyish things—play with dogs and have a penknife. That dreadful mother of his does her level best to change all that—making him wear crushed-strawberry dungarees and so on—but he keeps reverting to type. No, Matthew: gender is our destiny, no matter how hard we may fight against it."

"I don't agree," said Matthew. "I don't see myself like that."

"None of us see ourselves the way we really are. None."

He looked at her in astonishment; had Elspeth had too much to drink, he wondered. Not that inebriation made any real difference; he had always thought that the maxim *in vino veritas* was entirely true. We revealed our true personalities when we took too much drink: nice people were nice drunks while nasty people were nasty drunks. It was as simple as that. So if Elspeth after a few glasses of wedding reception champagne expressed the view that human life was biologically determined, then that was what she really thought. And that, perhaps, should not be a surprise. At heart, Matthew thought, everybody was conservative, even if they identified themselves as being the opposite. Scotland, he was firmly convinced, was deeply conservative but did not realise it, or, if it did, chose to deny it.

But now the taxi had reached the top of India Street and was slowing down to disgorge them. He looked up; he could see that the lights in the flat were still burning. He pointed this out to Elspeth. "The boys must still be up. I hope that they haven't been running rings round Anna."

They went upstairs and let themselves in. From somewhere within the flat there drifted the sound of music; inane, repetitive lyrics: boom-pa, boom-pa, boom-pa, boom-pa-pa; la, la, la.

"Abba!" said Elspeth.

At first Matthew bit his tongue. He liked Abba, but realised that he could hardly say that openly—not in Edinburgh; not in India Street. Perhaps it was a bit like harbouring conservative thoughts: one couldn't express them openly in Scotland, but one could at least think them in the privacy of one's room.

"Ha!" he said disdainfully. "Abba!"

The door of the drawing room was ajar and Matthew pushed it open.

La-la boom, la-la boom, hoop, hoop, hoop! went the music. And there, sitting on the couch, was

Anna, and at her feet, his back against the couch, legs sprawled out, staring up at the ceiling, was a man of about Matthew's age, fair-haired and wearing a pair of narrow rectangular black spectacles.

"So, here you are," said Anna. "Was the wedding a good one?"

Elspeth began to reply, but the young man now rose to his feet and introduced himself.

"I am Bo," he said. "I am a friend of Anna's."

They shook hands.

"Did you dance at the wedding?" asked Anna. "I hear that Scottish weddings are very turbulent affairs."

Matthew smiled. "Turbulent? I think that might not be the best word. Spirited, perhaps."

"I danced quite a bit," said Elspeth. "Matthew isn't so keen. But I think he still enjoyed himself."

Bo now joined the conversation. "I am very

interested in filming some Scottish country dancing," he said. "They would be very keen to watch Scottish country dancing on Danish television."

"Bo makes films," said Anna. "And he'd like to talk to you."

## 23. A Danish Proposal

Tired though he was, Matthew decided that he was getting his second wind.

"Would you like a dram?" he asked Bo, and then, sensing the Dane's confusion, he explained, "A whisky?"

Bo's face lit up. "That is very generous of you," he said. "We are very fond of your whisky in Denmark. We drink it all day."

"I think he means every day," corrected Anna. "Every day, Bo, means one whisky a day; all day means many whiskies, all the time."

Bo nodded. "We are not like you Scottish people," he said politely. "You are drunk all the time."

Again Anna explained. "I don't think that's quite what Bo means," she said. "He means that sometimes people in Scotland drink at different hours from people in Denmark."

"That is correct," said Bo. "When I went through Glasgow Airport at eight in the morning there were people in the bar drinking whisky and beer at the same time. I was very depressed."

"Impressed," corrected Anna.

Bo shook his head. "No, depressed."

Matthew thought it time to fetch the bottle of twelve-year-old Laphroaig that he kept in the kitchen. Returning with two glasses—Anna and Elspeth having declined—he poured a generous amount of the highly peated whisky into each and handed one to Bo.

"This is a very earthy whisky," he explained. "It's very popular."

Bo raised the glass to his lips and took a sip. For a moment his face was impassive, but then he gasped.

"Like it?" asked Matthew.

Bo nodded. "It is very interesting. In Denmark we have something very like this that we apply to the chest for colds."

"Some people find it slightly medicinal," said Matthew. "I'm sure that one can equally well apply it to the chest for colds. But tell me, Bo, what sort of films do you make?"

They sat down at each end of the couch vacated by Anna, who had gone off with Elspeth to check on the triplets.

"I make a special sort of documentary," said Bo. "You call them fly-on-the-wall films, I think."

Matthew nodded. "Where you observe people going about their ordinary lives?"

"Exactly. My last film was made on a Danish offshore patrol frigate, the *Hvidbjørnen*. Have you heard of it?"

Matthew shook his head. "No, I can't say I have."

"I went to sea with the men for two weeks and showed them going about their work, writing letters home and doing all the things that sailors do on boats. Tying knots. Scrubbing the decks. Eating their dinner. One of the young sailors was very homesick and I filmed him crying in his berth. It was very sad."

"It can't be easy, being a sailor," said Matthew. "Being away from home for long periods."

"Yes," said Bo. "But the sailors were all very kind and polite. And after a while they forgot that I was there with my camera—they just accepted me. That's the key to filmmaking—or any sort of photography. The subjects must forget that you're there. They must be quite natural."

"I can understand that," said Matthew. "Isn't that what the physicists say about experiments: the presence of the observer changes the event?"

"That's true," said Bo. "People certainly change when you point a camera at them. Have you noticed how everybody in photographs today is smiling?"

Matthew had not thought about it, but saw what Bo meant. "Yes, they do smile, don't they? I suppose that's because they feel they have to.

And of course photographers tell them to smile."

"That is smiling under orders," said Bo. "But the interesting thing is this: in older photographs people never smiled. You saw their faces just as they were. They didn't feel that they had to smile."

"So it somehow just started?"

"Yes. Perhaps it came from America—I don't know. The Americans feel that you have to be happy, you see. Look at their politicians: they have to smile all the time or they won't get elected. Do these people smile in bed too, do you think? They lie there asleep, perhaps, with a smile on their face. We Scandinavians never felt that: we allowed people to be melancholy. Indeed, we expected people to feel that way. I suspect that people in Scotland are a bit like us in that respect. You're very happy to be miserable, I believe."

"Oh, I don't think so," said Matthew. "There are those who put that sort of image about, but I'm not sure that absolutely everybody in Scotland is miserable. Our politicians tend to be miserable, I suppose—and our writers, artists, and singers too. And our financiers and manufacturers and farmers and policemen and delivery men and nurses and journalists and teachers and lawyers and bus-drivers and people you see in the street—they're all pretty miserable, but the rest certainly aren't. Or not all the time anyway."

Bo looked thoughtful. "I shall be very interested

to find out if that's true," he said. "Which brings me to the question I have for you."

Matthew looked at him expectantly. "Yes?"

"I would like to make a documentary film about your daily life," he said. "It would be one month in the life of a typical Scottish family. I would observe, but you would soon get used to me and my camera. I would be like that fly on the wall—you never notice him, you never worry about him."

Matthew frowned. "A typical Scottish family? An art gallery director with triplets, living in . . . living in a Georgian flat in Edinburgh? I'm not sure whether that's exactly typical."

Bo seemed ready for this objection. "I know what you mean," he said. "But that's nothing to worry about. I meant typical in the sense of typical documentary material. Actual ordinary people—people leading average lives, people without triplets and art galleries and Georgian flats—are really pretty much unfilmable. You, by contrast, will look very good on film, as will your wife, and your three sons. It will be very popular on Danish television—there is no doubt about that. It will give us Danes a window into Scottish life." He paused. "And will there be a chance that you will do some of this Scottish country dancing? Perhaps you and your neighbours could dance out on the street, on those pretty cobblestones. That would be very nice for people in Denmark to see, I think."

# 24. The Man from Mains of Mochle

Big Lou had had two invitations for that wedding Saturday—one, which took clear precedence, was to the wedding itself, at which she was to act as bridesmaid; the other was to go to the Farmers' Market, held weekly immediately below the towering rampart of the Castle. That invitation came from Alex Macphail, who farmed a farm called Mains of Mochle, just outside Arbroath, and who had now obtained a stall at the Edinburgh Farmers' Market.

Big Lou had known Alex forever, or so it seemed. They had been in primary school together, although she found it impossible to remember him at that age. In her class of twenty-two children, there had been slightly more boys than girls, and all the former seemed to merge into one vague, composite boy undistinguished for anything but an ability to disrupt the class, annoy the girls during interval play, and copy from others during tests. It was only later, when they started at high school, that Big Lou became aware of the quiet, rather soft-spoken boy who, like her, came from a farm. There was no question of romance, but an undemanding, casual friendship developed between the two of them. Like many school friendships, the separation that came with leaving school allowed for a fading of what bond there was. And that, of course, can be a blessing. There is nothing but disappointment in store for those who seek, after many years—sometimes almost a whole lifetime—to rekindle a friendship of early childhood. The one we admired so much for his litheness, for a smile, for amusing opinions and sense of fun, has become thick-set, dour, and dull. Time—and gravity—have done their work and we wonder how we could possibly have been so admiring, so taken with the person we now see before us. Of course we ourselves have changed— we, too, are thick-set, dour, and dull—but do not see ourselves as such. Eighteen or nineteen is the age at which most of us are permanently stuck— at least in our own eyes. And why the world should not see us thus is a mystery.

Big Lou and Alex met again at Crieff Hydro, where Big Lou had gone for the weekend with her then friend Darren, an Elvis impersonator. The occasion had been a weekend Elvis imperson- ators' conference—a trying event, as it turned out, for Big Lou. Darren had more or less ignored her in favour of Elvis discussions and she had felt hurt and rebuffed. By sheer chance she had found herself sitting next to Alex, who was not there for Elvis-related reasons, but had come to the Hydro to spend a quiet weekend by himself. He was a widower, his wife having died a little more than a year ago, and his pleasure at bumping into Big

Lou had been manifest. They had talked about all sorts of things—Mains of Mochle, rare-breed pigs, the agricultural affairs of the east of Scotland, and so on—all subjects which Big Lou continued to find interesting, no matter how long she spent in the city. His company was the catalyst that prompted her to detach herself from the rude and ungracious Darren, and she and Alex had subsequently enjoyed dinner together in the Hydro dining room. Since then there had been telephone calls, a visit by Big Lou to the Mains of Mochle, and a trip to Glasgow to listen to a Jethro Tull concert. "Those boys are gey musical," was Alex's verdict on that.

Big Lou was not quite sure where she stood with Alex. If there was going to be a romance, then she wondered why it had not already started. The answer, she decided, was that he was not ready: Alex had married at a young age—he and his wife were both twenty-two—and they had had twenty years of marriage before her death. A year was too short a time for the grief that followed such a long time together. She had read somewhere that the typical period needed to recover from such a loss was eighteen months. If that were true, then Alex would not be quite ready to embark on another relationship. He would need time—and she was perfectly prepared to give him that. After all, there had been nobody else as remotely suitable as Alex. Big Lou had been unlucky in her affairs—

the seedy chef, the unrepentant Jacobite, the secret Elvis impersonator—it was not an impressive list. Alex Macphail was a different matter altogether, and if she had to wait until he was ready, then wait she would.

"I'm going to be at the Farmers' Market every Saturday from now on, Lou," Alex had said. "You could drop in maybe."

"I'll try," she said. "But it's difficult, Alex. I have to get somebody to look after the coffee bar. And Saturday can be an awfy busy day."

"Please try, Lou," he said. "You could keep me company."

There was something pleading in his invitation, and she decided to ask Pat Macgregor whether she would mind relieving her in the coffee bar for a few hours on the Saturday after the wedding. Pat, who was a student, worked part-time in Matthew's gallery and regularly called in for coffee at Big Lou's. In spite of their difference in age—Big Lou was at least twenty years older than Pat—they got on well; indeed they had become friends.

Pat agreed to cover for as long as was needed, and so Big Lou found herself walking along Queen Street towards the West End, ready to spend a couple of hours with Alex in his stall at the Farmers' Market. When she arrived, he greeted her warmly, planting a kiss on her cheek. He had never kissed her before, and this chaste peck made her blush. When was I last kissed—by anyone? she asked herself. With Darren she had not got that far—and his greasy hair would have made it an unpleasant experience; the Jacobite was too preoccupied with history to kiss; the chef too crude to bother with such preliminaries. So this kiss, delivered in full view of the shopping throng and under Alex's sign that read *Mains of Mochle Country Bacon*, was as romantic an encounter as Big Lou had enjoyed for how many years . . . ten? Twelve? One kiss every dozen years. That was not very much, but there were people, Big Lou reminded herself, who had not even that. She looked at the bacon. Kisses and bacon. "Bacon and Kisses." It could be the title of a song, or of a reel perhaps, to be danced at a ceilidh. She closed her eyes. She could hear the music.

## 25. The Cuddliness of Thistles

Big Lou returned to the coffee bar an hour later. She had not spent much time with Alex, as the stall had been busy and he had not had the time to talk to her very much. He had promised, though, to come down to see her in Dundas Street once he closed up at lunch time. He would bring her some bacon, he said, so that she could make bacon rolls for any customers who might like to try them. "They'd love them, Lou," he said. "This saddleback bacon isn't like the ordinary stuff you get in the supermarkets. That's full of brine, and it comes out as white scum. You seen that, Lou? Horrible white scum."

She had returned to the coffee bar in a state of near-elation. Pat was dealing with a customer when Big Lou came down the steps—those very steps on which Christopher Murray Grieve, more widely known as the poet Hugh MacDiarmid, had stumbled all those years ago, when Big Lou's coffee bar had been a bookshop. And they were the same steps too down which the late Lard O'Connor (RIP) had fallen and expired not all that long ago on a visit to the capital from his native Glasgow. There were doubtless other steps in Edinburgh that had claimed more than one victim, but none perhaps as distinguished as these two;

distinguished for very different reasons, of course: MacDiarmid for his fierce championing of the Scots language and his rambling verse—sublime at times, and on other occasions contrived and also unforgiving; Lard O'Connor for his egregious espousal of a lethal diet and his embodiment of the bourgeois nightmare. Both came from a Scotland that was uncompromising; from a Scotland that could be perverse, awkward, and as cuddly as a thistle. Big Lou came from an entirely different place—from a hinterland of neat farms and hard-working people—but she understood what MacDiarmid meant, even if she had little time for Lard. She had read the poet, as she had read her way through shelf after shelf of the books she had bought when she had acquired the shop premises, and she had glimpsed, and understood, his vision.

Down those distinguished steps of stone worn by generations of feet came Big Lou, and she pushed open the door of her coffee bar. Pat looked up and smiled a greeting. She was pleased that Big Lou had returned to relieve her, although she had been enjoying serving coffee and would have been happy to go on had she not had shopping to do.

The customer's coffee cup pushed across the spotless counter, Pat turned to Big Lou. "Everything obviously went very well," she said. "And you look pleased."

Big Lou joined Pat behind the counter. "Aye, it

wasn't bad. Lots of people there." She poured herself a glass of water. "But he's keeping some bacon for me. He's bringing it down later."

Pat studied her friend. Her instinct for this sort of thing was usually reliable. Something significant had happened.

"This chap, Alex," she said. "Tell me about him."

"He's a friend," said Big Lou.

"I gathered that." She paused. "A close friend?"

Big Lou looked at her. "Close enough. I knew him when he was a wee boy. We were at school together—all the way through."

"And then?"

"He got married. She died. He's a farmer."

One needs few words, Pat thought, to sum up a life. We all grew up. We worked. We lost the people we hoped not to lose.

There was a silence. Then Big Lou said, "Did you have friends you knew as a child and then didn't see for a long time?"

Pat nodded. "Most people have friends like that."

"And did it work? Did the friendship start up again?"

Pat thought for a moment. "Sometimes." She looked at Lou. "Lou, I hope that this one works for you. I really do."

Lou stared down at the floor. "It would be nice."

"I know that you're happy by yourself," said Pat,

"but there are times when it's just nice to have . . ."

"To have a fella? Aye, it is." She reached out for the cloth with which she habitually polished the counter and set to the task, with wide, circular sweeps. "By the way," she went on. "Talking of fellas, I saw somebody I know when I was coming back here a few minutes ago. Walking up towards Queen Street. That fella."

"Which one? Matthew?"

"No, not him. Matthew's not a fella, if you see what I mean. Matthew's just Matthew. No, that good-looking fella. You used to know him. The one with the hair and the face."

"With the face?"

"With that braw face. I cannae mind his name . . . Bruce. Aye, that was it."

Pat stood quite still. "Here?" she asked.

"Yes," said Big Lou. "He said hallo and I asked him what he was up to. He said that he's just moved in round the corner. Albany Street. He asked after you."

Pat's heart skipped a beat. "Me? Bruce asked after me?"

"Yes. He said he hoped to see you some day."

Pat made a conscious effort to control herself. She shrugged insouciantly. "Oh, him. I haven't seen him for ages. I thought he'd gone away."

"I wouldn't get involved with him, if I were you," said Big Lou. "He made you unhappy before, didn't he?"

Pat took a few moments to answer. Then at last she said, "He did. But I got over him."

"Did you?"

"I hope so."

Big Lou looked doubtful. "Boys like that are very dangerous," she said.

"I know that," said Pat. She spoke too forcefully, and the determination in her answer made it apparent that even as she knew of the danger that Bruce presented, she was equally aware of her weakness. If she had got over him as she claimed, then she would not be closing her eyes now and picturing Bruce standing before her, the top two buttons of his shirt undone, his jeans low on his hips, his hands tucked into his pockets, and smiling at her, and smiling. She knew that she would have to see him again. Just to look at. She had to.

Pat opened her eyes and looked directly at Big Lou. There was perfect understanding between them. Both knew then exactly what it was to be a woman, and how hard it was. They might also have understood—had they thought about it—just how hard it sometimes is to be a man.

# 26. On Psychotherapy and Freedom

Cyril's first session with Dr. St. Clair was not a conspicuous success. It took place a couple of days after that initial discussion between Irene and the psychotherapist in which the possibility of treatment for Cyril's behavioural problems had been raised. Irene had immediately been attracted by the idea, which might not only bring the dog under control and stop his irritating creeping around the flat, but would also give her the opportunity to spend more time talking to the intelligent and, when viewed in a certain light and from a particular angle, rather handsome young Australian.

From Dr. St. Clair's point of view, taking on Cyril as a patient would allow him to practise some of the skills he had been taught on that early attachment to an animal behaviour specialist in Melbourne. Irene herself was another matter; he was not quite sure what to make of her. At one time he had thought that she was no more than an over-anxious middle-class mother, the sort that any person—any teacher as much as any psychotherapist or psychologist dealing with children—was very familiar with: the mothers who were firmly convinced their child was uniquely talented or simply uniquely interesting.

There had been plenty of those in Melbourne and he had discovered that they were equally prevalent in Edinburgh, where Irene, it seemed, was perhaps their standard-bearer. But this initial, somewhat dismissive view did not last, and gradually he had come to think that here was an intensely interesting woman—a woman who was thoroughly familiar with the works of Melanie Klein and who, moreover, had a way of listening to him that was both flattering and reassuring. So it had not been long before he found himself looking forward to her visits and not worrying if she tended to take up an increasingly large part of the hour nominally allocated to Bertie for his therapy.

For Bertie, of course, it was quite otherwise. He had been appalled when his mother had revealed to him, on their return to the flat, that the subject of therapy for Cyril had been raised and that she had decided it would be a good thing.

"But Cyril's a dog, Mummy," he had protested. "Dogs don't get psychotherapy."

Irene had smiled. "But there we're wrong, Bertie! We think dogs don't need therapy because most dogs don't get it, but that doesn't mean to say that dogs might not benefit from it, does it, Bertie? No, it does not. Some dogs are fortunate enough to get it, and I'm sure it makes them much better dogs. It's really just a form of dog training—that's all."

Bertie stared at the ground. He felt responsible for Cyril. Mr. Lordie had said to him, "I think you'll look after Cyril very well, Bertie. And I also think that Cyril will really enjoy staying with you." Those, he now remembered, had been his exact words, and Bertie interpreted them as a conferring on him of an obligation of trust. And what had happened? Cyril's life had been made a misery by all those ridiculous rules about what he could do in the flat and what he could not do. Now, to add insult to injury, the poor dog was going to have to go up to Dr. St. Clair's consulting rooms and . . . and what? Bertie tried to imagine Cyril sitting on the patient's chair and being asked endless questions by Dr. St. Clair. And Cyril would not understand any of it. As far as Bertie knew, the only words Cyril understood were sit, biscuits, walk, and, possibly, cat. You wouldn't get far with free association with that vocabulary, thought Bertie. Dr. St. Clair would say sit and Cyril would bark. Then Dr. St. Clair would say biscuits and again Cyril would bark. Bertie did not see the point of that exchange.

He looked at his mother; he had had an idea. "Wouldn't it be better for Ulysses to get therapy, Mummy? Wouldn't that be better?" He felt slightly disloyal in offering his brother as a substitute victim, but he had always thought that Ulysses had absolutely no idea of what was going on and it would make no difference. In fact,

Ulysses would probably be grateful to have Dr. St. Clair looking at him rather than his mother; it would give him a bit of a rest from bringing up his food, which is what he seemed to do whenever Irene tried to pick him up or addressed any remarks to him.

"Ulysses doesn't need therapy at present," said Irene briskly. "He's too young. Everything in good time, Bertie."

Bertie had realised that it was hopeless; once his mother decided on something, then it was almost always impossible to budge her. So, with great reluctance and with a heavy heart, he had accompanied Cyril to Dr. St. Clair's rooms and had sat staring miserably out of the window while Irene recited a litany of Cyril's problems.

"He's only with us for a short time," she said. "But it really is impossible. He barks far too much and sneaks around the flat in a most disconcerting fashion. He also comes creeping up to me in the kitchen and stares at my ankles for some inexplicable reason."

"I see," said Dr. St. Clair, looking with interest at Cyril, who was seated beside his desk, grinning. "He seems a well-enough behaved fellow right now." He paused, peering intently at Cyril. "And what's that he's got in his mouth?"

"Believe it or not," said Irene, "it's a gold tooth. It's ridiculous, but that dog's got a gold tooth. Heaven knows how he got it."

"Mr. Lordie told me," interjected Bertie. "He said that a friend of his who's a dentist put it in Cyril's mouth in the Scottish Arts Club one night. He said that the original tooth had worn away and Cyril was very pleased when he got this new tooth."

"Interesting," said Dr. St. Clair. "It was probably a very traumatic experience for him. That may have some role in the aetiology of his disturbed behaviour."

Bertie sat back in his chair. He wondered if, by closing his eyes hard enough, he could will himself to be somewhere else altogether—somewhere where there were no psychotherapists, no mother, no yoga lessons, no Tofu, no Olive—just a wide beach of golden sand along which a dog and a boy might run, with the wind all about them, and the sun high in the sky above their heads. Or even in Glasgow.

## 27. The Benefits of Self-Government

It seemed that one session of psychotherapy was quite enough for Cyril. Although he was, of course, unaware of what was going on, he could sense, as dogs often can, that what was happening in the room pertained to him. He felt acutely uncomfortable as he sat in Dr. St. Clair's consulting room while Irene talked, occasionally looking down and pointing her long finger at him to emphasise some point. And when that happened, and the finger was pointed, Cyril felt an overwhelming urge to bite it. It would be so easy simply to lunge forward and snap at it when it was so close to his snout, wagging disapprovingly. Dogs understand a wagged finger—somewhere deep in the canine mind that gesture spells out hostility and blame. He had done something wrong, then, but what? He had looked at her ankles, it was true, and he would have loved to sink his teeth into them, but he had not, understanding full well what the consequences would be. In that, Cyril was Pavlovian through and through. Biting ankles meant that he would be beaten with a rolled-up copy of *The Scotsman*, the punishment that Angus had traditionally meted out to him for any truly egregious piece of wrongdoing—eating a visitor's hat, for instance, as had happened one day when his master had been visited by Sir Angus Grossart, who had been seeking his opinion on a painting he was proposing to acquire for the entrance hall of his bank. This painting—a scene of people waiting by the harbour at St. Andrews for the fishing fleet to return—had been discussed at length by the two men over a cup of coffee in Angus Lordie's studio, while all the time Cyril had been chewing his way through the visitor's hat in the hall.

When Sir Angus emerged to take his leave, it was to find only a small fragment of his hat uneaten, and Cyril looking at the same time deeply satisfied and guilty, waiting for the punishment that he knew must follow. Angus Lordie's apologies had been profuse, and the visitor had been gracious. "I believe I have another hat," he said. "And what your dog has just done relieves me of the responsibility of ever having to do in metaphor what he has just done in reality!"

Now, having resisted the temptation of Irene's ankles, Cyril was not sure why he seemed to be in disgrace. He had tried smiling at Dr. St. Clair but it seemed to have little effect, and now he looked up at him mournfully. In return, the psychotherapist stared down on him, once or twice even leaning forward slightly to peer more closely and more intently at the embarrassed dog. Confused, Cyril looked over his shoulder towards Bertie, but there was no comfort there. And things did not improve. As they returned to Scotland Street, Bertie was silent: he knew what

Cyril was feeling and felt a bit that way himself.

"It's not working, Cyril," Bertie whispered to the dog once they were back in the flat. "You can't stay here. Your life will be ruined."

Cyril looked up at Bertie. He licked his hand gently, as one friend will touch, will comfort another.

"So I'm going to take you somewhere else," Bertie went on. "I'm going to ask if I can take you to the gardens, but I'm really going to take you to a new home."

Bertie obtained permission to take Cyril for a walk. As a truthful child, Bertie did not like to deceive his mother, but he felt that the dog's position was now so desperate that minor deception was justified. He was indeed taking Cyril for a walk—it was just that the walk was going to be rather longer than his mother might imagine.

"Be careful, Bertie," said Irene. "Just to the gardens, no further, remember."

Bertie said nothing. If you remained silent when your mother said something to you—if you gave no indication of consent, or even of hearing her— then it would not be wrong to do the opposite of what she told you to do. Tofu, he knew, took a similar view, perhaps even a more liberating one. Tofu said that you could say what you liked, no matter how untruthful it was, as long as you crossed your fingers when you said it. He had also explained that there was an alternative available if you did not believe in the permissive power of crossed fingers. This was to add, under one's breath, the words "or not." That meant that what you said was not a lie and that anybody who took exception to it had only himself to blame. Tofu had demonstrated this one day by telling Olive in the playground that she was wanted in the office because a message had been received that her house had burned down. Olive, who did not hear the muttered "or not" that followed this alarming news, had run tearfully into the school office, accompanied by an anxious Pansy, to emerge shortly afterwards to confront Tofu. He simply gloated. "You should listen more carefully," he said. Bertie, of course, had been appalled. There was so much wrong with the world, he thought. There was Tofu, and there was Olive, and there was his mother . . . and now there was this awful conspiracy to inflict psychotherapy on poor Cyril, who had never done any harm to anybody—or very little.

He made his way out of the flat and into the street. Cyril, who would normally be cheered at the prospect of a walk, seemed dejected and listless, barely keeping up with Bertie as they made their way up Scotland Street.

"Cheer up, Cyril," said Bertie. "You're not going back in there, I promise you."

Bertie, who received 37 pence pocket money a week, had saved enough for his bus fare. In

Dundas Street he waited patiently until a No. 23 bus lumbered along the road towards them. A worrying thought occurred to him: what if Cyril would be required to have a ticket? Would he have enough money for that?

He had a plan for that contingency: as the bus neared the stop, Bertie all but closed his eyes and stepped uncertainly through the door, his arms stretched out before him, as if feeling his way into the bus. If there were to be any problem, then he would claim that Cyril was a guide dog, and that, he knew, would entitle him to travel free.

The driver looked at him in astonishment. "You on drugs, son?"

Bertie opened his eyes wide, and shook his head.

"Well, you and your dug hurry up, I've no got all day! One child fare? Single?"

"And my dog?" asked Bertie in a small voice.

"Dugs go free," said the driver. "Thanks to Mr. Salmond. Benefits of having oor ain government."


## 28. At the Home of Ranald Braveheart Macpherson

Travelling by himself on the 23 bus, or almost by himself—Cyril lay at his feet, under the seat—Bertie experienced the full thrill of doing something significant all on his own. He was no stranger to the 23 bus, that finest of Edinburgh buses that connects the low-lying swamps of Canonmills with the breezy altitudes of Morningside and the Braids, but he had never been on it alone, and in pursuit of a journey that he himself had planned. So might a student microlight pilot at East Fortune Airfield feel when his instructor, that reassuring presence who has been with him on every training flight, suddenly says to him: "You're ready to go up by yourself"—and allows him to climb into the cockpit alone and taxi out and head down the runway, throttle open, and then, oh heavens, nudge the nose of the aircraft up and see the ground fall away beneath him, parted from the earth without the umbilical presence of an instructor who can take the controls and deal with an emergency; and the Firth of Forth is suddenly there and the North Sea stretching out like a wide blue field and Cockenzie Power Station and the hills and . . .

Such experience of freedom can be heady; can intoxicate; can set the heart thumping as fear and exhilaration fight with one another; and so it did with Bertie. Suddenly the normal sights of Edinburgh streets seemed at the same time to be exciting and frightening. And it appeared, too, that time itself had speeded up, and within what seemed to Bertie to be no more than a couple of minutes the bus was approaching Holy Corner and he would have to alight. Rising to his feet, he pressed the button that would signal the driver to stop: for him an act of immense significance—he, Bertie, was sounding a bell that would make this entire bus, with all its souls aboard, actually stop!

Cyril seemed to be in better spirits now. Perhaps he sensed that something was changing; perhaps he appreciated the distance that had been put between him and the restrictions of his temporary lodging in Scotland Street. Perhaps, as was most probably the case, he had merely forgotten what had happened before; dogs are not ones to linger on the past if there is the prospect of investigating new smells and marking out new territory. Now, as they made their way up towards the Church Hill theatre, Cyril gave every appearance of enjoying himself, wagging his tail enthusiastically, and even managing a small bark to register his more elevated state of mind.

Their destination was a house a short distance from the theatre itself. This house, which lay on a side street off the busy thoroughfare of Morningside Road, was the house of Ranald Braveheart Macpherson, Bertie's spindly-legged friend from cub scouts. Ranald, with whom Bertie had shared the adventure of the abortive trip to Glasgow—cut short when the two boys got off the train at Haymarket Station in the mistaken belief that they had reached Glasgow Queen Street—was perhaps Bertie's greatest friend, and it was natural that he should turn to him now. Ranald had always been so obliging, offering to show Bertie the money that his father kept in his safe and even offering to share some of it with Bertie if he so desired. And Ranald's parents seemed equally agreeable, having taken Bertie for a Christmas train ride and then to the German Market on the Mound. Ranald, it seemed to Bertie, led very much the life that he, Bertie, would love to lead. He had a rope hanging from the bough of a tree in the garden; he was given chocolate pudding for his dinner—not that this seemed to make much impression on his thin legs—and the adults in his house seemed to smile and laugh a great deal, rather than to preoccupy themselves with Melanie Klein and yoga and all the rest. It was, Bertie thought, just the sort of house in which Cyril—or any other refugee for that matter—might expect to be received with warmth.

Ranald's mother answered the door. "Well, well, Bertie, this is a very nice surprise. And who have we here with you? What an interesting-looking dog!"

Bertie introduced Cyril and then asked if Ranald was at home.

"Ranald is always at home," said his mother. "And I imagine that he'll be at home for the next twelve years or so."

Bertie smiled weakly at the joke. It was not really a joke as far as he was concerned: he, too, was destined to be at home for the next twelve years until that magical date—the day of his eighteenth birthday when the law of Scotland dictated that one could move to Glasgow if one wanted to and even if one's mother had other plans.

He went inside. Ranald Braveheart Macpherson, having heard the door being answered, now appeared from within the house to greet Bertie warmly and express his delight at seeing him with a dog.

"Where did you find him?" Ranald asked. "He's a really good dog, Bertie!"

Bertie looked over his shoulder. Ranald's mother was still standing directly behind him, and he was not sure he could reveal his plan in her presence.

"Boys' business, I see," said Mrs. Macpherson. "Why not go off to your room, Ranald?"

Bertie followed his friend with relief. "I've not got anything against your mother, Ranald," he started to explain. "It's just that . . ."

"Don't worry, Bertie," said Ranald. "She's not my real mother, you know. I told you that I was adopted, didn't I? So I sometimes call her my carer. She doesn't mind. She says it makes her laugh."

"She's very kind," said Bertie.

"No, she's not bad," said Ranald. "And my dad—that's the carer's husband—he's very rich. I told you about all his money, didn't I, Bertie?"

Bertie nodded. "I want to ask you a favour, Ranald," he said. "A big favour."

"Fire away," said Ranald.

"I want you to look after Cyril for me," said Bertie.

"Fine," said Ranald Braveheart Macpherson. "No problem." He paused. "Anything else, Bertie?"

## 29. Malt Does More

Matthew lay awake trying to identify the line that had come to him in that curious state halfway between sleep and wakefulness. It was a zone in which an idea, a quotation, or even a vision of events can become fixed in the mind, nagging at one's consciousness until sleep is dispelled and the mind realises that what one was thinking about was very little, or somewhat banal, or complete nonsense. In this case it was poetry; a couplet: "Malt does more than Milton can / to justify God's ways to man." It came to him at the end of a dream when somebody, familiar and yet unfamiliar—Matthew's father, perhaps, or his English teacher from the Academy, Dr. Marsh— was standing before him advising, Malt does more, Matthew; malt does more . . . And then, emerging through layers of consciousness, the quotation was completed and he found himself awake and muttering it softly—not loudly enough to disturb Elspeth in bed beside him and in a totally different stage in her cycle of sleep. She had been up to deal with the triplets: to settle Rognvald, change Tobermory, and comfort Fergus, who was niggling over something—some small issue of a blanket or a sheet. She had then returned to bed, still half asleep, in that virtually somnambulistic way that parents know very well and parents of triplets know three times better than most.

Of course, thought Matthew, as he focused on the ceiling, mostly dark, but lit here and there with small points of light from India Street outside; of course it was Housman and he was talking about ale rather than whisky. Matthew knew that because . . . well, he was rather uncertain as to why he knew that. He had had a good poetic education—thanks to Dr. Marsh—and they had looked at "A Shropshire Lad" at some point, but he had never really liked Housman because it seemed to him that it was strangely lugubrious. And, yes, it descended into doggerel at times, or something that came perilously close to doggerel.

He sat up in bed. "I tell the tale that I heard told. / Mithridates he died old." That came from the same place, he thought, more Housman, and had been lodged in his mind as well. That was all about homeopathy, was it not? Mithridates took small doses of poison to season himself against the various substances that his enemies put into his food—and survived their attempts at assassination. Perhaps if one took very small quantities of whisky . . . Matthew slipped out of bed and ruffled his hair vigorously, as if to clear his head. He had drunk too much—that was the problem. He and that Danish filmmaker, Bo, had drunk too much twelve-year-old Laphroaig while they had sat and talked about his films and the difference between Copenhagen and Edinburgh, and trout fishing in northern Sweden and in Scotland, and whether Scottish midges, which attacked you when you were trout fishing, were more or less aggressive than Swedish mosquitoes. They had then moved on to the brown bear (called, Bo revealed, brun bjørn) and the wolf (ulv), both of which might be encountered—albeit very rarely—while fishing in the extreme north and which therefore made, on balance, trout fishing in Sweden slightly more dangerous than in Scotland. Ulv, Matthew had declared, was a very good word for a wolf. Bo agreed, but said that the Swedish word, varg, was even more frightening than ulv, and that wolves, if they had the choice, would probably choose to be known as vargs on public relations grounds: "Wolves," he said, "are intent on frightening us. They've always taken that view and I see no sign of their changing now." He had then gone on to say that a Finnish friend had told him that in Finland a wolf was called a susi, which was altogether different; almost cuddly, said Matthew. "In Polish," said Bo, "a wolf is a wilk, which seems to me to be all wrong." Matthew agreed. "More appropriate for seafood, I would have thought."

It had been a rather absurd conversation, but it had seemed exactly the right thing to discuss at the time and had further cemented the friendship that had sprung up so quickly and so naturally between them. While this was going on, Anna and Elspeth had busied themselves with some triplets-related matter, and had then announced that they, at least, would be going to bed as they would be required to get up at a reasonable hour even if Matthew and Bo appeared to have no such need. If the remark had a critical edge to it, then that was missed by both men, who responded by refreshing their glasses with a further dose of Laphroaig.

Eventually Bo had looked at his watch and said that he needed to get back to the small flat in Stockbridge where he was staying. He thanked Matthew profusely for introducing him to Laphroaig, which, he said, became easier to drink after the initial shock.

"Thank you for agreeing, by the way," he said, as he stood up to go.

"To what?" asked Matthew. He was not sure whether Bo was referring to agreement on the naming of wolves, or to something else altogether.

"To the filming."

"Oh, that," said Matthew airily. "That will be a pleasure."

He vaguely remembered that they had talked about some documentary that Bo wanted to make about life in Edinburgh—and particularly life in India Street. That was fine by him, he thought: perhaps Bo would even engage him as some sort of assistant—Matthew had always been interested in filming and it would be useful to know how to operate one of these advanced pneumatic cameras, or were they really called pneumatic . . . Perhaps he could be the best boy, that wonderful term that you saw at the end of a film. What exactly did the best boy do on the film set? And then there was the gaffer: what on earth was the gaffer's role?

"I should like to start quite soon," said Bo.

"Whenever," said Matthew.

Bo reached out to shake his hand. "Matthew, my old friend, this will be a very important film. Fly on the wall."

"Mosquito on the wall," quipped Matthew.

Now, as he rose from his bed, Matthew remembered that he had agreed to something, but it was not until he reached the bathroom, and looked into mirror, that he remembered what it was.

## 30. Navy Envy etc.

Elspeth's recollection of the previous evening's events was somewhat clearer than Matthew's.

"You and Bo enjoyed yourselves last night," she remarked as, clad in dressing gown and slippers, she joined her husband in the kitchen. "I heard you talking about wolves. You were going on about what they were called in different languages. Very strange. You've never talked about wolves before and suddenly it all seemed to come out."

She glanced at the half-empty bottle of Laphroaig as she spoke, and wondered how many glasses of whisky had been consumed. Not that she minded: Matthew was fairly abstemious in most things and usually had nothing beyond a glass or two of wine. Whisky was for special occasions—a drink of hospitality that he would bring out when there were special guests.

Matthew grinned—rather sheepishly, she thought.

"We talked about all sorts of things," he said. "He's an interesting person."

Elspeth nodded. "Yes, I liked him." She lowered her voice; the door to Anna's room was still closed and she was presumably still asleep. "Do you think that he and Anna are . . . an item?"

Matthew shrugged. "Difficult to say. Has she said anything about boyfriends to you?"

"She hasn't mentioned anybody current."

"Well, he didn't say anything to me about it. I formed the impression that he was here in Scotland to do some filming. I don't think he came to see her." He paused. He knew that sooner or later he would have to talk to Elspeth about the film he had discussed with Bo.

Elspeth filled the kettle and plugged it in. "What's he want to film?" she asked.

Matthew hesitated. "Well, he's quite keen to make a documentary about everyday life." He looked at her. "In Scotland. Everyday Scottish life. He does that sort of thing."

"Oh yes?"

"Yes. He made a film about the Danish navy, apparently. He went off on some ship and filmed the sailors eating their dinner and, well, I suppose, sailing the ship." He looked out of the window. "What do you think the Danish navy actually does?"

Elspeth thought that they did more or less what other navies did. They sailed round and round and then returned to port.

"It's just that you don't associate the Danes with throwing their weight around," he said. "Or at least not in quite the same way as . . . as we do."

Elspeth frowned. "Do we throw our weight around?"

Matthew nodded. "I would have thought so. If you think of how we start lecturing people all over the world about this, that, and the next thing. Telling governments to behave, and so on. Do you see the Danes doing that?"

"They don't have a seat on the Security Council," Elspeth retorted.

Matthew shook his head. "It's not just that, surely."

"And they don't have a very big navy, do they?"

Matthew was not sure exactly how large the Danish navy was, but he assumed that it was large enough for its purpose—whatever that was.

"At least they've got a navy," he said. "There are some people who'd love a navy, you know, but who haven't really got any sea. In fact, they definitely don't have any sea. That's really tough if what you really want is a navy."

Elspeth raised an eyebrow. "Navy envy?"

"I suppose so. I remember reading somewhere about landlocked countries that would just love to have navies. In fact, some of them actually have navies, even if they don't have any sea. Bolivia, I think, is the biggest one of these. They've got a navy made up of thousands of sailors—with no sea. The Argentinians are kind to them and let them keep a ship in one of their own ports, but it can't be the same, can it?"

Elspeth agreed it was kind of the Argentinians. "I think that shows real sympathy," she said.

"And they've got bags of admirals," Matthew went on. "That's often the case with these things. When you don't have something, you will it into existence by having lots of people in uniforms who are in charge of the thing you don't have. It's interesting. Look at the Italian forestry service."

"What's wrong with it?"

Not everybody knows about the problems of the Italian forestry service—at least not everybody in Edinburgh—but Matthew happened to be one who did. "They have some forests—not many, but some. Most of these are up in the north, in the mountains. But apparently they have thousands and thousands of forestry officials—probably in pretty nice uniforms—down in the south."

"So what do they do?"

Matthew shrugged. "Not very much, I imagine. It's something like one tree per official."

"The trees will be very well looked after then," said Elspeth.

"No doubt."

The kettle had now boiled, and Elspeth poured

the water into the teapot. She looked at Matthew enquiringly. "This film he mentioned—the one about day-to-day life in Scotland. Where's he going to film it?"

Matthew stared at his hands, and Elspeth noticed it. A couple of years of marriage had taught her to read her husband. "Matthew?"

He sighed. "Well, I'm sorry, maybe I shouldn't have agreed, but I said that he could use us if he wanted."

"Us?"

"Yes. He wants to follow us about. He wants to record our lives. Looking after the boys. Going to work. That sort of thing." He watched her reaction. "It'll be a fantastic film."

Elspeth said nothing, but poured herself a cup of tea and then sat down at the table opposite her husband.

"I hope you don't mind," said Matthew lamely. And then added, "I imagine that we'll have subtitles when they show it in Denmark. Won't that be nice? To be subtitled?"

"Matthew . . ." Elspeth began.

"And we might win an award," Matthew continued. "We could be invited to one of those occasions where you stand up and thank your mother. And then cry. You could cry just a little perhaps . . ."

"Matthew . . ."

"And I doubt if it'll be any trouble. He seems

very discreet. And he can't have been any trouble on that Danish boat or they would have stopped him filming . . ."

Elspeth stared at him directly. "Listen," she said. "Listen, Matthew. Did you commit us?"

Matthew bit his lip. "I think so," he said.

# 31. *The Doppelganger*

Bruce was not one to open a door hesitantly. When he answered his door that morning, shortly after he had moved into his new flat in Albany Street, he did so with the confidence of one who knew exactly who would be standing on the other side. He expected to see the two young women he had encountered at the intersection of Queen Street and Frederick Street and with whom he had had that delicious, unambiguous, and fleeting exchange. He had expected to say, "Girls! Come in!" and usher them into his sparsely furnished hall, bowing slightly—women loved that, Bruce had discovered—even if the act of bowing risked loosening the towel that formed his only clothing at the time, as he had just stepped out of the shower. That would be a good welcome—to lose the towel altogether! They would avert their eyes and giggle, but they would be thrilled—there was no doubt about that.

That is what Bruce expected; he did not expect

to see, instead of the two young women, whom he had, for purely operational purposes, christened Delia and Dahlia, a young man of about his own age, and his height too, looking at him in mild astonishment.

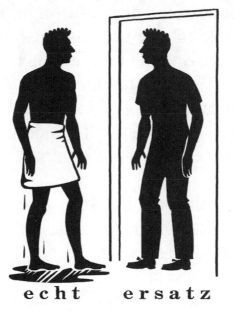

echt          ersatz

"Oh," said the young man. "Sorry, I didn't . . . ."

Bruce recovered himself quickly. "No, I was in the shower, but I'd finished. I thought you were somebody else."

The young man smiled. "We often think that, don't we? We think somebody is somebody else altogether, and then we find they're . . . well, they're not the person we thought they were."

Bruce shrugged. "Well, I suppose that's true."

The young man put out his hand. "I'm Jonathan," he said. "I actually live two doors down."

Bruce nodded. He was beginning to feel slightly cold, standing half-naked in the doorway, exposed to a cool breeze that seemed to be coming up the stair. Perhaps Jonathan had left the door open down below; even in summer, it could be chilly in Edinburgh, out of the direct sunlight. He looked at Jonathan, making one of those instant judgments that we make on meeting another for the first time. Facial clues as to intention? A smile. Not hostile or disapproving. Clothing? Casual, same as everybody else. Jeans. Topsiders. T-shirt that announced CREW in large letters. Yachting type? Maybe.

"I thought that Jenny still lived here," said Jonathan. "I knew she was going, but I didn't realise it would be so soon."

"She's gone," said Bruce. "I got the keys this morning. I've just moved in, actually." He paused for a moment—the most important, decisive pause in his life, not that he was to know it at the time. And then he said, "Come in. I need to go and get dressed."

"Thanks," said Jonathan, stepping into the hall: the most important, decisive step of his life—not that he was to know it either.

Bruce gestured towards the living room door. "Make yourself at home," he said. "I haven't got much furniture yet but I can do coffee. I'll be with you in a mo."

He walked off. He was aware, though, as he

made his way into the bedroom, that Jonathan was looking at him. It was an extraordinary feeling—an instance of perception that relies on none of the usual senses and yet can be as acute and reliable—sometimes even more so—as vision or hearing, and, *a fortiori*, smell. Words struggle to describe how it works: we feel the eyes upon us and there may even be a tingling sensation akin to the prickling, tickling impact of a strong magnetic field on the skin. Pick up a telephone and place it to your ear: feel the slight touch of the earpiece magnet, like the play of a feather on skin. Feel it. Bruce did.

He hesitated, looking back over his shoulder towards Jonathan, who was halfway through the living room door at that moment but whose head was also turned. Bruce saw the smile; nothing odd about it, just friendly. He continued into the bedroom. And then the thought struck him. Jonathan looked strikingly like him. Like Bruce. Like me, he thought. Just like me. My double.

He moved towards the window. There was no mirror in the room, as there were only the few sticks of furniture that Bruce had negotiated to be included in the sale, and that did not include a dresser. But the window-pane would do, and he stood before that now, catching his reflection in the glass—an insubstantial, fluid reflection, as one on the surface of water. He focused on his face, and thought: is there somebody else who shares that? It was a strangely unsettling question, and the answer could be even more so. Yes. There was. And that person was there in the living room, wearing a shirt labelled CREW.

He moved away from the window. So what? So what if somebody looked like him. We're not unique—not really. Nature is generous with her DNA, spreading it around, even between species, and if, in the small gene pool that was Scotland, there was another who had that particular sequence of genes in just the place on the genome that dictated facial features (and life, in those terms, was such a chemical lottery), then nobody should be surprised; his good fortune, thought Bruce—the his being his not mine.

He suddenly remembered what Jonathan had said. He could not recall the exact words, but they were something about thinking that somebody was a person other than the person they really were. What had he meant by that? Did he just mean to say that you could be surprised by who opens the door, or did he mean that you could be wrong about what somebody was underneath? Was he talking about the inner person? But then, who made remarks like that to somebody he has just met?

He went over to his opened suitcase of clothes. There was a green and yellow rugby shirt that was slightly crumpled, but would do. Black chinos. Great, he thought. Great.

And then he thought: why am I bothering? What am I trying to do? Why do I care what I wear when it's not Delia and Dahlia, but Jonathan, about whom I know nothing? Competition, he thought. He's a rival. If Delia and Dahlia were to turn up—and they might still do so—then there would be competition.

Bruce smiled. He was not afraid of competition. Even if there were two of him in Edinburgh—and that rather odd possibility now presented itself—one would be echt and one would be ersatz. Great words, he thought; and there was no doubt which he would be.

## 32. Rugby Types

Crossing the hall to return to his guest, Bruce hesitated before the living room door. The realisation that had come to him in the bedroom that Jonathan, his unannounced and unexpected visitor, bore a striking resemblance to him had unnerved him rather more than he would have anticipated. While most of us, if pressed on the matter, would concede that we cannot be all that different from others, within ourselves, deep in that region of consciousness where the sense of self resides, there is the belief that there is nobody quite like us. And of course that is true: just as we have yet to disprove the assumption that no two people will have the same fingerprints—and that applies even to identical twins—so too do we find it difficult to imagine two people who have had precisely the same experience of life as each other. That means that our assumption that each of us is special is, in that respect, entirely justified.

So there could not be another Bruce, even if Bruce was a type, with tastes and attitudes that could be found in any number of young men of his age and background. And that, of course, became very evident in Edinburgh on any Saturday when an international rugby match was being played at Murrayfield. If one went out on the streets of the capital before such an event, there would be no shortage of such young men in evidence: hundreds, indeed thousands of them, milling about looking vaguely benign, as rugby enthusiasts look; solid young men wearing the uniform of their caste—green waxed jackets (some of them) or heavy sweaters—their minds firmly fixed on the muddy, physical conflict ahead when a similar set of young men, distinguished only by their physique, their broken noses, cauliflower ears, and thick-set necks, would grapple enthusiastically with another set of such men, but of a different tribal affiliation, egged on by a cheering and excited, although almost always good-natured, crowd. Few of these young men, and certainly none of the players, would be mistaken for aesthetes, at least in appearance, no matter what sensitivity lay behind a robust exterior. And what of the women? They were there too, although in much smaller numbers, attracted by the sheer heady thought of being admitted to and participating in a male mystery as old as any ancient hunting party or sacrificial rite. And what could be more satisfying for the female spectators than to see thirty muscular men running backwards and forwards and occasionally bending over, head to head, and pushing one another backwards and forwards in the mud? Many women, in fact, swoon at the sight, and are regularly carried out on stretchers by first aid attendants, who revive them outside the stadium with cups of tea before sending them back in to witness further developments in the physical spectacle.

In such a rugby crowd Bruce would have passed unnoticed. And indeed that was where he belonged. He had played school rugby in Crieff and would have been a reasonably good player were it not for his concern about getting his hair messed up. That had led to several sharp exchanges with the coach, who had lost patience with Bruce's preening himself both on the field and in the changing room afterwards. The final straw had come when, in an under-16 match against Merchiston, one of the strongest school rugby sides in Scotland, Bruce had combed his hair when he was meant to be throwing the ball in at a line-out, much to the fury of players on both sides who were jumping up and down and lifting each other into the air in anticipation of the ball's re-entering play.

"You're behaving like a . . ." stuttered the almost speechless coach, "like a . . . like a girl."

"You can't say things like that these days, Mr. Wilson," Bruce had retorted.

That had been the end of his career as a player, but not as an enthusiast. Now, standing in the hall, momentarily hesitant, he was still wearing a rugby shirt—but as a fashion statement rather than a sporting garment. And he thought: why did I invite him in? Because he was at the door, he decided. Because he appeared to have known the girl I bought the flat from. Perhaps because I had already seen that he was . . . that he was me. The words came to his mind unbidden—and their effect was chilling. He can't be me, he thought. He isn't me.

He decided to go into the kitchen first and make the coffee that he had offered Jonathan. That done, he picked up the two mugs—the only ones he had in the yet unequipped kitchen—and took them back into the living room. At the door he again hesitated, but only briefly, and then entered the room.

Jonathan was standing with his back to Bruce, staring out of the window. When he heard Bruce come in, he turned round and smiled. "You have the same view as I do, only . . ."

He did not finish. With a sudden clatter, one of the mugs fell from Bruce's hand, somersaulted through its brief drop, and then landed, unbroken, on the floor. Coffee, in tiny flying droplets, splattered across the bare floorboards and against the legs of Bruce's black chinos.

Jonathan moved forward spontaneously, picking up the mug. "Bad luck," he said. "Are you all right? Not burned?"

Bruce took the now empty mug from Jonathan and handed him the full one. "You have that," he said. "I'll make myself another later on."

As he handed over the mug of coffee, Bruce noticed that his hand was shaking. "I've only got two chairs," he said. "As you can see. But let's sit down anyway."

He now looked at Jonathan. His first glance, given as he came into the room, had had that disastrous effect. Now he looked with trepidation, afraid of what he would see. And it was true. He was looking at his own image—his twin.

He was not sure if Jonathan had noticed the same thing: surely he must have. And how would he raise it with him? Could he say, outright, Do you know, we're identical? The trouble with that was the very strong taboo that exists—at least in Scotland—against one male's commenting on the appearance of another. You do not say it, and certainly not on first meeting.

But Jonathan did. "I've seen you somewhere before," he said, a smile playing about his lips. "In the mirror."

# 33. *The Red Hot Chili Peppers et al.*

For once Bruce, who normally was not stuck for a response, had no idea what to say. For a full minute or so he stood quite still, staring at Jonathan, his mouth slightly open, without a word on his lips.

"Go on," prompted Jonathan. "Sit down."

It might have struck Bruce as odd that his visitor was inviting him to sit, as if he, not Bruce, were the host, but everything about this encounter was so unusual that this thought did not occur to him.

Bruce sat down. Opposite him, on the only other chair, Jonathan continued to smile. "I saw you get out of your car," he said. "When you arrived . . . I happened to be looking out of my window and saw . . . saw myself getting out of the car."

It took Bruce a moment to appreciate what was being said. He smiled wanly.

"For a moment I thought I was seeing things," Jonathan went on. "You know how you sometimes get things wrong on first glance? You know that feeling?"

Bruce nodded silently.

"But when I looked again and you were about to go in the door I got a clear view of your face and realised that I hadn't been mistaken. It was a shock—a real shock."

Bruce had been studying Jonathan's face as he spoke. It was a disconcerting exercise, and now his gaze moved upwards to the hair, which was almost exactly the same as his, cut in roughly the same way. At last he managed to speak. "It's very odd," he said.

"That's putting it mildly," said Jonathan. "Would you mind if I took a photograph of us standing together? I'll hold my mobile out in front of us and get our heads."

He rose from his chair and Bruce, after hesitating for a moment, stood up too.

"It will be easier for us to compare ourselves in a photo," said Jonathan. "Come over here. Stand next to me and I'll take a snap."

Bruce approached the other man. He felt uncomfortable in getting so close, and when Jonathan inclined his head so that they were almost cheek-to-cheek, Bruce held his breath involuntarily.

"It's all right," Jonathan said. "You can breathe if you like."

"I am breathing," Bruce muttered.

"You're very tense."

Bruce said nothing. Jonathan was now holding his mobile phone out before him at arm's length. A moment or two later there was a flash and a clicking sound.

"Gotcha," said Jonathan. "Now let's take a look."

Bruce was shivering as he looked at the picture on the screen.

"You're nervous," said Jonathan. "You don't have to be."

"It's so strange," said Bruce. "I mean, you and me . . ." He was not sure what he wanted to say, and so he left the sentence unfinished.

"Of course it's strange," said Jonathan. "That's what makes it so exciting."

Exciting? Bruce was not sure why Jonathan should find it exciting. Unsettling? Creepy? Yes to both of those, but exciting?

They looked at the picture. Bruce asked Jonathan to brighten the screen, which he did.

"Better?" asked Jonathan.

Bruce nodded. He reached out and touched his image with a finger. "My chin's a bit different," he said. "I think it's different here . . ."

Jonathan turned to him in astonishment. "That's me," he said. "That's not you, it's me."

The photograph was of their heads and necks: their shirts, which would have distinguished them, did not show.

"No," said Bruce. "That's me on the left— you're on the right."

Jonathan shook his head. "No. You were standing on the left facing the camera. Remember? That means that you're on the right of the picture on the screen."

Bruce was silent. Jonathan was right: he had mistaken the picture of the other young man for himself. He caught Jonathan's eye; the latter's

166

expression was challenging—the look of one who was expecting a response.

"Right," said Bruce. "So we look the same. So . . ."

"So what?" interjected Jonathan. "Is that what you were going to say?"

"More or less."

"Well," said Jonathan, "it's interesting—to say the least. How often do we find our double?"

Bruce shrugged. "For most people—never."

"Exactly. Unless . . ." Jonathan paused. "Tell me, what do you do?"

"For a living? I'm a surveyor. Property work generally."

Jonathan looked thoughtful. "I almost did that. I applied for a land economy degree in Aberdeen, but I didn't take it up. I work for a PR agency now."

Bruce frowned. "Funny," he said. "I almost did that."

"And what sort of music do you like? Favourite band?"

Bruce looked out of the window. "Red Hot Chili Peppers."

Jonathan shook his head in amazement. "Snap!"

"Haven't heard them," said Bruce.

Jonathan laughed. "No, they're not a band. I mean snap in the sense of me too. I like the Peppers. Flea."

"Flea's great," said Bruce. He paused before continuing, "But why are you asking?"

Jonathan took a sip of his coffee, and grimaced. It was cold. "You know, some time ago I came across this book. It was by somebody called Wright. Somebody I knew was reading it and I picked it up. I couldn't put it down." He took another sip of the cold coffee. "It had a simple title, *Twins*. And that's what it was about."

Bruce was listening intently. "It was about real twins? Actual twins? Not just people who look like other people?"

"Yes," said Jonathan. "There's a place in the States where they study these things. Minneapolis, or somewhere like that. Anyway, they look for twins who have been separated at birth—given up for adoption, and so on. Years later, they're traced and they're studied before they're introduced to one another. They discovered amazing things."

"Such as?"

"They had the same tastes . . ." Jonathan left the sentence hanging in the air.

Bruce felt his heart beginning to thump. Adrenalin, he thought.

"And?"

"And a whole lot of other things. Same political views. Same hobbies. Marriage to the same sort of person—including, in one case, two women of the same name. And so on. It was uncanny."

Bruce decided to bring an end to a conversation

that he was finding distinctly unnerving. "We're not twins. I'm my parents' only child."

Jonathan drained the last of his coffee. "That's what all these separated twins thought," he said quietly.

## 34. Out of the Mouths of Pre-Teens and the Non-Formula-Fed . . .

Although Ranald Braveheart Macpherson had readily agreed to look after Cyril, not even asking why there should be a change in the dog's care arrangements, Bertie felt duty bound to explain to his friend what lay behind his request.

"I don't want you to think that I'm trying to get out of something I promised to do," he said to Ranald. "Scout's honour I'm not doing that, Ranald."

Ranald assured him that nothing could be further from his mind. "I know you'd never do a thing like that, Bertie. You needn't worry."

"It's just that Cyril was having an awful time in my house," Bertie went on.

Ranald nodded; he understood. "Your mother?" he asked.

Bertie bit his lip. He was a loyal little boy, and did not like to run his mother down. And yet at the same time . . . "I suppose so," he said apologetically. "Something like that."

Ranald reached out and put a reassuring hand on Bertie's shoulder. "I can imagine what it's like, Bertie," he said. "No dog would like to live in the same house as your mother."

"She does her best," said Bertie. "She really does."

Ranald shot him a sympathetic glance. "Of course, Bertie. Of course she does." He paused. "Tofu says your mum's a cow, you know. Have you heard him say that?"

Bertie did not reply. He had heard it, of course—on more than one occasion. It was only Tofu, whose views counted for nothing, being largely composed of fabrications and provocations, but it had still been hurtful.

"Tofu's wrong about most things," said Ranald.

Bertie nodded his agreement. It was kind of Ranald to support him in this way; but no more than he expected from such a good friend.

"But maybe he's right on this one," continued Ranald.

Bertie looked away.

"Not that it matters, Bertie," said Ranald. "There are plenty of people whose mothers must have been cows, and yet they've managed to have quite a nice life." He paused. "I'm trying to think of one right now, but I can't, I'm afraid."

Bertie decided to change the subject. "Cyril won't be any trouble, Ranald," he said. "You only have to feed him once a day and make sure that he's got lots of water in his bowl."

"I'll be very careful about all that," said Ranald.

"Good," said Bertie.

They discussed further arrangements. Would Ranald need to ask his parents, Bertie wondered. Adults were odd about that sort of thing—they seemed reluctant to allow pets to be looked after even if there was to be very little work involved.

Ranald looked at his watch. "I'll leave it another half an hour," he said. "They start drinking wine round about then and they usually say yes to anything you ask them after they've had a glass or two of wine."

"Good idea," said Bertie.

"And I've got the ideal place for Cyril to stay," Ranald went on. "There's a shed in the garden that has some old sacks. I'll make him a bed out of the sacks and he can spend the night in there. During the day he can come inside and sit in the kitchen."

The details of Cyril's boarding having been agreed, Bertie said goodbye to the dog. "You'll be very happy with Ranald," he whispered into Cyril's furry ear. "And I'll come and see you from time to time. I promise I will."

Cyril looked at Bertie and licked his face. He was aware that something was happening, but he had no idea what it was. It could be something to do with food, or walks, or it could be about something else altogether, but Cyril would have no idea of any such further possibilities. Dogs are capable of envisaging lists of two things;

beyond that, they become intellectually stretched.

Bertie thanked Ranald and was shown to the front door. From within the kitchen, he heard a murmur of voices, followed by a high-pitched giggle. Ranald Braveheart Macpherson raised an eyebrow in mock tolerance.

"I don't know what they talk about," he said to Bertie. "It's sad, really, but I think they're harmless enough."

"They're nice parents," said Bertie.

Ranald considered this solemnly. "On balance," he said, "yes."

Bertie ran the short distance from Ranald's house to the bus stop. He was glad that he had done this, as a 23 bus lumbered into sight coming up Morningside Road only a minute or so later. He felt more confident about making the journey on his own now, and he asked for his ticket with as deep and mature a voice as he could muster.

"You got something wrong with your throat, son?" asked the bus driver. "Smoking too much?"

Bertie shook his head. "I don't smoke," he began. "I never . . ."

"That's OK," said the driver. "I was only pulling your leg, son."

Bertie sat towards the back of the bus. As the journey progressed, he went over in his mind what he could say to his mother when she upbraided him for being out so long. He could try to slip in unnoticed—he had attempted that on several occasions before—but he knew that he was unlikely to be able to get in undetected. Could he say that Cyril had run away? That would be a convenient and easy answer, but the problem was that it was a manifest lie, and Bertie liked to tell the truth. Well, could he do just that? Could he simply tell Irene the truth?

He rehearsed what he imagined would be his conversation with his mother. "Cyril was unhappy, Mummy. And I knew that you didn't like him all that much."

And Irene would look at him with that look that she sometimes used when looking at Stuart. Bertie was not sure if he could face that look—as captured members of the French Resistance had wondered whether they could face the interrogation of the Gestapo. Bertie had seen a film about that and his heart had gone out to the brave men who refused to tell their questioners where a downed British airman was or where the cache of weapons was hidden. He had asked his parents about the Gestapo, and they had explained that it was all a long time ago and Germany was a very different place today.

"Would you have been in the Gestapo, Mummy?" Bertie asked innocently. "That is, if you had been alive when all that was going on?"

The question had caused consternation.

"Certainly not, Bertie!" exclaimed Irene.

"I don't think that's a very nice question to ask

Mummy," Bertie's father had interjected. But even as he spoke, Stuart could not help but let the tiniest of smiles—invisible to the naked eye—play about his lips. Out of the mouth of babes and sucklings, he thought.

## 35. Ranald Braveheart Macpherson's Mother Receives a Telephone Call

Bertie need not have worried. Having decided to tell his mother the truth, the disgrace in which he then found himself had nothing to do with the transfer of Cyril but was focused on his having made the bus journey to see Ranald Braveheart Macpherson entirely by himself. That, said Irene—and with some justification on this occasion—was not to happen again. Bertie might think that he was old enough to undertake such a trip, but he should remember that he was still six, and six-year-old boys did not get on buses by themselves.

"I really don't see why I should still be six, Mummy," Bertie complained. "I seem to have been six for an awful long time."

"That's the way things are, Bertie," said Irene. "And just enjoy being six. There'll come a time when you'll wish that you were six again. Birthdays are not quite the same thing when you get a bit older, I can tell you!"

A telephone call was made to Ranald's mother,

and Irene extended a half-hearted offer to take Cyril back. Ranald's mother, however, expressed the view that her son seemed to have formed an attachment to their new boarder and that it would be perfectly in order for Cyril to stay. "A boy needs a dog," she said over the phone.

At first Irene received this remark in silence. Then came her response. "Some boys, perhaps. Not all."

"Oh, I think most boys want the same sort of thing," said Mrs. Macpherson. "You know that, of course . . ."

This led to a further silence. War undeclared can be more bitter, more fraught with danger, than war declared.

"Naturally," said Irene, "having two boys, I feel that I certainly know their little needs. You only have the one, don't you . . ."

Ranald Braveheart Macpherson's mother let out an involuntary gasp—slight, but not slight enough to mean that Irene did not notice that her dart had gone home. With this knowledge, Irene followed up with a low-flying missile. "Of course dogs are easier to look after in suburbia," she said.

The stressing of the final word was accomplished with consummate ease—only the slightest inflection was needed to convey disdain, and Irene applied that with the delicacy of a great chef seasoning his signature sauce. But there was more to come.

"And I suppose that living in Morningside," she continued, "a dog is perfectly all right."

Again, the choice of words was perfect. Morningside may be a perfectly pleasant part of Edinburgh, a suburb of douce villas and comfortable flats, but it also stands for everything that is Edinburgh about Edinburgh. Comedians traditionally used Morningside as a target for wit directed against respectability: the word Morningside, preferably pronounced with a distortion of side into sade, could reduce Glaswegians to guffaws, in the same way as the mere mention of Glasgow could cause seemingly endless mirth at an Edinburgh pantomime. Of such stock references is humour made, but here it was not mirth that was Irene's objective. Her observation that the Macphersons lived in Morningside was tantamount to outright ridicule—at least in her book—and that inference was quickly and correctly picked up by Ranald's mother, who again gave a short, involuntary gasp.

"We're in Church Hill, actually," she said. "But I suppose you weren't to know."

That equalised things—but only temporarily.

"I find it difficult to distinguish these places," said Irene. "Please forgive me."

A short silence, and a perilous one: Irene was unaware of the mortal danger into which she had wandered.

By now, Ranald's mother had collected her

skirts and was ready to respond. "Be that as it may," she at last said to Irene. "Returning to the subject of that poor dog: he must have felt so confined in that small flat of yours, poor creature. I'm sure you'll be pleased to see the back of him—it'll give you all a bit more room. We have quite a large garden, you know—that'll give him some space to romp about with Ranald." She paused. "Bertie so enjoyed it when he came to see Ranald a few weeks ago. He loved the garden, with its lawn and so on. Bliss for a child who's never had any of that."

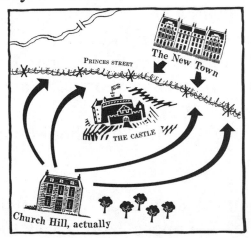

Irene was unable to say anything. The sheer force of this onslaught and its overt hostility had taken her by surprise and she was having difficulty marshalling a counter-attack. But there was more to come, and even as the echoes of this last bout of artillery fire from the South Side were reverberating in Scotland Street, Mons Meg was being wheeled into position.

"I mustn't detain you," said Ranald's mother, thereby signalling that this was exactly what she proposed to do. "I mustn't detain you—you must be so busy, even if you don't have a job."

There was a short pause while this comment was allowed to sink in. Ranald's mother did have a job, and she knew that Irene knew that, as Irene had once come into the small gift shop in Bruntsfield where she worked four mornings a week.

Realising that if she were to recover any ground, she would have to act quickly, Irene seized the opportunity that had opened up.

"Thank heavens I don't have to work in a shop," she said. And then, "Oh, I am sorry, I forgot for a moment that you were a shop assistant yourself. I really am very sorry."

There! thought Irene. That should put her gas at a peep.

But no.

"Not exactly an assistant," said Ranald's mother calmly. "Oh, I suppose I do assist the manager there, but . . . well, you see, we own that shop."

The only sound from Scotland Street now was that of breathing, and it was irregular. Like a matador preparing for the final dispatching of the victim, Ranald's mother, with perfect timing, administered a final lance—resplendent in ribbons like the weapon of a cruel Spanish bullfighter; and in the background, ominous and insistent as a funereal drum, might have been heard the lines of Lorca: *A las cinco de la tarde. Eran las cinco en punto de la tarde.* "At five in the afternoon. It was exactly five in the afternoon." Of course, Lorca's bullfighter came to a sticky end: not so the mother of Ranald Braveheart Macpherson.

"One of our many shops," she said casually. "But where were we? Oh yes, our little canine refugee . . ."

## 36. *A Memory of Foxes*

It took Cyril some time to realise that Bertie had gone and that Ranald Braveheart Macpherson was now in charge of him. Most dogs are fairly adaptable when it comes to accepting changes in human authority and will adjust to a new command structure; Cyril was no exception, and once he understood that Bertie was no longer there, he readily obeyed Ranald in the plans that he had for him. It was not ideal, though, and he became particularly unhappy when Ranald led him out into the garden and into the garden shed that was to be his new sleeping quarters.

"This is where you're going to spend the night, Cyril," explained Ranald, spreading a small pile of old hessian sacks on the floor. "I'll bring you a bowl of water and some food. You'll be very comfortable."

Cyril sat on the hessian sacks and waited for something to happen. He was not sure what was expected of him, but when Ranald returned with a bowl of Irish stew and pieces of bread, he at least understood that. Ranald waited for him to finish his meal and then took the empty bowl away.

"That's all, Cyril," he said. "Now you can go to sleep. I'll see you in the morning."

And with that Cyril was left alone in his unfamiliar shed, with the last light of the day fading outside and a whole library of new smells filling his nostrils. Some of these were not all that dissimilar to smells he had encountered before—mice, for instance, smelled roughly similar whether they infested the cellars and cupboards of the New Town or the gardens of South Edinburgh. That smell, at least, was familiar, but lawn seed was entirely new to Cyril, as was the smell that came off a bundle of green garden string, and the smell of a dead bat that had been trapped somewhere up in the shed's roof. But most disturbing of all was the powerful evidence of the proximity of another creature—something that Cyril had frequently picked up in the Drummond Place Gardens and was firm in the canine memory: the smell of fox.

Cyril attempted to take no notice of it; those creatures left trails of scent everywhere, and a dog that became too anxious about it would soon have no peace of mind. But after a while the smell became too powerful to ignore and was now accompanied by a scraping noise directly beneath the floorboards of the shed. Cyril had no alternative but to leave his bed of hessian and place his moist, receptive nose to the cracks between the boards. Now it was very close—and overpowering. The enemy—which was what a fox was—was right beneath him.

Cyril was at a loss what to do. He could hardly allow a fox to flaunt its presence immediately beneath him—what dog could countenance that? And yet there appeared to be no means of getting out of the shed, the door of which had been tied shut by Ranald Braveheart Macpherson after he had brought him his food. He scratched at the door with his paw: had Angus been there this would have brought an immediate response, but there was no Angus. He scratched again, and then, realising that his request would go unanswered, began to howl.

It was a prolonged, mournful howl, into which Cyril put all the sorrow of the canine condition: a howl that seemed to express deep nostalgia for the woods, for the snowy wastes of his lupine ancestors' ancient homelands, for all the sense of loss and separation that a dog feels when his master, his reason for living, his sun, is no longer there.

Inside the Macpherson house, Ranald Braveheart Macpherson's father heard Cyril's howling and remarked to his wife that perhaps it was not a good idea to leave Cyril outside. "These creatures don't like to be by themselves," he said. "He could sleep in the kitchen."

Ranald Braveheart Macpherson's mother, who had opened a bottle of New Zealand white wine to celebrate her recent telephone victory over Irene—"that unspeakable Pollock woman" as she called her—was now in a state to agree to anything.

"Sure," she said. "He can sleep in the kitchen, poor little soul. And what a pity that we weren't able to take Bertie as well, don't you think? I'd love to kidnap that little boy and bring him over this side of town. Do you think we'd get into trouble with the law if we did that? Did it discreetly, I mean."

"Naughty sweetheart!" said Ranald's father, shaking a finger at his wife. "Naughty, bad girlie! Tut tut!"

Ranald's mother took another sip of wine. "Yes, wicked moi! But you married me, didn't you, Buffalo Bill?"

The origin of the nickname was lost in the mists of time, but she had always called him that.

"I'm going to fetch him," said Ranald's father. "The neighbours will think we're harbouring a banshee."

"A good name for that woman, come to think of it," mused Ranald's mother, reaching for the bottle of wine. "Irene Banshee. It somehow sounds so suitable, don't you think?"

"Don't overdo it, sweetness," said her husband, glancing at the bottle. "Do leave some for me."

He left the kitchen and went out into the garden. The howling emanating from the shed was continuing and, if anything, had become louder and more plaintive.

"Don't despair, Cyril," Ranald's father called. "Help is at hand."

The door of the shed took a moment or two to open, as it was secured with twine, Ranald Braveheart Macpherson having employed his knowledge of knots recently acquired under the instruction of Rosemary Gold, Akela at the First Morningside Cub Scouts. But once the knot was untied and the door could be opened, it was possible for Cyril, filled with relief at his rescue from durance vile, to dash out, completely forgetting, for the moment at least, the provocative presence of a fox underneath the floorboards of the shed.

It was impossible for Ranald Braveheart Macpherson's father to catch him. All that he could muster was a cry of "Hold on, there!" which Cyril, in the first headiness of freedom, completely ignored. Out of the garden he went and then, heading off with no real sense of where he was going, he dashed headlong down the road towards the neighbouring suburb of the Grange.

And it just so happened that once he had put a good half mile between himself and Ranald Braveheart Macpherson's house, Cyril rounded a corner to come up against a man going out for an evening walk. The dog had not expected the man and the man had not expected the dog, and so they both stopped short in their tracks. Cyril looked up at the man. He knew immediately that this man would be kind to him; he might not be Angus, but he would be kind to him.

"Hello, young fellow," said Cardinal Keith O'Brien, head of the Roman Catholic Church in Scotland. "Just where are you heading at such a pace?"

## 37. Student Life

Pat Macgregor had recently moved flats, even if not areas. After some months in one corner of Marchmont, the area of Edinburgh most popular with students—or with those students who could afford to live like students—she had moved to another corner of the same quarter, to a flat on the top floor of a Victorian stone tenement in Warrender Park Terrace, which snaked round the edge of the Bruntsfield Links, an undulating urban golf course that had once been part of an oak forest surrounding the town. The town had consumed the oak forest and gone on to swallow the farmland beyond, but the links and the Meadows remained, green lungs serving the cobbled arteries and stone chambers of the growing city. Which was so beautiful; for all that it was a city, it was so beautiful, with the good fortune to grow at a moment when people still believed—could believe—in whimsy, and were prepared to adorn their roofs, their skyline, with stone thistles and castellation and spikes; all things that are useless except as a means of lifting the spirit or answering our longing for the beautiful—whatever we think that to be.

So now Pat, who was pursuing her studies for a degree in the history of art, found herself in the fifth flat of her student existence. She had started off in Scotland Street, where for a brief time she was the flatmate of Bruce Anderson, surveyor and Narcissist-About-Town, progressing to a flat in Union Place, where subterranean subsidence had caused the floors to incline to such a degree that the furniture—and the inhabitants—would lurch or roll across the room if not fixed to the floor; a disconcerting experience that created in visitors unused to it a sensation of seasickness. Pat, and the two people with whom she shared, had become accustomed to it, jokingly calling their flat La Maison de Mal de Mer, but had not renewed their six-month lease when it had come to an end. "Nobody renews," complained the landlord. "What's wrong with the place?" The reply, of course, was, "It slopes." To which the landlord had retorted, "But that's the way the country is. Look at a map, for heaven's sake. Scotland goes down the way—it always has." With such a world view there was as little point in arguing, of course, as with those who believe in astrological destiny (Pat was Aries), or alien abduction (most likely to occur in Scotland near the town of Bonnybridge), or alchemy (which, delightfully, forms the basis of so many political promises).

From there she had gone to a flat in Tollcross, not far from the Rootsie-Tootsie Club. That had not been a success. Although the floors, unlike those of her flat in Union Place, were level—or close enough—the flat's proximity to the Rootsie-Tootsie Club had meant that there was a great deal of noise at nights, including frequent disturbance from courting couples who would enter the stair— the lock on the common front door being ancient and not having worked since the nineteen fifties— to pursue their conversations in the back green, directly outside Pat's window. The disadvantages of this flat had been compounded by the nature of the neighbours in the flat opposite them on the landing; these were all Goths, noted for their dark clothing, pallid complexions, and staring eyes. Pat and her flatmates—two nurses from the Infirmary—were not sure how many Goths there were, and which Goth was which, and found it unsettling to be climbing the usually unlit lower stair and to discover that one was not alone, but sharing the ascent with a silent, shadowy, and wraith-like figure, one of the Goths.

The Goths never spoke, presumably because they were either beyond speech, or because they had nothing to say to those who were not Goths. The patrons of the Rootsie-Tootsie Club were not similarly afflicted—they had plenty to say, and usually said it in loud voices after being ejected by the club, or denied entry by the doorman. Their language was colourful—full of quaint and traditional expressions intended to emphasise the point, not without their particular charm, perhaps, but developing a certain monotony after a while.

It was a relief to leave Tollcross and move to the first of her flats in Marchmont. No Rootsie-Tootsie Club there; rather lace curtains, teacups, and aquatints of Edinburgh Castle, or traditionally so; now the lace curtains had given way to blinds, the teacups had become coffee mugs, and the views of Edinburgh Castle had been replaced with posters of a beret-wearing Che Guevara, or, amongst those who felt that Che had become slightly passé, reproductions of paintings of butlers dancing on the beach in evening clothes, or long-legged women blowing smoke into the air in bars: Fife Realism, in other words. Both Guevara and Fife Realism gave artistic pleasure, and that, Pat believed, should not be sneered at. We put on our walls what we think is beautiful or inspiring, and if others think that it is manufactured or shallow, then they need not have it on their walls.

The decoration of the walls of Pat's room had been very much the same in each of the flats. She had three reproduction prints that she had arranged to have framed by a small picture-framing shop in Brunstfield: a picture by Cézanne of a statuette that the artist had kept in his studio, David Hockney's *Mr and Mrs Clark and Percy*, and Raeburn's *The Reverend Robert Walker Skating on Duddingston Loch*. The Cézanne and the Hockney had been approved of by her friends on her course. "Two giants," said one of these, a boy called Tim, who was hoping to study at the Courtauld in London after graduation from Edinburgh. "But the Skating Minister? Pat, my dear, what were you thinking of? Bourgeois Edinburgh personified!"

"But that's what I am," said Pat. "That's where I come from."

Tim had raised an eyebrow, and shrugged. Then he moved his hand carelessly, half gesturing dismissively to what lay outside the window: Edinburgh, and a large slice of Scotland. "Well, at least you're honest," he said. "Not that that's much compensation for being so ineffably respectable."

# 38. T. Eliot Top Bard . . .

It was not a long walk from the flat in Warrender Park Terrace to Pat Macgregor's father's house in the Grange—ten or fifteen minutes at the most. In spite of this proximity, Pat found that she did not go home very often—something that made her feel vaguely guilty. There was no reason for this guilt, though: her father might have lived on his own but he gave no appearance of being lonely. And when she did call round at the house unannounced, he was often not there.

"Where do you actually go?" she asked him once, after she had found him in on none of three consecutive calls.

"Go?"

"I come round and you're not there. You must be somewhere."

He considered this. The logic behind it was impeccable. He was tempted to use the famous reply of the Orcadian who had suddenly left his home and his island without any explanation and been away for eight years. On his return to the house, when asked where he had been, he had simply said, "Oot"—which was true, of course, but was hardly revelatory. Not that one should always use more words than are necessary, as Dr.

189

Macgregor had occasionally pointed out to his daughter.

"But just how many words are necessary then?" she retorted.

Dr. Macgregor, who had flirted with psycho-analysis, and in particular the Lacanian school, was interested in language. He had seen the frustration of many of his patients who had sought to say something to him but had failed because the words to express their distress were simply not there. "Take away the words," he had said, "and the capacity to share goes. I've seen people sit and weep—just weep—because they can't tell me what they feel inside."

Pat listened. She knew how her father helped people, and she was proud of him for it. He was a kind doctor—that most precious of people. And now, it seemed he wanted to talk.

"How many words do you think you use in a day?" he asked.

Pat shrugged. "Two thousand? Ten thousand? More? Some days, I suspect, there's a lot to say; other days there's . . . well, not quite so much."

Dr. Macgregor nodded. "Fair enough. The truth of the matter is that we can't be sure. There are a lot of figures bandied about, but I've read that they're all unsubstantiated guesses. And memes. This is particularly so when they claim that women use three times as many words a day as men. I simply don't believe that. Where's the evidence? Look at the figures. Some of them say twenty thousand as opposed to seven. Others say eight as opposed to four. It's pure speculation." He paused. "Except when it comes to teenagers, apparently."

"Teenagers?" Pat was close enough to her teens—having escaped from them only a few years previously—to feel threatened by the word.

"Yes. Apparently there has been some very concrete research on the words used by teenagers."

"And the result?"

"Grave," said Dr. Macgregor, with a certain mock theatricality. "Some long-suffering professor of linguistics went through ten million words of speech transcription—teenage talk—and came up with the conclusion that the average teenager knows forty thousand words."

Pat said that she thought that was not bad at all. If one had forty thousand words, there was a lot one could say, other than LOL and :-)

"Yes," said Dr. Macgregor. "If one used forty thousand words one would sound like . . . Who would one sound like? T. S. Eliot?" He paused. "Was T. S. Eliot ever a teenager?"

"Not a very convincing one," said Pat.

Dr. Macgregor smiled. "Mention of Eliot always makes me think of Auden's palindrome. Do you remember my telling you about it? 'T. Eliot, top bard, notes putrid tang emanating. Is sad. I'd assign it a name: gnat dirt upset on drab pot toilet.'

Yes, read it backwards and it says exactly the same thing. It's a most remarkable achievement."

T.S. Eliot

"Teenagers . . ."

"Yes, the thing is this: although they know forty thousand words, they actually use very few—we're told. Eight hundred a day."

"That sounds quite a lot . . ."

"It isn't. Think about it. This little conversation of ours has used . . . what? Six hundred words—something like that. Auden's palindrome alone was twenty-something words. So, make up five long palindromes and you've already used one eighth of what you can say a day."

"Perhaps palindromes should count double," suggested Pat. "Backwards and forwards."

"Perhaps. Like trams . . ." Dr. Macgregor became thoughtful, even melancholy.

"Trams?" said Pat.

"Let's not go there," said Dr. Macgregor. "The trams certainly aren't."

"Aren't what?"

"Aren't going there."

"Eight hundred words . . ."

"Yes. But here's something else: of those eight hundred words, there are twenty that they use rather a lot. In fact, those twenty words make up one third of their daily speech. And these top twenty words include words like yeah, no, and but, as well as a few slang expressions. So it doesn't leave much room for more . . . nuanced expressions, shall we say?"

They were both silent for a moment. Then Dr. Macgregor continued, "I sound like a typical middle-aged grouch, don't I?"

Pat nodded. "Maybe. :-) But typical middle-aged grouches may have a point. The fact that the person who says something is middle-aged doesn't mean that it's rubbish. That's as bad as condemning what teenagers say because they're teenagers. LOL!"

"You're very kind," said Dr. Macgregor.

He looked at his daughter. They had been sitting in the kitchen of his house, waiting for the kettle to boil; and it had done so, but was ignored because they were talking about words and the decline of words. Now he rose to his feet and switched it on again. The kettle made a noise, an agitated noise, as the already-hot water steamed up again, like an argument, an old fight, that had been rekindled. Did middle-aged kettles huff and puff more than young kettles, he asked himself. Will I huff and puff as I grow older, sitting here in my house in the Grange, reading and thinking about how life leaks away?

Eliot came back to him. T. Eliot top bard . . . But not the palindrome, rather the line about growing old and wearing the bottoms of one's trousers rolled. He looked down. His trousers had turn-ups. J. Alfred Prufrock, he thought.

## 39. The Caravaggio Within

We go in—just as we always do, thought Dr. Macgregor as he led his daughter into the dining room of what John Gifford and his co-authors of *The Buildings of Scotland* would have described as a polite villa. That description had struck him forcibly when he had opened the copy of that work given to him by Pat as a birthday present some years earlier, and discovered that his house in Dick Place, along with others like it, was a polite villa. It was at the same time both dispiriting and reassuring; dispiriting in the sense that to live in a polite villa implied that one's life was rather dull: the connection between building style and personality type may not be a necessary one, but it nonetheless exists in many cases, whether as cause or effect—that might be difficult to tell. People who live in small, neat houses may be big-hearted and large-souled—few people can afford large houses, the sorts of houses in which high-ceilinged and spacious thoughts might be imagined to flourish; we may, after all, have to live in some small town in central Scotland rather than Paris but that does not mean that the inner Parisian cannot flourish wherever we are. The danger, of course, is that we spend time imagining that we would be happier elsewhere, and forget to cultivate happiness where fate has placed us. Auden's image of the child, scolded in France, wishing he were crying on the Italian side of the Alps came to his mind, and he thought: we are all that scolded child.

So while the size of one's house said nothing about oneself—except in those cases where people buy ostentatiously large houses to impress others with their grandeur, and there are many of those—the state of living quarters spoke volumes about the one who lived there. Untidy people lived in a state of disorder, and this reflected their personality and their mental habits. Ordered people lived neatly: cut their hedges, did their washing-up regularly, made their beds in the morning. It was so obvious. Send me a picture of your room and I will tell you who you are. Somebody had said that once at a seminar Dr. Macgregor had attended at the Royal College of Psychiatrists, and some present had laughed at what they saw as an excessively simple aphorism;

and yet sophisticated laughter, he thought, was so often misplaced.

Physical untidiness and the untidy mind . . . were they always linked? Every proposition, it seemed, could look less than universal when subjected to close examination; every rule had those glaring exceptions that made it look much weaker. Auden was famously untidy; his suits were dishevelled, bore on their fabric soup stains, cigarette ash, detritus of indeterminate origin; his flat in New York was piled high with books and manuscripts and brim-full ash trays; he kept chocolate puddings on the bathroom floor as that was colder than the fridge; and so on. And yet of all twentieth-century poets he was the one who paid most attention to metre, and ran his life with great, almost obsessive attention to punctuality: Martini time was at the appointed hour itself, not five minutes early nor five minutes late. So order could exist in the midst of disorder, and people who lived in polite villas might not necessarily be timid or unadventurous, but could have lives full of passion and excitement, even if they were not necessarily . . . "Caravaggio," he muttered.

Pat, taking her accustomed seat opposite her father at the table, looked up with concern. If one's father started to mutter Caravaggio à propos of nothing it was potentially worrying. "What was that?" she asked.

He shook his head. "I was thinking," he said. "I

was thinking of the sort of life that I lead now and comparing it to the life of Caravaggio."

She looked at him wide-eyed. "But why would you compare yourself to Caravaggio? Surely chalk shouldn't be compared with cheese."

He thought about this for a moment. While one would not want to be thought to be too similar to Caravaggio, it was not very flattering to be put at the absolutely opposite end of the Caravaggistian spectrum. Most men, if pushed, would like to be thought to have at least a little bit of Caravaggio within them . . .

"No," he admitted. "You're right: I shouldn't compare myself with Caravaggio."

Pat smiled. "Good. I like you just as you are, Dad. Solid, dependable, predictable . . ."

She realised, as she spoke, that to be described as predictable was not necessarily complimentary. She apologised. "Sorry, Dad. I didn't mean to say you're predictable. I didn't mean it. Not really."

He smiled back weakly. "My darling, maybe I am. Look at the table—look at what I've prepared for you. Do you even have to remove the covers from the dishes to see what it is? Do you think Caravaggio gave his guests the same dish every time?" He looked at her, and then said, "Don't answer."

She stared down at her place mat. It was a picture of Stirling Castle. Their place mats had always been the Castles of Scotland, and when one set had eventually worn out, another set had miraculously appeared from somewhere with the same limitless munificence as that with which St. Catherine of Siena's remarkable water barrel had filled and refilled itself. Who made place mats of the Castles of Scotland? Who stocked them? Who got them from the central warehouse where the Castles of Scotland were stored in their presumed thousands to all those polite villas where they were put into daily use? And what conversations took place over these pictures of the Castles of Scotland? What same things were said, by the same people, in the same tone, time and time again?

"Stirling Castle," she said, looking up from the mat.

Her father nodded, and looked down at the place mat before him. "And I've got Balmoral."

He spoke as one might comment on an allocation of gifts by some generous donor: you shall have Stirling Castle; you shall have Balmoral; you shall have Glamis; and you, my dear, shall have a polite villa, no more.

No, he would have to speak in a way that took them beyond all this.

"Pat," he said. "I've made a decision. It's a big decision, my dear, and I want you to be the first to hear about it."

# 40. Ethics of Filming Giraffes . . . and People

If Matthew's recollection of exactly what he promised Bo was clouded—this being the result of a more than minimal dose of Laphroaig—then the same was not true of Bo's own recollection of what was agreed. A few days after their first meeting and the enthusiastic conversation that it had entailed, Bo arrived at the flat in India Street bearing his filming equipment.

Matthew and Elspeth had already discussed the matter over breakfast.

"You could tell him that you've changed your mind," Elspeth had suggested. "You don't always have to do everything you agree to do."

Matthew shook his head. "I don't like doing that," he said. "And, anyway, it won't be too bad."

Elspeth was incredulous. "Having a filmmaker follow us around all the time for a couple of weeks? Not too bad?"

Matthew shrugged. "I don't think it will. And if you like, he can spend most of his time with me."

They had left it at that. Nothing was specifically agreed, but the clear expectation was that Bo and his documentary film would be the principal responsibility of Matthew and, to an extent, Anna. It was Anna, after all, who had invited him to the flat and she should therefore bear some of the burden that his subsequent presence entailed.

Now, opening the door to Bo, Matthew winced when he saw the camera case and the various bits of equipment that accompanied it.

"Here I am!" said Bo brightly. "And what a good day it is outside for filming. Bright, but not too bright: just the conditions filmmakers like."

Matthew glanced up at the cupola above the stairs. Broad slabs of sunshine penetrated the glass and cut at an angle through the still air of the interior, illuminating floating specks of dust. "Yes," he said flatly. "Of course."

"Well then," said Bo. "I'll set things up and then . . . well, then you can simply get on with your lives! You mustn't mind me—that's what you say in English, isn't it? You mustn't mind me?"

Matthew stood aside to allow Bo to enter the hall. "I'll be going to the gallery this morning," he said. "You're very welcome to come with me and film that."

Bo nodded enthusiastically. "That's just the sort of thing I want," he said. "I shall film you walking along Heriot Row and then down Dundas Street. That will be very interesting for people in Denmark."

Matthew managed a weak smile. "Do you really think so?"

Bo did. "The whole point about a documentary film of this nature is that it involves what we call the uninterpreted recording of activities and events. If I started to select only those things that are more dramatic in your life, then I would be interpreting your life—I would be changing it. But I shall not do that. I shall merely show, and in that way the audience of the film will see your life in its natural context, for what it is." He paused, and looked at Matthew, as if to confirm that he understood. "It is the same as making a wildlife documentary."

Matthew frowned. "Not very flattering . . ."

Bo laughed. "Oh, I don't mean to compare you to a giraffe or anything like that. But the analogy is appropriate. Making a wildlife film involves many ethical issues relating to observation. That man who chased the animals . . . what was he called? He did not follow these rules, I'm afraid."

"The one who . . ."

"Yes, the one who went and ran after wild creatures. I saw a film of him chasing a black mamba in Africa. Chasing it! That was very unwise, not only because black mambas do not like to be chased and have the means of showing this disapproval, but also because you should never chase wild animals you're filming. You should never stress them. It also encourages people who watch these things to go and chase creatures themselves. It is not very good."

Matthew agreed. He had seen that man in action and had been unhappy about the way he disturbed the creatures he filmed. "He meant well, no doubt," said Matthew. "Perhaps he felt the end justified the means. Perhaps he thought it was the only way to get people to relate to wildlife."

Bo looked up from his task of screwing a lens into the body of his camera. "Perhaps. And I'm sorry about what happened." He twisted the lens in further until there came a satisfying clicking sound. "There, that's fixed. But of course there are many interesting issues in filming people. There is that very amusing man who pretends to be from somewhere remote and goes and speaks to all those people in America and gets them to say embarrassing things. I'm not happy about that, you know. They are simply being polite to him, and he takes advantage of that politeness. That is bad."

Matthew was silent. He wondered whether he said embarrassing things himself. It was perfectly possible that he did. Or even if he did not say embarrassing things, then might some of the things he said simply be silly, or inconsequential? Most of our conversation was like that, he thought. We don't speak as if our lines have been written for us by a dramatist. Did Oscar Wilde speak with the sophistication of an Oscar Wilde character? He doubted it. But then Oscar Wilde did come up with some very apt remarks in his ordinary exchanges with people. What had he said to the customs official on entering the United States? Have you anything to declare, Mr. Wilde? Only my genius. What a thing to say! What would happen if one tried that these days? Matthew doubted whether customs officials today would appreciate it. And he doubted, too, whether the customs official to whom it was originally said was all that pleased either. Would he have gone back to his colleagues and reported, "You know what that Oscar Wilde said to me when I asked him whether he had anything to declare? Well, you'd hardly believe it but . . ."

Oscar Wilde was so funny, Matthew thought. A fly-on-the-wall account of his life would be quite a thing . . . well, not of all his life, just bits. And what was attributed to him on his deathbed in Paris? He had not liked the room's decoration and had announced: "Either that wallpaper goes, or I do." He probably did not say that—but he could have.

He looked at Bo. What does he expect of me, he wondered. And what if he were . . . sending me up?

## 41. Observation

Matthew had not envisaged how difficult it would be to appear natural when walking under the unremitting gaze of a camera. As he made his way up India Street that morning, with Bo walking backwards in front of him, his lens trained unblinkingly on his embarrassed subject, Matthew found himself uncertain what to do with his hands. In a normal walk, the hands find their place naturally, hanging by one's side, perhaps moving slightly with the rhythm of the walk—not moving piston-like, as the hands and arms of a runner will move; that is how it is when we don't think about what we're doing. But once we start to think about those ordinary movements we perform when doing some everyday task, then the looseness and fluidity of the body is lost and an awkward rigidity may take over. And even more so, when we think about such movements and are at the same time observed by a camera: then not only may our gait become truly awkward but the facial expression we assume may reflect this state of discomfort too.

Public figures—those who regularly find themselves under the scrutiny of crowds or cameras—have their ways of dealing with this: a fixed mask, perhaps, or little movements that absorb the body's restless energy, that give it something to do. Some people, although seemingly at ease in the space they occupy, adjust the cuffs of their shirt as they walk, a small gesture that must make it easier for them; Mrs. Thatcher had her handbag to grasp—in her case, both a shield and a weapon to be used on opponents; Mr. Brown sucked in his cheeks and, it seemed, chewed them thoughtfully—perhaps a way of keeping himself awake, a substitute for pinching himself, in the many moments of mind-numbing tedium that a prime minister must endure. All of these were entirely understandable devices that those who have to put up with us—the public—at our most inquisitive and demanding must be forgiven for employing. But such techniques are not easily learned, and Matthew, who could not recall ever having been filmed before—let alone for a Danish documentary—had not had an opportunity to acquire them. Now, as he turned the corner into Heriot Row, he felt that lack acutely. And not only did he not know how to walk when observed by a camera, he also had no idea where to look. Bo had asked him not to look into the lens of the camera, and Matthew was trying to follow that instruction. But tell yourself not to do something, and that is exactly what you will feel drawn to do. Those who encounter Medusa know all about that. Skiers also know it, having had it drummed into them at ski school: do not look down at your skis but keep your gaze focused on where you want to be; funambulists too: they know that should they glance down at those curious, ballet-type shoes they wear, then they will lose their balance and fall; and so they look steadfastly ahead, their eyes focused on some point just beyond the end of the singing wire, as Matthew now focused his gaze on the junction of Heriot Row and Dundas Street, never before studied with such longing intensity.

"Just relax," called out Bo from behind his camera. "Pretend that I'm not here."

Matthew made a non-committal sound and tried, for a few moments, to think of something that would distract him. A completely detached thought—something that had no bearing on his current situation—could make him look normal, or so he thought. But the thought that came to him was an inadmissible one: one of those embarrassing, intrusive thoughts that arrive uninvited and make one blush, which is what Matthew now did. This is hopeless, he thought. I'm going to look ridiculous.

Bo appeared not to share this view. After they had eventually arrived at the gallery, and Matthew had made a show of extracting the key from his pocket and opening the door, he switched off his camera, lowered it from his shoulder, and clapped his hands enthusiastically.

"You're a natural," he exclaimed, patting Matthew on the back. "This is going to be a great film!"

Matthew looked puzzled. "But nothing's happened," he exclaimed. "All you've done is to film me walking to work."

"But you walked so well," said Bo. "The way you . . . the way you moved, your whole walk—people in Denmark are going to go wild over that."

Matthew frowned. He had no idea why people in Denmark should find his walking to work—or indeed his walking anywhere—of the remotest interest. If he were ever to see a documentary film showing Danish people walking to work in Copenhagen, he was sure that he would find it very dull; why should it be any different when the subject of the film was him?

"Just go ahead with your normal routine," said Bo. "Just ignore me."

Matthew went to his desk and sat down. Bo picked up his camera again, turned it on, and moved slowly towards Matthew. "Don't look into the camera," he whispered. "Just do what you normally do."

For a few moments Matthew stared blankly at the surface of his desk. What did he normally do when he sat at his desk? Now that he had to think about it, he found it difficult to remember. He read the mail, of course; that would give him something to do.

He reached for the small pile of letters he had picked up as he had entered the gallery. There was not much to the pile that morning: two white envelopes, one brown, and an advertisement for an Italian restaurant.

"You could open the letters," Bo suggested helpfully.

Matthew resisted the temptation to give him a scathing look. He did not need to be told what to do; he would open the letters because that was what he normally did. "I don't need prompting," he muttered sotto voce.

He slit open the first of the white envelopes and extracted a typewritten page from within. It was an enquiry from a dealer in London who wondered whether Matthew had any Anne Redpaths in stock. Matthew put the letter to one side and opened the second. This was handwritten, and consisted of no more than one line.

*You,* it said, *are being watched.*

There was no address at the top of the letter and no signature at the bottom.

# 42. Jonathan Makes a Proposition to Bruce

Jonathan stayed for no more than half an hour before he looked at his watch and explained to Bruce that he was expecting a visitor in his own flat, on the opposite side of the street.

"I'll have to go," he said. "But I imagine that we'll be seeing one another again."

He smiled, and looked at Bruce in a way that was not easily interpreted. It was not exactly an invitation, but it was more than one of those mere social niceties that we utter without meaning them: the "see you later" or "we must meet for lunch sometime" remarks that are not meant to be taken literally. The last thing one should say if somebody says let's meet for lunch sometime is when? It is even less appropriate to take one's diary out of a pocket and prepare to write; that quite justifies the response next year, perhaps.

Bruce nodded; he was thinking of what Jonathan had said about twins, and how twins separated at birth, brought up in ignorance of the existence of each other, sometimes reported a vague sense of incompleteness—a sense that there was something, somebody, missing.

"It's very strange," Jonathan had said. "I was

reading about somebody who was convinced he had a brother. He said that he just knew it. And then, when he was well into his adult years, he discovered that there was a brother, who had been handed over for adoption straightaway. He was there all the time." He paused, and fixed Bruce with a stare. "Imagine what it feels like to find that you have a brother you didn't know about? Can you imagine that?"

"I suppose it's rather satisfying," said Bruce.

"Mind you," said Jonathan thoughtfully, "children believe all sorts of surprising things. Some of them seem to be convinced that they've had other lives."

"Spooky," said Bruce.

Jonathan laughed. "I don't let these things worry me. I rather like hearing about them, in fact. I was reading about a child who was adamant that she had lived in a village in France over a hundred years ago. She gave the name of the village and mentioned people who lived there—by name."

"And were the details correct?"

Jonathan nodded. "Apparently so."

"Did she speak French?"

"That's the extraordinary thing. She spoke some, although she had never learned it. She wasn't fluent, but she knew the French names for some fairly obscure agricultural implements. That's called xenoglossy, by the way."

"What's called xenoglossy?"

"The ability to speak a language you've never learned."

Bruce was thinking of the girl who claimed to have been French. "She must have been exposed to some information about that place," he said. "Perhaps she read about it somewhere. You don't need to know much about a place to be able to pretend to be from there."

Jonathan thought about this. "Or a person. You probably don't have to know all that much about a person's life in order to claim to be that person. Remember all those films about people being sent off as spies, having to mug up on a false identity. They can't have known all that much about the person they were pretending to be."

Bruce shrugged. "You had to be careful about details. Little things—and one slip could get you shot . . ."

He did not finish. "Like us," said Jonathan.

Bruce looked puzzled. "How like us?"

"Well," said Jonathan, "we could find out a bit about each other and then . . . exchange existences. To get away with it, I suspect that we'd only have to know a few things: names of family members, where we went to school, the name of our boss, a handful of things like that."

Bruce frowned. "Are you serious?"

Jonathan got up from his chair. "Actually, I am."

"You mean I should step into your shoes, and you into mine?"

Jonathan nodded. "We'll take the same size," he said, and then laughed.

Bruce ignored this. "Why? Why should we do it?"

"Why do people do anything unusual? Why do they decide that they've had enough of their own lives and look at the lives of others?"

Bruce did not answer, and so Jonathan continued. "I have an interesting life, I suppose. But sometimes I think of how . . . how fulfilling it would be to be someone else. Don't you think that too?"

Bruce looked out of the window. He had always been entirely satisfied with his existence but . . . yes, he supposed that there had been times when it had occurred to him that other people's lives were more interesting than his. "Sometimes," he said.

Jonathan was studying him. "I thought of an amazing story, by the way," he said. "Imagine that you have an identical twin and your twin commits a crime."

Bruce thought about this. "I can see where this is going," he said. "The innocent twin is arrested and convicted of the crime committed by his brother."

"No," said Jonathan. "That could happen, of course, but what I had in mind was that the guilty twin is arrested and sent to prison. His brother comes to visit him and the guilty twin overpowers him . . ."

"Difficult under the eyes of the guard, surely."

"The guard is in on it," said Jonathan quickly.

"I see."

"Yes, and the prisoner dresses his brother in his prison clothing and gets into his. Then he walks out, leaving his twin in his place."

Bruce laughed. "It wouldn't work."

"Why not?" asked Jonathan.

"Because the one left behind would tell them. And they would check up and see that there was a twin."

Jonathan was prepared for this. "But they wouldn't be able to tell."

"Fingerprints?" said Bruce.

Jonathan considered this for a moment. "Maybe. But it's fiction, just a story, remember, and you don't have to be completely realistic." He paused.

"But what I want to ask you is this: should we do it? Should we swap?"

Bruce never understood why he gave his answer so quickly.

"Yes. Why not?"

## 43. *You Have My Life, I'll Have Yours*

"One thing," said Bruce. "One thing I want to ask you: how long for?"

Jonathan, who had been on the point of leaving before this conversation started, now sat down again. "Good question," he said.

"A couple of hours?" asked Bruce. "A day?"

Jonathan shook his head. "Oh, more than that," he said. "What would be the point of doing it for a short time? You wouldn't get the feeling of being me and I wouldn't get the feeling of being you."

Bruce looked at him doubtfully. "But what about work?"

Jonathan shrugged. "You tell me what you're expected to do and I'll try and do it. Your job isn't rocket science, I take it?"

"No," said Bruce. "But you still have to know a bit."

"I can bluff," said Jonathan.

"But what about the names of the other people at work? It'd become pretty apparent, don't you

214

think, that we didn't know who was who?"

Jonathan did not consider this to be a problem. "It's amazing how long you can go without knowing what to call somebody," he said. "Have people got their names on their doors in your office?"

"Yes," replied Bruce.

"Then I'd find out who's who."

Bruce thought for a moment. "Do you know anything about building?"

Jonathan said he did. He had a friend who was an architect and he had told him a lot about levels and detailing of walls and things of that sort. "And I bought a flat once," he said. "That taught me a lot about the way you people work." He looked at Bruce, a smile playing about his lips. "You'll have no difficulty with my job," he said. "PR is CS, which means common sense. CGW—can't go wrong."

"Except with the acronyms," said Bruce. "One could go wrong PDQ with those."

Jonathan was sanguine. "Don't worry—it'll be all right. Shall we give it a week? Ten days?"

Bruce hesitated. "My job's fairly responsible," he said. "People buy property on the basis of my reports."

Jonathan tried to reassure him. "I'll consult you," he said. "We could meet on the occasional evening and go over things. You could tell me what to do."

Bruce was still unhappy.

"Listen," said Jonathan. "It'll be a cinch. Haven't you heard of those people who pass themselves off as doctors? You read about them in the newspapers from time to time. Sometimes they get away with it for years—in fact, they can be rather good at what they do."

"They can't be," said Bruce.

Jonathan contradicted him. "No, they can be. If you've been a nurse or whatever for ages and seen what the doctor does, then you can probably do it just as well. Maybe the same applies to dentists. I suspect it does. After all, you don't really need to train for all those years to do those jobs."

"Are you sure?"

"Sure, I'm sure. Long training periods are all about professionalisation and restricting access. And they're also about the vested interests that colleges and universities have in keeping people on their courses for years. Take accountancy: six months intensive training and you can do most of the jobs done by accountants. You won't know everything, of course, but you'll know enough to do a lot of it. Plumbing: six months too. Max. Same for being an electrician. That's dead simple. Green wire here, brown wire here, earth over there."

Bruce found himself wondering whether Jonathan was joking. "But the earth is the green wire," he interjected. "Green and yellow, I think."

Jonathan seemed vaguely surprised. "Is it? Well, okay, you put the green wire in the earth socket and that's that."

Bruce listened.

"The only one I'd be careful about is being a pilot," Jonathan continued. "You need actual flying hours for that. Anything that requires feel needs quite a long training. But the rest . . ." He shrugged. He seemed to have second thoughts about pilots. "Actually, pilots don't really need much experience any more. Those big planes are flown by computers. You just sit there and switch on automatic take-off and landing and the computers do the rest. You don't have to touch a thing. If you can turn on a computer, then you can fly a jumbo. Simple."

"As long as everything goes well," Bruce said.

"Which it will do 99.9 per cent of the time. But do you think you're going to get the pilots' unions to admit that? Oh no, you aren't. And the reason for that is that if they admit that they just sit there and do nothing, then somebody's going to ask how come they deserve those big salaries? How much do you think the captain of a big passenger jet gets?"

Bruce was unsure. He thought that it was over one hundred thousand pounds, but he was not sure. "Over one hundred grand?"

"Yes," said Jonathan. "If he's senior and with a pukka airline. One hundred and twenty, and more.

So you're not going to get them admitting to the fact that their job could be done just as well by the cabin crew—let alone the passengers. Mind you, if you fly for one of those budget outfits— the real cheap and cheerful end of things—then you get minimum wage. And you have to take your own sandwiches. Did you know that? Those guys have to take their own lunch with them—or they buy the bacon roll for four quid like the rest of us."

Bruce decided to move the conversation on. "All right," he said. "So you go into my office and I go into yours. What then?"

"We take it from there," said Jonathan. "You lead my social life, and I lead yours."

"But what about our friends?"

Jonathan had his answer ready. "That'll be the fun part—the big test, if you like. If we can fool them, we can fool anybody."

"I'm not sure . . ." Bruce was beginning to feel doubtful.

"Of course, if you've got cold feet . . ."

This had the effect that Jonathan had imagined it would.

"Of course I haven't got cold feet," Bruce protested. "I'm just raising some of the practical problems we might encounter."

"Fair enough," said Jonathan. "So you're still committed?"

"Of course."

"Well then I'll tell you something about myself," said Jonathan. "Listening? All right. Here goes. First bit of information—not important, but you should know: first bit: I'm gay."

## 44. Shuggie McGrath and Other Memories

Bruce said nothing. He was aware that Jonathan was watching him, assessing his reaction to the disclosure he had made, but he had nothing to say about it really. Jonathan's preferences were of no particular interest to him, and were certainly not any sort of threat. Like all profoundly narcissistic people, Bruce imagined that everyone was as admiring of him as he was of himself, and it did not particularly matter to him whether this admiration was male or female in origin. So, after a brief moment during which he registered what Jonathan had just said, he merely shrugged and said, "I'm cool with that."

Jonathan raised an eyebrow, but only slightly. "You sure?"

Bruce shrugged again. "Yes, whatever."

"All right," said Jonathan. "So let's . . ."

But now Bruce had thought of something. "Are you in a relationship at the moment?"

Jonathan smiled. "I thought you might want to know that."

"Not that I care," said Bruce hurriedly. "It's nothing to do with me, but it suddenly occurred to me that if you were in a relationship then it could be awkward if . . ."

Jonathan continued to smile. "Yes? If?"

Bruce looked embarrassed. "If you had a friend, then the friend might think . . ."

"Yes?"

Bruce was now blushing. "He might expect me to . . ."

"Like him?" prompted Jonathan gently.

Bruce became flustered. "Well, I'm sure I'd like him. I'm sure he's great . . ."

"But he doesn't exist," said Jonathan. "I just told you."

"I mean, if he did exist, then he could think that I had suddenly gone off him."

Jonathan frowned. "But why would you do that? You just said that you were sure that he'd be great."

"Of course he'd be great," blustered Bruce. "I told you: I'm cool with people like that."

"Like what?" asked Jonathan.

"Like your friend."

Jonathan looked puzzled. "But how can anybody be like somebody who doesn't exist?"

Bruce tried to look amused. "Hah!" he said. "I see what you mean."

Jonathan looked thoughtful. "Let's forget about him," he said. "He doesn't exist, and so there's no problem. I live by myself."

"So do I," said Bruce. Then again a further thought occurred. "You'd live in my place then? And I'd live in yours?"

"Yes," said Jonathan. "I've got more furniture, of course."

"I'm not sure that I want to," said Bruce. "I thought we were just going to exchange jobs—that sort of thing."

"No," said Jonathan. "We exchange the whole deal. You wear my clothes, live in my flat, go to work as me. The whole deal." He paused, looked at Bruce with a mixture of amusement and something that struck Bruce as condescension. "Unless you are getting cold feet."

Whether or not it was intended as such, this remark was exactly the one to stiffen Bruce's resolve. He had never been able to take a loss of face, and even if he felt this exchange of identities was a pointless and rather hazardous exercise, he would be loath to say so.

"Of course I've not got cold feet," he retorted, rather too loudly. "I said I'd do it."

"Good," said Jonathan. "And now I'll tell you a bit more about myself. I'll give you my history so that you'll ring true."

Bruce sat back in his chair. "Fire away."

"I spent my first seventeen years in Glasgow," Jonathan. "Bearsden."

Bruce nodded. "I know Bearsden a bit. I've got cousins there."

"Good," said Jonathan. "So if somebody says something about Bearsden you'll know what they're talking about."

"Of course," said Bruce. "No problems."

"Right," continued Jonathan. "I went to school at Hutchy."

Bruce said that his cousins did so too. "Maybe you know them. There were two of them." He paused. "How old are you?"

Jonathan did not reply for a moment. Bruce stared at him.

"Twenty-seven."

"Same here," said Bruce.

"Birthday?"

Bruce hesitated. "Eighth of June." He knew what was coming.

"Same here."

There was another silence. Then Bruce cleared his throat. "Coincidence," he said. "Put a bunch of people in a room and there's always a chance you'll find two with the same birthday—a much higher chance than you'd imagine. I read about it."

"But there are only two of us in this room," Jonathan pointed out. "Not a whole bunch."

Bruce was not persuaded. "As I said, coincidence."

Jonathan made a gesture of acceptance. "All right, coincidence."

"So my cousins were called McGrath," said

Bruce. "Bob and Hugh. We called Hugh Shuggie. Still do. Shuggie's our age. He would have been in your year at Hutchy."

Jonathan laughed. "Shuggie McGrath? Of course I knew him. He was a runner, wasn't he?"

"Yes. A sprinter. And he played bass in a band, the Shugs. There were two of them called Hugh, you see."

"I remember them," said Jonathan. "And he was also in the Pipe Band, wasn't he?"

Bruce nodded. "He played the pipes at another cousin's wedding over in Ayrshire. Kilwinning."

Jonathan seemed to be mulling over a memory— a fond one. "Shuggie and I were quite friendly," he said. "I think he liked me."

Bruce shook his head. "He's not . . ." He stopped himself.

"Not what?" asked Jonathan.

"Not playing the pipes any more," said Bruce quickly. "But carry on."

Jonathan continued. There had been Hutchy, he said, and then there had been the bit that came after Hutchy, which was the world. "As between the two, I think I prefer Hutchy to the world."

Bruce looked unbelieving. "I didn't like being at school," he said. "All those rules. Being told: do this, do that. I couldn't wait to get out of it."

Jonathan said that he could not disagree more. "I loved it," he said. "We were a group of friends together. And I don't think I'll ever make friends like that again. Never."

"You can't live in the past," said Bruce.

"Maybe not. But when there was a time that you were really happy, then why shouldn't you think about it? Why shouldn't you keep memories alive?"

Bruce looked up at the ceiling. If Jonathan was unhappy now, was that the reason why he had suggested this exchange? Did he think that he would be happier leading somebody else's life—was that it? Or was it possible that Jonathan had a reason to escape his life, some reason that was pressing, undisclosed—and serious?

## 45. A Visit to St. Bennet's

It was with some relief that Cyril followed Cardinal O'Brien. The dog had been sure enough of the need to escape from the shed in which Ranald Braveheart Macpherson had locked him for the night. He had no sense of obligation to stay with Ranald—Bertie, by contrast, had been a different matter, Cyril having known him for years, as a companion with whom to romp in the Drummond Place Gardens and as somebody whom he occasionally met on his walks with Angus. He was also familiar enough with Scotland Street, as Angus had been accustomed to taking him there on his visits to Domenica—rather tedious visits, in Cyril's opinion, as he was often made to stay on the landing for long periods, his leash tied to the banister, while his master visited the person who, unknown to Cyril, had now become his mistress according to the law of Scotland—if the law of Scotland can be bothered to regulate such matters as the lives of dogs. Those lives are led somewhere below us, in a region of shoes and ankles and detritus, in a place of rich smells and rough textures of which we have only the faintest of ideas, but that for dogs constitutes the whole world; for dogs in Scotland don't know that England exists, or France, or America—or anywhere, really, and are none the unhappier for it.

Cyril followed the Cardinal that evening because he had no idea what to do otherwise. Some dogs are happy to follow their noses—one sees them in the street looking as if they know where they are going, but they do not. If their nose were to be pointed in a completely different direction then that is where they would go, with the same apparent sense of purpose as before—at that comfortable, relaxed pace of a dog who has all the time in the world. Cyril, though, was in a strange part of town and was feeling confused as a result; and here was somebody who had spoken to him kindly and had that vague sense of authority to which dogs, as pack animals, are so sensitive.

From Cardinal O'Brien's point of view, the dog

he encountered had clearly strayed from his home. While there were some of the neighbourhood dogs he recognised, Cyril was not one of them and could not be left to wander. There was, he thought, a council department that was concerned with strays—and in that he was right. These people used to be called dog-catchers but he doubted if such an insensitive term would be used these days. Dog-catchers had been redescribed as dog wardens, which was less threatening, even if catching dogs was what dog wardens actually did. (Traffic wardens, by contrast, had never been described as car catchers, even if that, as in the case of dog wardens, was exactly what they did.) But even dog warden had a dated feel to it now, and the hunt was on for a less custodial, less prescriptive name. Dog consultants was very much a favourite, and, it was widely believed, would probably win.

"You'd better come along with me," said Cardinal O'Brien, looking down at Cyril fondly. "Then we can try to get you home tomorrow morning."

He had examined Cyril's collar, hoping to find some indication of his address, but there was nothing. He had found, though, a small metal tag, rather ornately inscribed with the letters RSA. Those, he imagined, were the initials of the dog's owner, and it struck him as odd that somebody should put such information on a collar when a far more useful bit of information would be a telephone number or a street address.

Cyril looked up at the Cardinal and wagged his tail. He could tell that he was in safe hands here and when the Cardinal invited him to follow him, he readily acceded to the suggestion. So the two of them made their way back to St. Bennet's, the Cardinal's official residence. This house was one among many such houses in the area—substantial, but not in the slightest bit ostentatious; ostentation was for places like London and the flashier parts of Dublin, not for Edinburgh. All that marked this house out from its neighbours was a domed archiepiscopal chapel in the grounds—a charming building by R. Weir Schultz, and built in the early years of the twentieth century by the generosity of the third Marquess of Bute. The Butes, an illegitimate off-shoot of the Stuart dynasty, were great swells, having acquired a considerable fortune by inventive talent. While some Victorians contented themselves with inventing industrial processes, the Butes distinguished themselves by inventing Cardiff. That proved to be a good invention: inventing a port city can be profitable, and they acquired great wealth. This in due course came into the hands of the third Marquess, a man of broad interests and serious mind, who converted to Catholicism and became the model for the hero of Disraeli's novel *Lothair*. This marquess was to die rather early—he was in his early fifties—but he succeeded in building a large number of buildings, public and private, including this chapel. Today those who drive past it, and see its green copper dome rising above the high wall that marks the curtilage of the house, probably do not think of the high-minded Victorian who caused it to be built. In his time, people must have imagined that nobody could ever possibly forget the man who enabled its construction, but everybody is forgotten, no matter what physical reminders they leave behind them.

For Cyril, of course, the gates of St. Bennet's were like any other gates, the house like any others. And the kitchen into which he was taken was much like any other kitchen; and the dish of cold beef that was generously put before him was just like any other dish of cold beef—to be wolfed down greedily in spite of the fact that the last meal, the Irish stew given to him by Ranald Braveheart Macpherson, had been consumed less than an hour before.

The Cardinal then took Cyril into a small scullery where he placed an old cushion on the ground for his bed.

"Goodnight, my boy," said the Cardinal. "And God bless."

It was a kind thing to say to a dog, and a good thing. Because the least of us, the very least, has the same claim as any other to that love, divine or human, which makes our world, in all its turmoil and pain, easier to comprehend, easier to bear.

# 46. Pleasant Semi-Somnolence

Cyril slept well in the Cardinal's house, comfortable on the cushion that had been provided for him. By the time the scullery door was opened in the morning, he was ready for the day, his tail wagging in anticipation.

"You're looking cheerful," said Cardinal O'Brien. "Breakfast first, and then I might arrange a bit of exercise for you."

Cyril had no idea what was being said to him, but readily acceded to the suggestion. Dogs agree with us in all that we say to them, which is what makes them such agreeable companions. And their sycophancy is so complete, so natural and unforced, that we never really object to it.

He followed the Cardinal through to the kitchen, where a plate of porridge and gravy was placed on the floor for him. This did not take him long to polish off and then, while the Cardinal had his own breakfast of scrambled eggs and bacon, Cyril sat politely on the floor beside his chair, waiting for any scraps that might come his way. There were several of these: two bacon rinds and the crust from a slice of toast.

"You dogs are always hungry, aren't you?" said the Cardinal.

Cyril looked at his host and cocked his head. He

was pleased with his new guardian and wanted only to be noticed by him and secure his approval. But there were newspapers to read, and the Cardinal busied himself with these and with a steaming cup of coffee before a secretary arrived at the house with correspondence to attend to.

"I see Your Eminence has acquired a dog," said the secretary, reaching down to pat Cyril on the head.

"He acquired me," said the Cardinal. "And I think we'll have to get in touch with the council about him. They may be able to trace his owner." He paused. "You know that my immediate predecessor had a dog?"

The secretary shook his head. "Before my time, Eminence."

"Well he did," said the Cardinal. "Cardinal Gray had a dog called Rusty. And when he celebrated Mass in the chapel here the congregation was regularly three religious sisters and his dog, who used to sleep quietly in his basket near the altar and never uttered a whimper."

The secretary smiled. "I can just see it," he said.

"Yes," continued the Cardinal. "And the extraordinary thing was this: when Cardinal Gray returned from the Second Vatican Council with instructions that Mass should be said in English rather than in Latin, Rusty started howling in anger at the change in language! He left the chapel and never came back in—to the consternation of the nuns! It was quite astonishing."

"Rusty was a traditionalist?" said the secretary.

The Cardinal smiled. "That might be one conclusion," he said.

They passed on to a discussion of the day's business, at the end of which the Cardinal asked the secretary whether he would mind picking up some provisions at Valvona & Crolla if he was going down to the Cathedral. The secretary agreed to do this, and he also agreed to take Cyril with him for the outing.

"Dogs like to get out and about," said the Cardinal. "But be sure to remember to keep him on his leash. We don't want him running off into the traffic or anything like that."

Cyril set off with the secretary, walking off jauntily in the direction of Bruntsfield Place, where the 23 bus might be picked up. After the short trip to the centre of town, they got off just before Queen Street and completed the rest of the journey on foot. Cyril sniffed at the air, and then sniffed at it again. There was something very familiar about this air, and he felt that although he might not be able to find it exactly, he was now rather close to his home. And if he was close to home, then he should be close to Angus, and that set his tail wagging like the arm of an hysterical metronome.

Aware of the fact that food shops might not

welcome dogs, the secretary tied Cyril's leash to a lamppost outside the front door, instructed the dog to sit, and then went in with his shopping list. Mary Contini and her husband, Philip, happened to be glancing out onto the street at that very moment and could not help but notice Cyril outside.

"That looks awfully like Angus Lordie's dog," said Mary. "Remember, the one who stole that salami?"

Philip Contini peered out of the door. "I do believe you're right," he said. "I'll go and take a look."

Cyril greeted Philip Contini warmly—he knew this man and licked his hand enthusiastically as his jaws were gently prised open to reveal the tell-tale gold tooth. Returning inside, Philip confirmed his wife's suspicion. "It's him all right," he said. "I thought Angus was away on his honeymoon."

Overhearing this conversation, the secretary explained how Cyril happened to be there. This was followed by a brief discussion, and this discussion was followed by a brief telephone call to the Cardinal. Options were considered and a decision was taken: Cyril would be looked after by friends of the Continis who were believed to be well-disposed to dogs. When Angus and Domenica returned from Jamaica, then Cyril could be restored to them; for the time being it was deemed best not to disturb them in Jamaica.

Cyril sensed that he was being talked about, and followed the conversation closely—in so far as he could—his head turning left and right like a tennis umpire's. Then, a short time later, he was bundled into the back of the delicatessen's van and driven off to Ravelston, where he was handed over to Roger Collins and his wife, Judith McClure. Cyril explored his new surroundings quickly, and then settled down to sleep on a rug in the study that Roger and Judith shared. It was a room as comfortable for the writing of books as it was for the settling down of dogs, and the rest of the day followed in pleasant semi-somnolence while Roger worked on his new book and Judith, at her desk, drafted a report on Scottish–Chinese educational co-operation. Cyril watched them both from the corner of an eye. He was tired and replete; there were, of course, smaller creatures he could be chasing outside in the garden, but why bother when one was so comfortable and secure? He saw no reason. Perhaps it was time to become relaxed about the world, even if one was a dog. Why fetch when people shouted Fetch? One grew beyond such things. Fetch! Hah! *Pourquoi*?

## 47. Cold Showers and Other Reactionary Preoccupations

Word reached Bertie of Cyril's fate when he and his mother next paid a visit to Valvona & Crolla.

"A very satisfactory solution," said Irene. "He'll be perfectly happy there . . . and we'll be perfectly happy here." For Bertie, who had been looking forward to having a dog, even temporarily, it was far from satisfactory, but his attention was now diverted by the announcement by his teacher that the school would shortly be holding a summer fair. This news led immediately to an excited buzz of conversation, curtailed, though, by the further information that there would not be room for everyone to have a stall.

"Obviously not everybody can have a table," said Miss Maclaren Hope. "We can't all have a table in this life, boys and girls, or there wouldn't be any room for anything else, would there? No, there would not."

Sensing a restriction, the class remained silent.

"So," continued the teacher, "we can only have three stalls for each class. Everybody else can have a nice time looking at the things for sale."

Olive's hand shot up. "I'll have one, Miss Maclaren Hope," she said. "Pansy and I don't mind having one of the tables, if you like."

Olive stared at the others while she made this offer, daring them to object.

Tofu raised his hand. "That's not fair," he objected. "Why should she have a table, Miss Maclaren Hope? What's she done to deserve a table?"

Olive shot a glance of pure hatred in Tofu's direction. "I asked first," she said. "If you ask first, you're entitled, so you just shut up, Tofu."

"Now, now," said Miss Maclaren Hope. "We mustn't talk to one another like that, boys and girls. We mustn't tell one another to shut up."

"Yes," said Tofu. "She should stop telling people to shut up just because she doesn't like what they say." He paused. "Or if she doesn't like their singing, either. You know what I heard, Miss Maclaren Hope? You know what I heard when you were singing us your Gaelic songs? Remember that time? I heard Olive say I wish she'd shut up. That's what she said, Miss Maclaren Hope. I'm not inventing it. Promise."

The teacher glanced at Olive, who looked away guiltily. "I don't think we need to go there, Tofu," she said. "I'm sure that Olive wouldn't say a thing like that. And, anyway, as far as tables are concerned, we're going to have a draw. Everybody should write their name on a bit of paper and then I'll pick three names out of a hat and those will be the lucky people to have a table. Each will be able to ask a friend to help."

The draw took place, with surprising results. Olive's name was first—which resulted in smirks from both Olive and Pansy; next came Tofu, who punched the air with satisfaction; and finally, Bertie.

"We shall all have such fun," said Miss Maclaren Hope. "I'm quite sure of it, boys and girls. Such fun!"

The announcement of the fair was made on Friday. Bertie had intended to tell his mother of the news that evening, but did not find the opportunity to do so until the following morning. The cub scouts met on Friday evening and he was reluctant to raise a controversial matter with her at a time when her co-operation was required. Bertie lived in dread of Irene's suddenly changing her mind on the issue of the cub scouts, which she barely tolerated and could so easily suddenly ban. In her view, they were a paramilitary organisation designed to inculcate militaristic, patriarchal values, not to mention the interest they might occasion in compasses and penknives and the like. Baden-Powell, founder of the Boy Scouts, was beyond the pale, she felt: a militarist, a reactionary, a corrupter of youth in much the same way as Socrates was alleged to have corrupted the youth of Athens by giving them the wrong ideas. "I would have administered the hemlock myself," she once remarked to Stuart. "I would quite happily have dosed Baden-Powell with a good long draught of hemlock—wretched man!"

"It was quite some time ago," said Stuart mildly. "He was a child of his time—as we all are. He thought he was doing the right thing." So many people, he felt, thought they were doing the right thing; in fact, it was difficult to think of anybody who actually thought otherwise. Did anybody get out of bed in the morning, look in the mirror, and say: I shall be really malevolent today?

"Nonsense," snapped Irene. "Baden-Powell was a reactionary."

Stuart looked at the floor. "If you say so," he said.

"Well, I do. And he was." She paused. "And John Buchan too."

Stuart looked up. He rather liked *Sick Heart River* and *The Thirty-Nine Steps*, but he felt that perhaps he should not confess to that—at least not to his wife.

"What's wrong with John Buchan?" he asked mildly.

"Everything," said Irene. "Absolutely everything."

Stuart frowned. "Have you read Buchan? I didn't think that he was to your taste, really . . ."

"Of course I haven't read him," said Irene. "That's not the point. But I've certainly read critiques of his work, and that's quite enough for me. I'm with Gertrude Himmelfarb when it comes to Buchan."

"Gertrude Himmelfarb? But she's . . ."

Irene cut him short. "She has some blind spots—I'll admit that. She believes in Victorian values, but the least said about that the better. Yet she's quite right when it comes to John Buchan, with all that going on about the clean, sporting life: cold showers, early rising and so on. Shameful stuff."

Stuart looked thoughtful. His showers were often cold because Irene, who used the shower before him, tended to spend rather a long time there and used all the hot water. He usually felt rather invigorated after a cold shower and he was not sure that this was too bad a thing. Perhaps if more people had cold showers then they would be more productive and energetic and less inclined to laze about. But these, he thought, are reactionary thoughts and quite unworthy of the progressive thoughts my wife wants me to have.

## 48. Tablet Is Full of Sugar

Bertie eventually broke the news of the school fair to his mother as they were walking up Dundas Street for his Saturday morning appointment with the psychotherapist. Irene was propelling the pushchair in which Bertie's younger brother, Ulysses, was slumped, held in position by an elaborate system of straps and buckles and dressed in a tiny blue sailor suit. Bertie was puzzled as to why Ulysses should wear a sailor suit and had raised the matter with his mother, pointing out that she often said that she disapproved of uniforms. "Sailor suits are not military uniforms," Irene had replied. "They are civilian outfits, Bertie, and there's an important distinction. Ulysses is in the merchant marine in his little outfit."

"Then why does it say HMS *Jolly*?" asked Bertie. "Look, it says that on his front pocket. HMS stands for Her Majesty's Ship, which means it's the Royal Navy. I read that. If Ulysses were in the merchant navy it would say MV, Mummy."

"You mustn't be too literal, Bertie," muttered Irene. "People have all sorts of things on their shirts these days. They don't really mean what they say, you know."

"Do you mean that people put fibs on their shirts?" asked Bertie.

Irene laughed. "Well, they're not really fibs, Bertie. They just say ridiculous things. Nobody pays much attention to what shirts say. Post-modernism, you see, Bertie. Mummy will explain all that a little bit later. Not now."

But this was not the time for discussion of sailor suits. "There's something very exciting going to happen at school, Mummy," he announced as they prepared to cross Great King Street. Bertie had discovered that it was a good tactic to broach tricky subjects while his mother was trying to negotiate a street-crossing as she was usually distracted at such times and seemed to lack enthusiasm for argument.

"Oh yes, Bertie," said Irene, glancing up the road to check for oncoming cars. "Careful now, Bertie, that driver looks as if he's going to be inconsiderate. A male driver, of course."

Bertie persisted. "It's a fair," he blurted out. "There's going to be a school fair, Mummy."

Irene frowned. "Come along, Bertie. We can't stand in the middle of the road like this."

"And I'm going to have a table, Mummy," Bertie continued. "I'm going to ask Ranald to help me. We can sell bags of things."

Irene was non-committal. "We'll see," she said.

"I wondered if you'd make me some tablet, Mummy," Bertie went on. Tablet would go down well at the school fair, he thought. And if they charged ten pence a piece, then they would get a whole pound for a bag of ten pieces, and if they sold ten bags then that would be five pounds for him and five pounds for Ranald. That was a lot of money, Bertie thought, although perhaps not for Ranald, whose father, his friend had explained, had a great deal of money that he kept in a safe in his study. Ranald Braveheart Macpherson had offered to show this money to Bertie, as he had discovered the combination number and was able to open it himself. "There's heaps of money in it," he said to Bertie one day. "You should see it, Bertie. Heaps."

They had reached the other side of the road. "Tablet is full of sugar, Bertie," said Irene. "An occasional piece, yes, but you do know what happens if you have too much sugar?"

"We wouldn't eat it ourselves, Mummy," said Bertie quickly. "We'd sell it to other people. They'd eat it."

"And their teeth?" Irene asked. "What about their teeth, Bertie? Do we want other people to get holes in their teeth? Is that what we want?" She waited for an answer, but none came. "So maybe we can make some carrot-men for you to sell. You remember those little figures we made out of carrots—with cloves for eyes and a little bit of red pepper for their mouths. People would love that."

Bertie was silent. Nobody would buy a carrot-man—at least nobody in his or her right mind would. And he could imagine the reaction of somebody like Tofu, who had told Bertie that he was planning to sell some stolen property at his table. "I'll make loads of money, Bertie," Tofu had said. "I know what sells, you see."

They arrived at Dr. St. Clair's consulting room. Because they could not take Ulysses' pushchair up the stairs, that was left in the hall at the bottom, and Ulysses was carried up by Irene. This provoked loud screams from the young infant, who struggled with his mother and was copiously sick.

"He's always sick when you pick him up, Mummy," said Bertie. "Are you holding him the right way up?"

"Of course I am, Bertie," said Irene. "His little stomach is just a bit sensitive, that's all."

"But he's never sick when I pick him up," said Bertie. "It's just you, Mummy."

"Nonsense, Bertie," said Irene, wiping Ulysses' face with a small cloth, and producing further howls of rage. "And we mustn't keep Dr. St. Clair waiting. He has lots of patients to see, Bertie. You're not the only one."

Bertie was not sure about that. He had never seen another patient in the psychotherapist's waiting room, and he doubted if there were any.

They began to go upstairs. Bertie reached out to touch Ulysses, who immediately stopped crying and smiled at his brother.

"There," said Irene. "His little stomach is obviously settling now."

They rang the bell and a few moments later were admitted to the waiting room by Dr. St. Clair himself. "Well, Bertie," he said. "Here we are. And your little brother too! My, he's getting big. Going to sea already, I can't help but observe." He paused. "He's a handsome little fellow, isn't he?"

"Yes," said Bertie. "And he looks really like Dr. Fairbairn, don't you think? See his ears there? They're just like Dr. Fairbairn's."

Dr. Fairbairn, of course, was Bertie's previous psychotherapist, the one who had suddenly gone to Aberdeen. Irene had been fond of him, Bertie knew, and was upset when he had gone. Very upset.

## 49. The Wolf Man Again

Bertie's psychotherapy appointment followed a familiar pattern. For the first forty-five minutes of the hour-long session, Irene closeted herself with Dr. St. Clair while Bertie was left to his own devices in the waiting room. Even although he suspected that he was the subject of discussion within, he appreciated the fact that this dramatically curtailed the amount of time he had to spend with the psychotherapist talking about his dreams. In Bertie's view, Dr. St. Clair was a considerable improvement on Dr. Fairbairn, who had been, he felt, certifiably mad. It was only a matter of time, he thought, before Dr. Fairbairn would be taken off to Carstairs, where all the most dangerous disturbed people in Scotland were kept; for the time being he was on the loose in Aberdeen, but he was sure that that would not last.

Dr. St. Clair was much milder, although still quite capable of sounding off for long periods on the subject of wolves. Bertie knew, though, that this was a deep-seated obsession of psychotherapists, as he had come across a book in his mother's library all about a Wolf Man whom Dr. Freud had treated. That was the origin of it all, Bertie decided: one psychotherapist began to talk about wolves and soon they were all talking about them. It was very strange, and the only thing to do was to humour them. That was why Bertie had made up a dream about wolves sitting in a tree, which had thrilled Dr. St. Clair, who had written copious notes during Bertie's narration.

Ulysses accompanied Irene into the consulting room, which meant that Bertie was alone in the waiting room. This suited him; he liked his little brother, but he did not like to have to supervise him for too long, and Ulysses had a tendency to eat magazines. The last time he had been under Bertie's supervision in the waiting room, he had eaten an entire section of *Good Housekeeping* that he had subsequently regurgitated over Irene's shoulder on the way down the stairs. No, it was much better for Bertie to be left on his own and able to immerse himself without interruption in the latest copy of *Scottish Field*.

Bertie liked *Scottish Field* for several reasons. Principally he liked it because his mother disapproved of it. "It's all right for people who bury themselves in the countryside, Bertie," she had said. "Those country types with their dogs and Agas and so on. That's not really who we are, Bertie."

Bertie frowned. "But I like dogs, Mummy. And what's wrong with the people?"

Irene smiled. "It's difficult, Bertie . . . I suppose they tend to be conservative in their views, Bertie. That's all."

"That means they want things to remain the same?"

"Precisely, Bertie. They want things to remain the same. That's what conservatives are like."

Bertie thought about this. "And we want everything to change?"

Irene smiled. "You could put it like that."

"So if everything changed, then I wouldn't have to have psychotherapy, would I? Or do yoga?"

"No," said Irene. "That's not what I meant, Bertie. And anyway, we don't have time to discuss these things at the moment. Some other time, I think."

Now, opening the pristine copy of *Scottish*

*Field*, Bertie carefully looked through the pages of the magazine. His favourite section was the social section at the back. This was where there were photographs of various events throughout Scotland—of charity balls, of horse shows, of parties at big hotels. Bertie liked these photographs because he recognised some of the faces that seemed to crop up in these settings. There was Mr. Roddy Martine talking to a group of people at a fundraising party for the Scottish National Portrait Gallery. There was Mr. Charlie Maclean conducting a whisky tasting for a group of visitors from the United States of America. The visitors all looked happy, not to say drunk; everybody looked as if they were having a good time, although presumably all of these people were conservatives. They certainly did not look as if they wanted anything changed, Bertie decided.

He was about to put the magazine down when his eye caught an article that he had missed on first perusal. It was all about a boy of fourteen who was planning to sail from Scotland to Iceland, single-handed. Bertie looked at the photographs. The boy, who did not appear much older than twelve, was pictured standing on the deck of a gaff-rigged cutter of not much more than twenty feet. The sails were stiff in the breeze and there was wind in the boy's hair. He was holding on to the boat's tiller with one hand and waving with the other.

Bertie read the text of the article aloud, following the lines with his index finger. "Angus McLetchie (14) is planning to be the youngest single-handed sailor ever to navigate his way between Scotland and Iceland. This plucky pupil at George Watson's College in Edinburgh has been sailing since he was five and is looking forward to the technical challenges of the passage . . ."

There was another photograph of Angus McLetchie, this time from much closer up. " 'We are not nervous about this trip,' said Angus's mother, Angela McLetchie (39). 'Boys should be allowed to do what they want to do, as long as they take sensible precautions. Angus is very sensible,' said his father, Hugh McLetchie (42)."

Five, thought Bertie. Five. He had been sailing since five. He looked out of the window. My life is passing me by, he said to himself. By the time Angus was my age he had been sailing for a year. Perhaps he had already sailed to Skye or to Ireland. Soon it will be too late for me and I will never have done any of those things.

He put the magazine down and sat for a moment deep in thought. The school fair was his big chance to make some money, and if he made some money, then he could go somewhere. He could buy a ticket to Glasgow, perhaps, or even to Dunstaffnage, where this boy Angus McLetchie kept his boat. He could meet him and ask him if he had room on the boat for him, as a member of the crew. He could hold the tiller for Angus while he trimmed the sails or cooked sausages in the galley down below. Or Bertie could cook the sausages himself while Angus steered, because he presumably knew the way to Iceland.

When the time came for him to go in to talk to Dr. St. Clair, Bertie mentioned that he had heard there was a boy of fourteen planning to sail to Iceland by himself. Dr. St. Clair looked at Bertie sceptically. "Oh yes, Bertie?" he said. "All by himself?"

"Yes," said Bertie.

"And would you like to do that, Bertie?" asked the psychotherapist.

Bertie nodded.

Dr. St. Clair scribbled a note on his pad. *Fantasies of escape,* he wrote. *But why Iceland?*

## 50. *A Fiscally Responsible Boy*

For some reason unknown to Bertie, his mother was in an unusually good mood as they returned from the psychotherapy session with Dr. St. Clair. Bertie liked his mother to be happy, or at least to be less concerned about things than she usually was. In his opinion she worried far too much about matters that really were none of her business, and that if only she could stop thinking about Melanie Klein and what Melanie Klein might have made of a situation then she would be much more content. It seemed to him that his mother was somehow angry with the world, which she wanted to be fundamentally different from the way it was. Would one not be happier if one accepted that there were a very large number of people who not only thought differently from oneself, but also did things of which one strongly disapproved?

Bertie had reached a similar conclusion about dogs. By observing Cyril he had decided that there were certain matters that dogs would do well to accept rather than to rail against. There was, for instance, the question of sticks: most dogs seemed to believe that sticks were in the wrong place in this world, and simply could not resist the temptation to pick them up in their mouths and deposit them elsewhere. Or, curiously enough, if one threw a stick, a dog would normally rush after it, pick it up, and bring it back to where it had been before. That, of course, rather disproved the theory, unless one took the view that the dog was not content to leave the stick in its new setting and wanted to put it elsewhere, that elsewhere just happening to be the place where the stick had started in the first place.

More pressingly, perhaps, dogs needed to accept that cats existed, and to leave them be. Yet there were very few dogs—none, in fact, thought Bertie—who were prepared to take a philosophical, accepting attitude towards any cats they encountered. Rather than attempt to chase cats, Bertie felt, dogs would do better to ignore them, in much the same way as a cat will ignore a dog whom it knows to be securely attached to a leash. Dogs, by contrast, would pant and strain to get at the cat and waste a lot of energy in the process, rather than doing something better with their time . . .

But what was that? Bertie had puzzled over what there was for dogs actually to do, and had decided that there was nothing. Perhaps it was the same with his mother. Perhaps Irene's problem was that she had very little to occupy herself with, other than to look after Ulysses and to tell Bertie what to do. Looking after Ulysses was not easy, Bertie conceded, as he was always being sick over things and that inevitably involved a lot of washing and cleaning.

"Try not to be sick over Mummy quite so much," Bertie had whispered to his small brother one day. "I know it may be hard, but Mummy doesn't really mean it most of the time. Just pretend that you can't hear her."

Ulysses looked up at Bertie with mute, adoring eyes. The tiny child loved his brother; he loved him so much; he was perfect in his eyes.

"You don't understand me, do you?" Bertie continued, tickling the baby under his chin. "You don't speak English yet, I suppose."

Ulysses let out a small chuckle, followed immediately by a small burp. He reached for one of the buttons on Bertie's shirt, but Bertie gently pushed the tiny hand away.

"Try not to be sick so much," Bertie whispered. "Try and be kind to Mummy. You'll be eighteen one of these days. Try to remember that."

Now, as they walked back from psychotherapy, with Irene in a good mood, Bertie decided to raise again the subject of the school fair. This time, there was what seemed like a firm commitment by Irene to allow Bertie to take part. "But what are you going to spend the money you earn on?" she asked. "I don't want you spending it on unhealthy sweets."

"Of course not," said Bertie, who had been hoping to spend it on chocolate. "I'll save it, Mummy, I promise I will."

Irene smiled at him benevolently. "Mummy's little fiscally responsible boy!" she teased.

Bertie was not sure about the implications of all that, but he had been listening to the news on the radio and had realised that there was a problem with the government spending more money than it had. His father, who seemed particularly inter-ested in these matters, had told him about that and had shaken his head in a most foreboding way. "Future generations will have to pay for all this," Stuart had said. "That's the problem, Bertie."

Bertie had looked at Ulysses. As far as he

251

was concerned, Ulysses was a future generation, and so this really meant that Ulysses would be shouldering a large burden. He was not really sure how his little brother would cope with that, and he rather feared that he might be copiously sick—all over everything—once he discovered how deeply he was in debt. But there would be time enough to worry about such matters in due course—not now.

A much more pressing concern than the national debt was the issue of what he would sell on his table at the fair. When the question arose a few days later, on the Friday before the fair, which was to be on Saturday afternoon, Irene repeated her suggestion about making carrot-men and indeed showed Bertie a bag of carrots she had bought for that express purpose. Bertie realised he was trapped. He was very eager to participate in the fair, but he had the gravest doubts as to whether anybody would want to buy such carrot-men as he made.

"Of course they'll want to buy them," enthused Irene. "You just listen to me: your carrot-men will go like hot cakes."

"But couldn't we sell actual hot cakes then, Mummy?" he asked.

"No, Bertie, *carissimo*," said Irene. "Sugar is poison."

"But I see lots of people eating sweet things," protested Bertie. "And they don't die. If it was poison, they'd all be dead."

Irene smiled. "Mummy doesn't mean poison like that," said Irene. "There are gentler poisons—things that are not good for the system, which actually do poison it, that aren't exactly cyanide or belladonna, Bertie. *Capisci*?"

Bertie sighed. It was no good arguing—it was going to be a case of carrot-men or nothing. Ranald Braveheart Macpherson, with whom he was sharing the table, had announced that he would be selling tablet that his mother was proposing to make, using what Ranald described as "loads and loads of condensed milk." Perhaps there would be enough for Bertie to sell some as well, or, if there was not, there was always the possibility of a profit-sharing agreement between them.

"I'm going to make loads of money, Bertie," Ranald had crowed. "And it's all going to be tax-free, you know!"

## 51. Like Tiny Carrot-Lepers

It was with some trepidation that Bertie made his way to the school that Saturday afternoon. He travelled on the 23 bus with his mother and Ulysses, his baby brother being dressed in his sailor outfit, the cap of which, instead of sitting at a jaunty angle, as the designer undoubtedly intended, had fallen over his brow, with the result that his vision was more or less entirely obscured. There was also a vague smell about him that Bertie hoped would not get any worse; he could not imagine any embarrassment greater than having to help his mother change Ulysses at school; although the entire day was in fact becoming quite embarrassing, irrespective of any contribution made by Ulysses. There was his own outfit to be taken into account—the crushed-strawberry dungarees that his mother had insisted he wear when he knew—he was sure of it—that all the other boys would be wearing jeans. Tofu, in particular, had a pair of black jeans with four zips that he would be certain to wear, and equally certain to make reference to while staring pointedly at Bertie's outfit.

"There's still quite a lot of wear in these," Irene had said, as she helped Bertie into the offending garment. "They were a very good buy, Bertie. They've done you for almost two years now. Waste not, want not."

"They're getting a bit small, though," said Bertie. "I think maybe we should throw them away now, Mummy. Or we could give them to some boy who hasn't got many clothes. I'm sure he'd like them." He was not sure, actually; in fact, if anything, he was convinced that there would be no boy in Scotland, or indeed elsewhere, who would thank anybody for the gift of this item of clothing.

"That's a very generous thought, Bertie," said Irene. "But don't worry: I think I'll be able to let them out a bit so that you get a bit more wear out of them. Then we can keep them for Ulysses, for when he gets bigger."

Bertie glanced at his tiny brother. It was a glance of sympathy; the sort of glance that those despairing souls, seen by Dante on his melancholy journey, might have given one another as they contemplated their hopeless durance.

"Yes," continued Irene. "It will be very nice for Ulysses to have your clothes, Bertie. And your toys, too, when you're finished with them."

"That's all right," mumbled Bertie. He paused. "Wouldn't it be nice, though, if you were able to cut these down for him right now? If you made the legs shorter then he could wear them straightaway. I bet he'd like that, Mummy."

Irene laughed. "I don't think Ulysses cares what he wears," she said. "Not at this stage. He's still so young, Bertie. He doesn't really care."

Bertie knew that this was true. As far as he could make out, Ulysses had absolutely no idea of what was going on. He had shown his younger brother a map of Scotland only the other day and had pointed to where they were, but all that Ulysses had done was to attempt to eat the map. If you didn't even know what country you were in, thought Bertie, then what else did you not know?

But now they were on their way and the whole

ordeal of the school fair lay ahead. It could have been different, of course. It could have been a treat, had Bertie been allowed to make what he wanted to make—tablet—rather than to have to make those ridiculous carrot-men that his mother was so keen on. They had made twenty-four of these, and they were all laid out in a baking tray that Irene had covered with foil and Bertie was now carrying. The carrot-men had rapidly become soggy, for some reason, and had lost the firmness of trunk and limb with which they had started. Some of them, in fact, had mislaid their facial features as well—the tiny pieces of clove that had served as their eyes, and the slivers of red pepper that had been their lips. Disfigured now, like tiny carrot-lepers, they slumped in their tray staring up—if they still had their cloves—at their ceiling of foil.

As the bus turned the corner at the Royal Scottish Academy and began its lumbering journey up the Mound, Bertie looked down Princes Street, at the fluttering flags on the flagpoles, at the blue Saltires, at the white flags with Edinburgh's castle symbol; at the people walking along the pavement; at the normal life that seemed to be going on outside his world. He imagined a carrot-man walking along the street, enjoying the sunshine, raising his hat to passers-by, strolling without a care in the world, blissfully unaware that carrot-men were made to be eaten . . .

They arrived at the school. There was a good crowd there already, and one of the senior pupils, who had a reputation as a juggler, was entertaining a group of admiring parents with his dexterity. There was a small table set up at the entrance to the school, where two sixteen-year-old girls from the senior part of the school were taking entrance money. Bertie recognised these girls, who had often smiled at him in a friendly way, but he was not sure of their names.

"Is that your little brother, Bertie?" asked one of the girls. "He's really sweet, isn't he? Look at his ears."

Bertie was about to say something about how Ulysses' ears looked very like Dr. Fairbairn's, but was silenced by a glance from his mother.

"I'm glad to see so many people, girls," said Irene. "Come on now, Bertie, you must get to your table. I think I see Ranald's mother, which means that Ranald must be here."

"What are you selling, Bertie?" asked one of the girls. "Are there cakes in that tray?"

"Carrot-men," answered Irene, on Bertie's behalf. "Bertie spent a lot of time making them."

"Carrot-men?" said the girl. "What do you do with carrot-men?"

"You eat them, stupid," said the other girl.

"And they're very tasty," said Irene. "Come along now, Bertie. Goodbye, girls."

They went into the hall where the tables had been laid out. There was already a fair number of people milling about, peering at and poking the offerings that the children had placed before them. Bertie found Ranald Braveheart Macpherson, who had already displayed his wares on his half of the table—four plates of delicious-looking tablet. Several people had bought some even at this stage, and Ranald excitedly showed Bertie the money he had taken. "And there's going to be heaps more, Bertie," said Ranald. "I think I'm going to make over twenty pounds."

## 52. The Tragedy of the Carrot-Men

The school fair now in full and noisy swing, Irene had left Bertie to his own devices and was inspecting a table loaded with house-plants. For his part, Bertie was busy taking the foil off the top of his baking tray, exposing the carrot-men to Ranald's scrutiny.

"They're very nice," said Ranald after a moment's hesitation.

"Thanks," said Bertie.

"But do you think anybody's going to buy them?" continued Ranald. From the tone of his voice it was clear what his own view of that possibility was.

"You never know," said Bertie. "There may be some healthy people here. You never know."

Bertie looked around him, to see what was being offered at the other tables. There were Olive and Pansy, standing behind their table, which was laden with small brightly coloured notebooks. They seemed to be attracting a lot of interest, as there were at least five or six people examining the books. And there, one table away from them, was Tofu, who had a large pile of what looked like CDs on the table in front of him. Again, he appeared to be doing a roaring trade, but found the time, nonetheless, to give Bertie a wave—a triumphant wave, it seemed to Bertie.

Noticing Bertie, Olive left the table under Pansy's care for a moment as she came over to talk.

"So, Bertie," she said. "What have we here?" She peered at the contents of the tray and then looked at Bertie. "Oh, Bertie," she said. "That's so sad. No, it's tragic, Bertie, really tragic."

Bertie looked away. "You don't have to eat them if you don't like them," he said.

"No, I won't," said Olive. She smiled. "Have you seen what Tofu's doing?"

Bertie shook his head.

Olive leaned forward and lowered her voice. "He's selling pirate CDs. I'm not making it up, Bertie. And some of them are stolen, Pansy says. I'm going to tell one of the teachers when they come to buy our notebooks. I'm going to tell them to go and phone the police to come and get him. It'll be his own fault. Tofu's been asking for this for a long time."

It had not taken long for the school hall to fill with people. Most of them were parents, accompanying their children. The children separated from the adults as soon as was decently possible: all children are thoroughly embarrassed by their parents, who are invariably too tall, too short, too dowdy, too badly dressed, too effusive, too out-of-touch, too poignant, too dim, too reactionary, or too posturingly progressive for any sensible child to bear. Olive, for example, never spoke of her parents at all, and almost went so far as to deny having any. She referred to the family's neat bungalow in the Braids as "this place I've got in the Braids," and when asked about her father, who was very much in evidence and a conscientious and hard-working breadwinner, she simply said "Yes, there's somebody." It was true that her mother was acknowledged, but usually with a sigh and the comment "Let's talk about something else."

As for Tofu, who was the son of two well-known Edinburgh vegans, one of whom, the father, had written a tome on nuts and had converted his car to run on olive oil, there was the continuing mystery of his mother. Tofu had said that she had been eaten by a lion in the Serengeti, but Olive had put about the story that she had simply died of starvation. Others, including Bertie, thought that she was still alive, and Olive's friend, Pansy, had said that she had seen her with Tofu in a shop in Princes Street buying him underwear.

Bertie's friend Ranald Braveheart Macpherson had come to the fair with both of his parents. Unlike the other children Ranald did not seem to be embarrassed to be seen with his parents, but this might have been explained by the fact that he was adopted. He had spoken very openly about this to Bertie, claiming to have been found in a basket by the side of the Water of Leith just before it goes under the bridge at Stockbridge. "I was jolly lucky the basket didn't leak," he had said. "If it had, then I would have been drowned, Bertie. But I didn't, you see." The discussion had continued into one of whether Bertie could get himself adopted, preferably in Glasgow, using eBay as a means of advertising himself. That had not worked, and Bertie was still stuck with Irene.

"Don't be too sad about that, Bertie," said Ranald. "It's perfectly possible that your parents will die soon, just like mine, and then you can get yourself adopted same as me."

"But did yours die?" asked Bertie. "I thought they put you in a basket in the Water of Leith."

Ranald shook his head. "They put me in the basket, and then they went off to Aberdeen and died," he said. "I think they froze. It's very cold up there and sometimes it happens that way."

Now Bertie stood at his table with Ranald Braveheart Macpherson and waited for people to come and buy the carrot-men he had made. A number of customers did present themselves, but they were interested only in Ranald's tablet, which he sold in small bags of three pieces, neatly tied with a red ribbon at the top. "It's very important to get the presentation right," said Ranald. "My dad told me all about that. He knows about these things. My mummy says that he could sell anything. That's what she said, and I'm not fibbing, Bertie." He paused. "That's why my dad's got loads of money."

Ranald looked at Bertie's carrot-men. "I don't think anybody's going to want those, Bertie. Perhaps you should have a sale. Perhaps you could make a sign that says seventy-five per cent off. Or you could write 'Closing Down.' People like closing down sales, you know. My dad told me that."

Bertie was tight-lipped. He did not want to close down; he wanted to be as successful as Ranald or Tofu, whose pirated CDs were selling briskly. And yet he knew that what Ranald said was right. The market place was the market place: if you wanted to sell something, then you had to offer something that people would want. And who would possibly want carrot-men?

He stared down at the floor and then looked up again. He tried to smile, but it was very hard.


## 53. *A Tiny Carrot Icarus*

And then something quite extraordinary happened—a development that might have been mundane in itself, but was utterly transformative. Roger Collins and Judith McClure, who had stepped in to look after Cyril, arrived with the dog on a lead. Cyril sensed Bertie's presence the moment he entered the room, and tugged on his leash until he reached the table where Bertie was standing. Then, with a final tug, he leapt up at the boy who had so briefly been his guardian, almost knocking over the tray of carrot-men in the process.

"I believe I know who you are," said Roger. "Cyril has effectively introduced us, I think."

Bertie greeted the visitors politely, and then introduced them to Ranald.

"We were taking Cyril for a rather long walk along the canal," Judith explained. "And then we noticed the sign outside that said there was a school fair. We thought we'd pop in for a moment and perhaps buy something."

Bertie noticed her glance at Ranald's tablet and his heart sank. Of course that was what they would buy. But Judith's gaze had moved on, and was now resting on the tray of carrot-men.

"Carrot-men!" she exclaimed. "That's interesting, Bertie. And how are sales?"

Bertie looked down at the ground again. "Actually, I haven't sold any. I don't think people want carrot-men."

Roger frowned. "People don't want carrot-men? Am I hearing correctly? What can they be thinking of?"

Bertie said nothing.

"Do you mind if I try one?" asked Roger, reaching to pick one up. "I'll pay for it, of course."

He popped the carrot-man into his mouth. Down went the tiny arms, the hat, the carrot legs; a whole carrot life consumed.

"Delicious," pronounced Roger. "And you know who would like one, too? Cyril."

At the mention of his name, Cyril wagged his tail. With that perpetual unsatisfied hunger that is the lot of dogs, he sensed that something was coming his way.

"There you are, Cyril, old chap," said Roger,

throwing a carrot-man in Cyril's direction. Through the air it fell, a tiny carrot Icarus. Snap! went Cyril's faithful jaws.

"Well, well," said Roger Collins. "He likes that. You know what, Bertie, I think we'll buy your whole stock—the lot of them. Judith and I will have some and Cyril will have the rest. Will twenty pounds do?"

Bertie nodded mutely. He was aware of the wide-eyed surprise that registered on Ranald's face. He was aware, too, of Olive glowering from the next-door table; she still had many unsold notebooks.

The carrot-men were scooped unceremoniously into a plastic bag and the money changed hands. Then Judith and Roger said goodbye to the two boys and moved off.

"You see," said Bertie, simply. It was all that he needed to say. You see.

Half an hour later, it was time for the tables to be cleared and unsold stock packed away. Ranald's tablet had almost sold out, with only two bags remaining. One of these he gave to Bertie and the other he pocketed himself. Money was counted up. Ranald had made twelve pounds and Bertie had the crisp twenty-pound note that Roger Collins had given him.

Tofu had made forty-two pounds, but was to keep none of it. Informed by Olive that Tofu was selling pirated, and possibly stolen, goods, a teacher had come to investigate. After examining the discs and interrogating Tofu for twenty minutes, the teacher confiscated the entire proceeds of the illegal trading and declared they would be given to charity.

Tofu was furious, and complained bitterly to Bertie about the injustice of it all. His position was serious: he had already spent fifteen pounds of his anticipated profit in purchasing a large model aeroplane from a boy in a higher class. He had taken delivery of the plane the previous day and crashed it shortly thereafter. Now the bill had to be paid.

Bertie felt the twenty-pound note in his pocket. He was a generous boy and would have given Tofu the money if there had been no other alternative; but there was one.

"I tell you what, Tofu," he said quietly. "Why don't you sell me your jeans? I'll give you twenty pounds and my crushed-strawberry dungarees."

Tofu wrinkled up his nose. "They're pink."

"No," said Bertie. "Crushed strawberry. How about it, Tofu?"

Tofu thought for a moment. He had another pair of jeans at home, and Bertie, after all, had none. He would only have to wear Bertie's dungarees to get home; thereafter he could throw them away.

"All right," he said. "We can go and swap trousers in the boys' loo."

They went off to do this, with Ranald Braveheart

Macpherson keeping watch in case authority, in any shape, should approach the scene of the transaction. Once bedecked in the jeans, Bertie walked out with a jaunty step. It did not matter what happened now. His mother could hardly take these jeans from him and make him travel home in the bus without any trousers. And once he was home, he could work on her to allow him to wear them at least now and then. Oh, life was wonderful; it was so rich, so exciting—if you had jeans.

He stood in the school grounds and looked up at the sky. It was blue and high and empty. And up there, crossing it in a great arc, was a tiny speck of silver, a plane, a thin pencil-line of white trailing behind it. The plane caught the sun, and flashed its message to Bertie. Freedom, it said. Freedom.

## 54. Svengali, EH3

Bruce stood by the telephone in the kitchen of his new flat in Albany Street, poised to pick up the handset and make the call. Jonathan had left his number, scribbled on a piece of paper produced by Bruce just before he had left after their first meeting. That had been a few days earlier; since then they had not been in touch with one another, although Bruce had seen him, or thought he had seen him, walking down the street when he had happened to look out. He had drawn back from the window, concerned that Jonathan might glance up and see him looking down at him. Then, after a few moments when he had sidled back up to the window and sneaked a glance down the street there had been nobody. Jonathan would have been going into his flat, of course, which was only a few doors away and where, unless Bruce made the call he was about to make, he himself was due to present himself that very evening to effect the exchange of identities—and of lives.

It was ridiculous; it was more than ridiculous— it was absurd. Taking the identity of another, even if that person was one's complete double, was a pointless and silly thing to do—the sort of thing that a child of ten might think amusing. And yet he had agreed to it—that was what both surprised and slightly unnerved him. He had agreed to make the exchange simply because Jonathan had presented him with the challenge and he had not been strong enough to resist it. He should have laughed it off; he should have scoffed at the whole idea, but he had simply agreed to it, fearing that the other young man would somehow think the less of him for declining. Well, if he had shown weakness then, he would show strength now.

He reached for the telephone—and at that precise moment it rang. Bruce hesitated for a moment, a sixth sense telling him who the caller was.

"Bruce?"

"Yes."

"Time to do it. You ready?"

Bruce drew in his breath. All he had to do was to say no. He had no need to give an explanation; Jonathan was nothing to him, he was a stranger . . . and yet, and yet . . . Jonathan was his double; Jonathan, in an extraordinary sense, was him.

"Fine." It was not what he had intended to say and yet the word had come unbidden. Suddenly it occurred to Bruce that he was being hypnotised. Could that be possible? Was that possible? Could Jonathan be one of these people who could exert a hypnotic power over another; who could somehow persuade people to enter a state in which they did his bidding—even something as peculiar as exchanging identities? Was he a . . . Bruce dredged up the term from the recesses of memory . . . a Svengali?

He might still have abandoned the whole enterprise in the hours that followed, but did not. And now it was time for him to go to Jonathan's flat, as planned, and step—metaphorically—into the shoes that would be vacated for him there. Locking his door behind him, he thought, You're doing something really, really stupid. It was an internal reproach to which he had given silent voice on several occasions in the past, but—and this was some consolation—on each occasion that he had said this to himself the outcome had been unexpectedly good. He had said it to himself when, in his early twenties and on a holiday in the United States, he had set out, quite against advice, to hitch-hike—starting at night—from Philadelphia to Oxford, Mississippi, and had succeeded in making the journey with two unbroken lifts, one with an attractive divorcee who fed him chocolates across several states, and the other with a church historian whose conversation focused on two subjects: the intricacies of baseball and Gnostic writings. So much else might have happened to somebody like Bruce, an innocent standing by the roadside at night; but it had not. Whatever divinity hedged him was on duty, and hedged.

He had similarly said it to himself when, egged on by raucous friends, at the age of seventeen he had run onto the pitch at Murrayfield and been rugby tackled by stewards and then bundled off for a brief half hour in a police van. Bruce's luck had held; but this plan was on a different scale from those earlier escapades. He hesitated, but only briefly, before walking downstairs and making his way purposively to Jonathan's flat.

Jonathan greeted him warmly. "I'll show you round," he said. "I've put stuff in the fridge. Milk. Some eggs. Ham. You like ham, Bruce?"

Bruce nodded.

"We seem to have the same tastes," said Jonathan. "Funny, isn't it?"

Bruce's response was non-committal. Jonathan had now opened the bedroom door and gestured for him to follow him in. He pointed towards a large wardrobe that stood against one of the walls.

"We'll take the same size of everything, won't we? Being identical, that must be the case."

Bruce said nothing, but watched as Jonathan opened the door of the wardrobe.

"Shirts here. Socks here." He paused, and looked at Bruce. "You don't have athlete's foot, do you?"

Bruce shook his head.

"Good," said Jonathan, obviously relieved. "I assume that washing destroys it, but you never know. And since you're going to be wearing my socks, I thought I'd ask."

Jonathan now bent down to reach for something from the bottom of the wardrobe. Standing up, he showed Bruce a pair of black brogue shoes. "These are really comfortable," he said. "I wear them to the office every day, so you should do that too. If you didn't . . ."

"Yes?" asked Bruce. "If I didn't?"

"Then they might notice and think it odd. That's all." Jonathan handed Bruce the shoes. "Try them. Go on."

Bruce tried not to wince. He did not want to wear these shoes; he did not want to be there at all. But there was something about Jonathan that made it impossible to resist his suggestions.

"In fact," Jonathan continued. "Put on these jeans over here. And this shirt too. Then try the shoes. We'll see the effect."

He smiled at Bruce, handing him a pair of neatly folded jeans that he had extracted from a shelf in the wardrobe.

"Go on," he said. "Don't worry, I'll go through to the kitchen."

Bruce closed his eyes. Perhaps if he didn't look at Jonathan he would be able to overcome this extraordinary, unsettling sense of being forced to do something that he had no desire to do. But he could not. The closing of one's eyes does not always make much difference in such circumstances, and it did not then. Acting almost as an automaton, Bruce slipped out of his own trousers and into the jeans provided by Jonathan. As he did so, he was aware of the gaze that had until a few moments before been upon him: cool, calculating, controlling.

## 55. *Young Spartans and a Moleskine Notebook*

Bruce woke up the next morning in Jonathan's bed—and Jonathan woke up in Bruce's bed— unlike most respectable Edinburgh people, who wake up in their own beds, rather than in the beds of others. Of course, sometimes even respectable people wake up in beds that don't belong to them, but then these are either (a) hotel beds, or (b) the beds of guest rooms belonging to those who are in their own beds (that is, the beds of the house in which the guest bed is located, but in a different room). Some say that this is because Edinburgh people have less fun than others; but Edinburgh people themselves do not see what fun has got to do with it.

For a moment or two Bruce was confused, and wondered why the morning light was coming into the room from the wrong direction. But then, opening his eyes fully, he saw the unfamiliar ceiling and the wardrobe and the Degas poster of young Spartan athletes exercising (which would not necessarily have been Bruce's choice of decoration) and he knew immediately where he was. He gazed at the poster: the young Spartans, five of them, were posed to the right of the picture, while on the left a small group of Spartan maidens, bare-topped but modestly wearing brief aprons of bright cloth, taunted them in the way that teenage girls will in groups observe teenage boys and laugh at them. The young men seemed indifferent to, or, at the most, only slightly surprised by the attention of the young women, and quite unconcerned by their own nakedness. They had races to run or hurdles to leap, and that for them was more important than any conversation with the maidens. A pleasant picture,

thought Bruce, with something in it for everybody.

His contemplation of the picture over, Bruce got
up out of bed, showered in Jonathan's shower, and
dressed himself in the clothes that Jonathan had
identified as his normal office outfit. It was a
very odd feeling putting on the clothes of another,
but as he did so, Bruce felt for the first time a
sense of anticipation over what lay ahead. This
might have been a ridiculous, irresponsible
escapade, but it was an extraordinary thing to do,
and extraordinary things certainly spiced up life.
After a few days they would give up the whole
thing—perhaps after a day or two, he suspected,
no matter that Jonathan seemed to want a week or
longer. Then they could talk about it and entertain
their friends with accounts of how they got away
with it. "And nobody suspected?" the friends
would ask. "You must be pretty good actors." And
Bruce would incline his head modestly and say,
"It wasn't too difficult. Not really."

Bruce was worried about going to Jonathan's
office, but had had an idea about how the dangers
inherent in that might be minimised. He would go
for one day, he decided, and then he would report
in sick for the rest of the week. He should be able
to manage a single day—longer than that could
expose him to a real risk of being detected. Yes,
one day would satisfy honour, and then, the
following week, they would bring the whole thing

to an end and Bruce could return to his own office and pick up any pieces that needed to be picked up. There was a limit to the damage that Jonathan could do in a week: there were no major transactions on the horizon and so he would not be able to do very much.

He had decided to eat the breakfast that Jonathan would have eaten, his double having helpfully left a small red Moleskine notebook in which he had written an account of his routines. "I have a bowl of muesli," he had written. "No sugar added type. Then a boiled egg and a slice of toast. I don't take milk in my coffee at breakfast, but I do during the day."

Bruce had found it strangely fascinating reading. "*The Scotsman* gets delivered before I leave for work," the notes had continued. "I do the Sudoku and I read Allan Massie and George Kerevan, if they're in. They've got it totally sussed. I look at the sports pages and the car ads

(I love car ads!). Then I walk to work along Queen Street (south side). When I get to the office I go straight to my desk. I always say hello to the receptionist, Jenny, and ask her about her boyfriend, who's in Saughton Prison but who's due out in about six months. He's a forger—quite a good one, apparently.

"My office is the second door along the corridor. It's got my name on it, so you can't go wrong. I go in, sit down, and look at the mail, which the secretaries will have opened and put in the in-tray. The letters I get are enquiries about our firm, acting for people. I look at them and arrange appointments to see them to discuss what we can do. You will see that there's a big lever-arch file on the shelf behind my chair—that has a whole stack of papers in it that describe what the firm can offer. Read through that, and then you can tell any of the prospective clients what we can do. It's totally easy. Totally.

"My immediate boss—or shall I say, your immediate boss—is Bill Fleming. You have to go and see him once a day—usually just after eleven—to tell him what enquiries have come in. You find out a bit about the firms and he will tell you anything he knows about them. Then you make contact with them, give them our literature, and arrange for them to come in and see Bill, or for him to go and see them. That's my job. The other bit of it is helping a woman called Andrea arrange events. I don't like her very much as she's homophobic, I think. But she may come in and ask you to do something about some publicity event she's organising. A product launch maybe. Just do what she says and she'll keep out of your hair.

"Finally, there are three other people there who are about my level. They're great. They share a large office at the back. Freddie does accounts, Grant does press liaison, and Janine is in charge of all office administration. Janine's secretly in love with Freddie, but he doesn't reciprocate. Grant likes Janine, but there's no chemistry as far as she's concerned. Sad, but they're a really nice group. You (i.e. me) like them and they like you (i.e. me).

"I leave the office at six on the dot and come home. Sometimes I go to the Blue Moon or Habana. You might not. Each to his own! Then I make a meal or eat out. I like Italian but can't stand Chinese food. I think I'm allergic to mono-sodium glutamate or noodles, or both. So if you tell anybody you're going to a Chinese restaurant they'll smell a rat. Mind you, if you go to some restaurants you'll be eating a rat! Only joking."

Bruce closed the notebook, and smiled. He was beginning to like Jonathan now that he was in his shoes, metaphorically and otherwise. He might be a Svengali, but he was an amusing one, as Svengalis often are.

# 56. The Hazards of Industrial Espionage

Bruce made his way along Queen Street, following the route identified by Jonathan as his morning walk to work. His double's shoes were comfortable, as were his clothes, which were less formal than those that Bruce normally wore to the office. When this was over, Bruce thought that he might perhaps buy clothes like this—comfortable navy chinos with a matching, loose-fitting jacket and open-neck sea-island cotton shirt—and wear them rather than the suit he habitually donned. The problem, though, was that everybody else at his firm, or at least all the men, dressed in the same dark suit: it was a uniform, really, although never described as such. There was no reason why he should not dress more casually, and more comfortably, but such attire would be bound to draw comments from the senior partner, who took a close interest in such things. These comments would be all about client expectations and confidence: "Clients simply won't trust chinos, Bruce." But what if clients wear chinos themselves? People do, you know; even clients. "The point stands."

At the junction of Queen Street and North Charlotte Street, where the road from Charlotte

Square dips down what would once have been a brae, a sloping meadow, somebody nodded to Bruce. He did not see the passerby properly, as he had half-turned his head to look out for cars turning at the traffic lights, and then the figure was gone; but he had nodded. Bruce had acknowledged the greeting with a nod in return, and then thought, Was that for me, or for Jonathan? Since he rarely walked that way—and certainly not at that hour—it must have been for Jonathan. And that realisation underlined the more worrying thought that his test had now begun in earnest. This, he imagined, was how a wartime spy must feel—dropped into enemy territory, so to speak, and on his guard against any slip of the tongue, any display of ignorance, even any grammatical error that would reveal that he was not who he claimed to be. Of course the spy would face the firing squad if exposed, and no such threat existed here . . . and yet, surely there would be some sort of consequence. Was it a criminal offence to impersonate another person? The answer to that must depend on whether one obtained any benefit from the impersonation. That would be fraud, Bruce assumed. He was obtaining nothing through this . . . this ridiculous exercise, other than a cup of office tea, perhaps, and access to office information.

But that worried him. What if he were to be exposed as an impostor and accused of industrial espionage? Were there virtual firing squads for industrial spies? Bruce smiled at the thought, in spite of his nervousness. He had read somewhere that there were people engaged in industrial espionage who went into rival supermarkets in order to note down the prices and the special offers. What if one of those intelligence gatherers were to be detained and bundled round to the parking lot at the back where a firing squad of cashiers and shelf-packers was lined up, ready to deal with the spy? The weapons, of course, would be those squeezy cleaning products that shot out a jet of window-cleaning liquid or something like that. Ready, aim, squeeze!

The absurd fantasy kept his mind off his situation until he had reached Queensferry Street. Now he was within yards of the office of Lothian Public Relations; he looked up at the windows of the Georgian building, at the neat panes of glass within their white astragals—one of those rooms was Jonathan's office, with its name on the door and its in-tray and its shelf with the lever-arch file of information.

Bruce took a deep breath and stared at the doorway. There was a large brass plate fixed across its central panel: *Lothian Public Relations Ltd.* He tried to open the door, but it did not budge. He pushed again, with the same result. Then he noticed the intercom, tucked neatly away to the side. The legend above a small silver button announced: *Reception: please push.*

Bruce pressed the button. At first nothing happened, and then a female voice came out of a small speaker built into the plastic intercom box.

"Yes. Who is it?"

"Bruce."

He spoke without thinking, but realised immediately what he had said. He opened his mouth to correct himself, but the receptionist was already saying something. "Bruce who?"

Bruce forced a laugh. "Fooled you! Jonathan."

There was a slight pause. Then the tinny voice replied, "Very funny! So we're Billy Connolly this morning."

A buzzer sounded and the door moved slightly inwards. Bruce pushed it open and went inside. Now he was in a shared entrance hall at the bottom of a stone staircase. His surveyor's eye, out of ingrained habit, ran over the décor. It was a well-maintained hall, and the stone treads of the stairs had been recently built up using matching stone composite. Nice.

He began to climb the stairs. On the first floor there was a landing exactly as described by Jonathan, and off this a door, once again marked with the name of the firm. This was unlocked.

Bruce went inside. There was the reception desk, and there was the young woman who must be Jenny. She was taking something out of a drawer and looked up to see him. She smiled.

"So," she said. "You're late."

Bruce was momentarily taken aback, but recovered quickly. "Traffic," he said.

"I don't see why traffic should hold you up when you're walking," she said.

He could tell that she was not from Edinburgh; somewhere further west, he thought, because there was the lilt of Glasgow there, that leaning into the final syllable as if its presence were somehow to be resented.

"You have to wait much longer to cross the road if there are lots of cars," he said. He decided to make a joke of it. "Even you must know that, Jenny."

She stared at him. "Jenny? Why did you call me Jenny?"

Bruce froze. He had been in the office precisely one minute and already he had made a terrible mistake. Jonathan had said that she was called Jenny, had he not?

He forced himself to respond. "Just a joke."

"Very funny," she said, sarcastically. "So you're Bruce, and I'm Jenny. Different names day, is that it? Like own clothes day, but different?"

Bruce gave a hollow laugh. "Why not? Anyway, where's Jenny?"

"She's helping Alice back there." She nodded towards the back of the office. "And Freddie wants to see you. He's got to go over to Falkirk at ten, and so you'd better see him before then." She paused. "He's got this great big boil on the back of his neck. He showed it to me. It's gross—really gross. And it's going to burst soon, I think. So don't stand behind him."

Bruce nodded, and began to make his way down the corridor. Offices were all the same.

People talk about traffic and boils and things like that. All the same.

# 57. The Tricks of the Documentary Trade

Bo looked at his watch.

"What happens now?" he asked.

From behind his desk, where he had finished examining the somewhat measly harvest of letters the morning post had yielded, Matthew looked back at the Danish filmmaker. Bo had trained his camera on Matthew's hands while he opened the mail, moving to his eyes while he read the contents, and then to the letters themselves—such as they were—as they lay on the desk before him. Then he had asked Matthew to pretend to read them again so that he could record the scene from a different angle, and after that he had suggested a shot showing Matthew looking out of the window, one of the letters in his hand, as if ruminating on the contents.

"Think of your reply," he said. "Think of the wording. Think of the . . . the subtleties."

Matthew had frowned. "But there aren't any," he said. "The answer to the question in this letter is simply no. They ask if I have any paintings by Anne Redpath in stock, and I don't. So there are no subtleties to be thought about."

Bo stared at him. "But surely there could be," he said. "If that letter said something different, then you might have to think quite intensely about what to say."

"But it doesn't," says Matthew.

"People in Denmark won't know that!" exclaimed Bo. "They won't see what's written in the letter."

Matthew looked puzzled. "But I thought this was a documentary," he said. "I thought that you were recording my life as it happens. Fly-on-the-wall stuff. I don't want to mislead the whole of Denmark."

"It is," said Bo. "Fly-on-the-wall. Exactly!"

"Then surely it should only show what really happens," Matthew said.

Bo laid his camera down on the catalogue table and walked towards the window. When he addressed Matthew, he did not talk to him directly, but spoke as if explaining something to an audience gathered on the pavement outside.

"Have you seen many documentaries?"

Matthew's gaze followed Bo's. Beyond the plate-glass window, light rain fell on the street, unexpected, a blip in an otherwise fine day. The rain, blown sideways by a puff of wind, touched the glass softly, ran in tiny rivulets downwards, lost momentum, welled.

Matthew thought. Had he seen many documentary films? How many was many? He had recently seen a film about a man who swam with crocodiles, which had struck him as a doubtful thing to do. And then there had been one about sumo wrestling that he had found strangely fascinating. "I've seen a few," he said. "There was a film about sumo wrestling and . . ."

Bo seemed not to have heard him. "You see, you have to realise that not everything in a documentary happened in the way it claims to have happened. You can't make films that way."

Outside, the imaginary audience of passersby, now gathered to listen to Bo, looked at one another and then opened their mouths to protest.

"No," Bo continued. "You see, the basic

message a documentary conveys needs to be accurate—nobody disputes that—but in trying to put this message across it is usually necessary to stage things a bit. That's all—just a bit of staging."

The imaginary audience looked distinctly disapproving. We don't expect to hear this sort of thing when walking down Dundas Street . . .

Matthew gave voice to their disapproval. "I'm surprised," he began. "I thought that . . ."

Again he was interrupted by Bo. "Let me give you an example. You may have seen in the newspapers recently that a certain politician shot a tiger with a tranquillising dart. The news footage of this event suggested that the tiger he tranquillised was dangerous and that the event took place in the wild—in fact it was a very tame one from a zoo."

"Oh."

Bo now turned away from his outside audience and addressed Matthew once again. "Yes. I think that particular leader likes to portray himself as a bit of a strongman. And there have been others before him who have done exactly the same. Mussolini once astonished the Italian public by going into the lions' den at Rome Zoo. It was later revealed that the lions had had their teeth taken out and had been given a heavy meal of macaroni. Then he was filmed courageously flying a biplane: in fact the real pilot was crouched down so that he couldn't be seen at the controls. And then there are those polar bears."

Matthew had heard about controversial filming of polar bears. "Oh, them. Weren't they in a zoo rather than on ice floes?"

"Yes," said Bo. "And when it came to filming the tiny, new-born polar bear, it was actually in a producer's ice-box." He paused. "I have never found myself filming in my own fridge."

Matthew laughed. "All right, I'll read the letter and pretend to think."

He picked up the letter and read it again before looking out of the window in what he hoped was a thoughtful manner. Bo watched him.

"I'm not sure, Matthew; I'm just not sure. You see, the people in Denmark like long, boring sequences in their films—that is what reality is for us—but I'm not sure if this is going to work."

Matthew felt a sudden pang of regret. Was Bo suggesting that his life was just not interesting enough to be a good subject for a documentary film? Was that the necessary inference?

Bo was now consulting his watch. "You said that you go over to a coffee bar at about this time. Could we do that instead?"

Matthew rose to his feet. "Yes, that should be fine."

"I'll film you crossing the street," said Bo. "And then I can film you drinking your coffee. The people in Denmark will be very interested in that."

Matthew was not so sure. I'm actually rather boring, he thought. That's the problem.

"Perhaps you can film Big Lou," he said. "You could film Big Lou making my coffee."

At the mention of Big Lou's name, Bo perked up. "Who is this Big Lou person?" he asked.

"She comes from Arbroath," said Matthew. "She is more representative of the real Scotland than I am."

"Ah," said Bo. "That's what we need. Arbroath. The real Scotland. That's what people in Denmark want—believe me, that's what they want."


## 58. Big Lou Remembers MacDiarmid

There was nobody else in Big Lou's cafe when Matthew and Bo came in. Big Lou watched in astonishment as Matthew ushered in Bo, who had his large video camera on his shoulder, the lens panning out to embrace a shot of the entire cafe. Big Lou's astonishment was matched by Matthew's embarrassment as he signalled to Lou that she should try to ignore what was happening. She took only a moment or two to pick up this message, quickly returning to what she had been doing when the two of them had entered—reading the book propped up on her counter. It was quiet time in the cafe—not a single other customer was present—and Big Lou, a voracious reader, usually

288

took the opportunity such spells presented to dip into whatever book she was immersed in at the time.

"Ah," said Matthew, trying his best to sound casual. "I see you're reading, Big Lou."

Big Lou looked up from her book, glancing briefly at the camera. "Aye, well, that's what it looks like, I'd say."

"Interesting," said Matthew stiffly. "What book is it, Lou?"

The camera lens whirred as it changed focus.

"*The Scots Kitchen*," said Lou, holding up the book for him to see. "Marian McNeill. You'll not know it, Matthew."

Matthew frowned. He resented it when Big Lou implied—as she often did—that there were gaps in his knowledge, and he found that he particularly resented that such imputation should be made on film.

"As it happens," he said, "I know all about that. I've seen *The Book of Breakfasts*. She wrote that, didn't she?"

Big Lou shrugged. "Maybe."

Matthew took the book from Lou and opened it at a random page. "My goodness," he said. "Listen to this quotation: 'Sir, I am above all national prejudices, and, I must say, I yield the Scots the superiority in all soups—save turtle and mulligatawny. An antiquarian friend of mine attributes this to their early and long connection with the French, a nation eminent in soups.' That sounds like Dr. Johnson—except he would never have said it. Well, there you are, Lou."

"Aye," said Lou, taking the book back from him. "As my old maw always said, 'A spoofu' o' stink will spoil a patfu' o' skink.'"

Matthew looked at her blankly and then turned to stare at Bo. "The people in Denmark won't know what all that's about," he said. "You'll have to cut that, Bo."

Bo switched off his camera and lowered it from his shoulder. "That was very interesting," he said. "People in Denmark will like that very much. They like to hear about soup—I am sure of that."

Big Lou put her book away. "You'll be introducing me to your friend, Matthew?"

Matthew looked apologetic. "Sorry, Lou, I should have given you some warning—coming in here like this with Bo. This is Bo. He's a very famous Danish filmmaker and he's . . ."

Bo raised a hand in protest. "Not very famous, Matthew, just a bit famous." He smiled at Lou. "I am a maker of documentaries, Mrs. Lou. Matthew has kindly agreed to appear in a film about his life here in Edinburgh. But I am also keen to film other subjects . . . and other people."

He did not finish his sentence, but looked meaningfully at Lou while the words hung in the air. She nodded in his direction and then asked him how he would like his coffee.

"I shall have it the way you have it in Scotland," he said.

Lou snorted. "I wouldnae dae that, if I were you. A bit of hot tap water over some instant is how most folk tak their coffee here."

Bo clapped his hands together in delight. "Oh, very amusing!" he said. "And so well put!"

"I don't think Lou was joking," said Matthew. "You weren't joking, were you, Lou?"

Lou shook her head. "We're not really into coffee culture yet, Mr. . . . er, Mr. Bo. Edinburgh is maybe—or parts of Edinburgh. But there's this big city called Glasgow and . . . well, they do things their ain way over there."

Matthew laughed. "That's a joke, Bo."

"No it isn't," said Lou.

"I have heard of that place," said Bo. "I must go over there, perhaps."

"I wouldnae take your camera with you," said Lou.

"Hah!" said Bo. "Very funny."

"Lou has a point," said Matthew. "You're safer here in Edinburgh. Less room for misunderstanding."

Bo placed his order. "Can you do me a latte, Mrs. Lou?"

Lou shot him a glance. "Aye, I believe I've heard of they things. Coffee with the coo's breeks."

"That's another joke," said Matthew quickly.

"The coo's breeks means the cow's trousers. It's the sticky bit that you sometimes get on the top of milk."

Bo smiled. "Very colourful." He paused. "I wonder, Mrs. Lou, whether you might agree to tell me something about yourself."

"Not much to tell," said Lou through the hissing of the coffee machine. "Born and grew up on a farm near Arbroath. Milked the coos. Went to school. Learned to read. Worked on the farm. Looked after an old uncle. He died. Went to Aberdeen. Worked in a nursing home. Came to Edinburgh and got this place, which was a bookshop. Took all the books out and put them in my flat down at Canonmills. MacDiarmid came here when it was a bookshop. He sat over there, where that table is."

"MacDiarmid was a famous Scottish poet," whispered Matthew. "Drank a lot of whisky. Wrote a lot of poetry."

"Same whisky as we drank the other night?" asked Bo.

"No. He liked . . . what did MacDiarmid like, Lou? What whisky?"

"Glenfiddich," said Lou.

Matthew did not notice when Bo quietly picked up his camera and began to film.

"He was a boy for his whisky all right," Lou continued. "And sometimes, when you read his poetry, you think, Maybe there was a bit of whisky in that line. But then, you read ither bits and you think, That's just so bonnie, that's just so true. And you go back and you read it again and you want to cry because it's so beautiful.

"Mind you, he was all over the place, you know. What did Norman MacCaig say at his funeral? That on the anniversary of MacDiarmid's death each year Scotland should declare three minutes of pandemonium. What do you think of that?"

The coffee machine hissed, as if in agreement. Bo smiled behind his camera. Matthew was out: the plot had changed.

## 59. Bursting a Boil Just Like Vesuvius

Bruce was dealing with the morning's mail when Freddie came into his office. Jonathan had explained that the day's crop of letters would already be in his in-tray by the time he came to work, and Bruce was relieved to find that this was so. After the encounter with Jenny—or the person who should have been Jenny—Bruce was wary; he had made two slips in the first ten minutes, and he would have to be careful if he were to avoid being exposed by lunchtime. Of course if that happened he had an escape strategy already worked out: he would simply disappear. One solution to being in a tight spot was simply turn on one's heels and walk away. He could do that if necessary, but it would be preferable to avoid it if at all possible.

Freddie did not knock, but pushed open the door, looked at Bruce, and said, "Yo, Jono!"

Bruce looked up to see a young man of about his age. He was well-built and had a pleasant, open expression. Bruce was not sure what to say, and so merely muttered, "Yo!" in return.

Freddie sauntered up to his desk and sat on it, swinging his feet.

"See my new shoes," he said. "How cool are these?"

Bruce glanced at Freddie's shoes with their elongated toecaps. "Pretty smart," he said.

"They were fifty per cent off," said Freddie. He winced as he spoke, reaching to touch behind his neck. "But, Jono, I've got this really serious boil on the back of my neck. It started last Friday. I thought it was just a bit of irritation, but it really got going and now it's agony. I can hardly turn my head."

Bruce made a sympathetic noise. "Boils can be really painful."

"Yes," said Freddie. "But I reckon it's almost ready. You know how these things eventually burst? All the pressure on the surrounding skin is relieved and the pain goes. It's like a volcano— Vesuvius or Etna." He paused. "Have you ever been to Naples?"

Bruce shook his head. It suddenly occurred to him that the real question was whether Jonathan had been to Naples.

"But you went to Sicily, didn't you? With your ex?"

Bruce had to think quickly. Obviously Jonathan had told Freddie about going to Sicily with his boyfriend, and so Bruce said, "Yes. Sicily. That was some time ago."

"I thought it was last year," said Freddie.

"Last year? Yeah, maybe. Time goes so quickly . . ."

". . . when you're having fun," supplied Freddie. "But not when you've got a boil. What was his name again?"

"Whose name?"

"Your friend."

Bruce looked down at his desk. "I'm sorry, but I don't like to talk about him."

It was, it seemed, an acceptable answer. "I

understand," said Freddie. "And I don't blame you. I feel the same way about Carly."

Bruce was emboldened. "I never liked her."

Freddie raised an eyebrow. "I thought you did. She liked you—a lot. I told her she was barking up the wrong tree, of course. No offence."

"None taken," said Bruce. "I suppose I did like her, come to think of it."

"I saw her the other day," Freddie continued. "She looked right through me. She was with that chap who works with Stu MacGregor. You know the one?"

"Oh, him," said Bruce. "What's-his-face?"

"Yes, him. I can't remember his name. Something stupid, I think. I don't know what she sees in him."

Bruce shrugged. "Women," he said. He glanced at the letters in the in-tray and wondered how long Freddie was going to sit on his desk, banging his new shoes against the side. "I suppose I'd better get on with my work."

Freddie sighed. "Yes, and I've got to go to see that chap who's complained about our campaign. Pain in the neck . . ." He paused. "You couldn't do something for me, could you, Jono?"

Bruce was cautious. "Depends," he said.

Freddie's hand went to the back of his neck again—gingerly. "I wondered if you wouldn't mind bursting this boil of mine. I can't see it and . . . well, it would be much easier for somebody else to do."

Bruce hesitated. "Go to your health centre. Get a nurse to do it."

Freddie shook his head, and winced. "I haven't got the time. And it'd be far easier to get it done here. It won't be difficult—it just needs a bit of pressure and it'll go. Just like Vesuvius, or whatever."

"I'm not sure," said Bruce. "You don't want these things to get infected."

"But I did that thing for you," said Freddie. "Remember?" He paused. "Are you feeling all right? There's something odd about you today. Your voice is a bit strange. Are you sure you're okay?"

Bruce decided that a distraction was necessary. "Your boil," he said. "I'll do it."

Freddie smiled. "Thanks. You're a real friend, Jono." He slipped off the desk and came to stand beside Bruce, who rose from his chair. "Take a look at it. I hate to think what it looks like."

Bruce moved round behind Freddie and peered at his neck. The boil was just below the hairline more or less in the middle of the nape—an angry red hillock on the summit of which he could make out a yellowish mass. "Sit down on my chair," he said. "It'll be easier for me to reach."

"Do it gently," said Freddie. "You don't want to tear the skin too much. What you really want is a hole in the middle to let the gunk out. What about using a paper clip?"

"I don't think that's a good idea," said Bruce. "You don't want to put anything in there. I think I should just squeeze it."

"Have you got a tissue?" asked Freddie. "You'll need something to mop it up."

"I've got a clean handkerchief," said Bruce.

"You haven't blown your nose on it?"

"No. It's quite clean."

"It soon won't be," said Freddie. "Still, all in a good cause."

Bruce leaned forward and placed a thumb on one side of the boil and his index finger on the other. He had taken his handkerchief—or Jonathan's—from the pocket of his jacket and was holding it ready in his left hand. "All right?"

"Do it," said Freddie.

Bruce began to exert pressure on the inflamed skin on either side of the boil. As he did so, the skin became redder, and he felt Freddie tense beneath him. "Are you sure about this?" he asked.

"Yes," said Freddie. "Just get it over with."

Bruce pressed harder. And then, with all the force and pent-up anger of a volcano that has been awaiting its moment, the boil discharged its burden. Freddie gave a cry—and so did Bruce.

# 60. The Life of Bacteria

The human body, we are occasionally reminded, consists largely of water. Many find that fact strangely reassuring; water, as Auden observed, is nowhere disliked; our company, he insisted, coarsens roses and dogs, but evokes from water only an innocent outcry when we force it through turbines or fountains. Others may find the idea of being mostly water a vaguely depressing thought; they would prefer to be made of firmer stuff, of substances with a more solid ring to them: iron, potassium, calcium; water for them is too . . . well, too liquid. At the heart of their unease, though, may be a simple rejection of this reductionist view: to reduce the human body to its constituents is a painful reminder that we are nothing much really, in spite of our pretensions; that all our grand notions of self-importance will never overcome the simple biological limitations of our existence—a sobering thought, and an important one. To be cut down to size is good for all of us, but particularly so for those who forget how transient are our cultures and institutions, how pointless and cruel our divisions, how vain our claims to special status for our practices and beliefs above those of others.

But if the thought of how watery we are is

disturbing, then how much more so is the contemplation of how many bacteria we host. Pursuing the reductionist approach, each human body contains sufficient bacteria to fill a half-gallon container, and these bacteria mill and congregate, hold riotous assembly, reproduce orgiastically, revolt and die right across the territory we so generously provide for them. We are so considerate: we go to great lengths to maintain our temperature at a level which suits them perfectly, even if they, by their activity, are occasionally rude enough to send that temperature soaring. We nourish them and allow them opportunities to meet and relate to their fellow bacteria inhabiting other bodies. Great are their celebrations when we kiss each other and introduce them to populations of their cousins; or shake hands; or even open a door.

The bacteria that Bruce encountered that morning in Jonathan's office had established themselves in a hair follicle on Freddie's neck. What had happened was that Freddie, who liked going to the Edinburgh City Council gym at Craiglockhart, had been exercising on a cross-trainer. This requires one to hold two handles on which there are rounded metal sections. These metal sections exist to monitor the user's heart rate, which is then displayed on an illuminated panel, encouraging the person exercising to go faster or to slow down, or informing him, in extreme cases, that his heart has actually stopped and that further exercise would be pointless. But anything that is grasped by a series of people—even for such a healthy objective as improving fitness and heart rate—can also harbour the bacteria we all carry around on our hands. To limit cross-infection, the gym had provided a bottle of mildly sterilising liquid that could be sprayed on all such surfaces after use—a nicety observed by some, but not all, users of the gym. And it was one of these non-observers who left on the handles of that particular cross-trainer a rather unpleasant variety of bacteria that been waiting for an opportunity to colonise pastures new.

When Freddie came, used the cross-trainer, and then touched the back of his neck, these tiny organisms leapt joyously into what must have seemed to them a great, welcoming cave: a tiny crevice around one of Freddie's hair follicles. Once in their new quarters, they established a civilisation, and multiplied, creating in the process a surprisingly large quantity of dead skin cells. These became a mound not entirely dissimilar to the mounds of rubbish that our own civilisations create—a mound of foul-smelling pus.

Then came the pressure that Bruce exerted around the site of this tiny ecological disaster, and in a sudden and spectacular outburst the pus was released out into the air, hitting the first solid object it encountered and covering it with tiny droplets of yellow, flecked with red. The red was blood; the encountered object was Bruce.

"Steady on!" cried Freddie. "Careful!"

Bruce shouted too, an indeterminate cry, a shout of disgust that required no word to make its meaning clear. Pushing Freddie away lest a further eruption occur, he wiped at his face with the handkerchief he had been holding. This handkerchief, until then white, came away with streaks of yellow and red—the colours that were now also evident on the front of Bruce's shirt, and on the lapels of his jacket.

Freddie stood up and gingerly felt at the back of his neck. "The pain's gone," he said. "It's just gone." He turned to Bruce. "You all right, Jono?"

Bruce's face was contorted with disgust. "No," he said. "I'm not. I'm covered with . . ."

Freddie smiled. "You do look a bit of a mess," he said. "Look, let me give you a wipe."

"Keep away from me," muttered Bruce. "Disgusting . . ."

Freddie looked affronted. "It's just pus," he said. "Everybody gets pus . . . now and then."

"What am I going to do?" said Bruce.

"Go home," said Freddie. "I'll tell Bill. Go home and get changed." He paused. "Look, I'll pay for your jacket to be dry-cleaned. How about that? Your shirt will be fine. Just bung it in the wash."

Bruce continued to wipe at his shirt-front and jacket with the handkerchief, but it seemed only to make the situation worse. Freddie was right, though, about going home. He could hardly go through the day covered in pus.

"By the way," said Freddie. "Sorry to mention it now, just after you've been so . . . so helpful, but you owe me twelve quid."

"Why?" said Bruce.

"The six quid I lent you last week—remember? For lunch, when you couldn't get to a cash machine? And then there's six quid for the syndicate."

Bruce almost asked what syndicate this was and then he remembered that Jonathan would know. "All right," he said. "Here."

He reached into his pocket and extracted his wallet, passing over a ten-pound note and two coins.

"Thanks," said Freddie. "Did you read about those people over in Ayrshire who won all those Euro millions? Could be us sometime, Jono!"

That answered Bruce's question. An office lottery ticket syndicate. He sighed. Boils. Pus. He should have realised; he should have thought about all this before he agreed to this ridiculous exchange of identities. Well, it was over now. He would go back to the flat and get changed—into his own clothes.

# 61. Jonathan's Doubts

Jonathan was rather enjoying being Bruce. The suggestion to exchange identities had come from him in the first place and it had not been an impromptu, spur-of-the-moment suggestion, even if he would never have anticipated stumbling into the conditions that would make such a change possible. There had been a background to it—a background of unease over who he was and where his life was going.

There was nothing fundamentally wrong with Jonathan's life in Edinburgh—he enjoyed what the city undoubtedly had to offer anybody in his late twenties and of a generally sociable disposition, and so he was certainly not bored; it was more a feeling of pointlessness. That can be a problem, and a major one. Believing that one's life is somehow without direction is undermining. The sense of a lack of purpose, like a strong weed-killer, destroys that which it surrounds, withering the satisfaction otherwise obtained from day-to-day pursuits, strangling not only excitement and joy but also one's basic appreciation of life.

This problem had started for Jonathan when he had read an essay in a Sunday newspaper about anomie, a concept of mismatch between the individual and society. Anomie, he was told, came into existence when social values failed to chime with the individual—a condition that the writer of the article felt was endemic. Jonathan liked the sound of the word, and felt that it somehow expressed his feelings about his life, and in particular about his life in the PR agency. Suddenly it occurred to him that a life that he had previously thought was perfectly satisfactory was far from being that. What did his existence actually mean? He went through the motions of going to work, seeing others socially, improving his material circumstances and so on, but at the end of the day he had no answer to the question: why am I doing all this?

He had raised the subject with a friend when sharing an after-work drink in the Filmhouse bar. "I'm not exactly sure why I'm here," he said. "Are you?"

The friend looked at him in mild astonishment. "Well, we're here to see a film," he said. "Or that's what I thought. Unless there's some other agenda."

"Oh, there's no other agenda," said Jonathan. "Have you got another agenda?"

The friend shook his head. "I haven't got an agenda. I thought maybe you had—the way you suddenly said that you weren't sure why you were here. That sounded like an agenda."

"No," said Jonathan. "No agenda." He looked about him, at the people seated in the bar. Did they have an agenda? It was hard to tell. Some people look as if they definitely have an agenda, while with others it's rather more difficult to tell. "It all seems rather pointless," he continued.

The friend looked into his glass. "I suppose it can seem that way. Do you think we're just filling time?"

Jonathan thought about this. It seemed an extraordinarily bleak conclusion that all that he was doing was filling time. What his life needed, he decided, was meaning. But how did one find that?

"Meaning?" echoed his friend, after he had raised it with him. "Where do most people find meaning in their lives? What are their options?"

This question, so simple in its expression, was not easily answered.

"Material fulfilment?" asked Jonathan.

"Maybe," said the friend. "That's probably it for just about everybody these days. People think that satisfying their material wishes will make them somehow happier. It doesn't, of course. It only makes them want more."

"Yet it does provide a goal," said Jonathan. "If you're on twenty-five thousand a year and you want to be on thirty thousand, at least you have an objective. If you've got an old car and you want a new one, then at least you have something to work for."

"Maybe," said the friend. "Maybe. But the goal

is always elusive, isn't it? And it's always just over the horizon."

"All right. Then comfort. Maybe that's what we're all striving for. Just to be comfortable. To be warm. Not to be hungry. To have somewhere comfortable to sit. Pretty basic stuff, but all understandable goals."

"To an extent. But . . ." The friend looked about him. "We've got somewhere comfortable to sit, and yet you're not happy, are you?"

Jonathan sighed. "No."

"Religion?" asked the friend. "What about that? A lot of people find the answer there, don't they? Religion answers your question as to meaning fairly definitely, doesn't it? Or most religions do. They tell you why you're here and what you've got to do. And they often keep you busy doing it by inventing all sorts of rituals to underline the point. All of that gives people a structure and a sense of purpose."

Jonathan smiled. "If you accept the basic premise," he said. "But I'm not sure I do."

"That there's a divine purpose?"

Jonathan nodded. "I can't," he said. "That's the problem. I look at where we are and . . ." He shrugged, in sheer helplessness. "I see our real situation. I see us as tiny specks of life that happen to have come into existence on a lump of rock hurtling through space. We're tiny—really tiny. And yet we somehow claim that our ant-like existence is special and that the creator of all this is actually listening to us. I can't, I'm afraid."

The friend listened. "If you think that," he said quietly, "then there's absolutely no point in continuing. Nothing has any meaning."

"But that's the whole point," said Jonathan. "Maybe it hasn't."

"Except in a limited context," said the friend. "We can still identify happiness and unhappiness. We can still identify pain and the absence of pain. Even those basic things give us a . . . a reference point for all the rest. It creates value—value for us."

Jonathan listened intently. The friend, who had rather surprised himself by the direction the conversation had taken, now drained his glass and smiled. "You know your problem, Jono? You need a change. Simple."

## 62. Encounter in Dundas Street

The conversation that Jonathan had with his friend in the Filmhouse bar proved to have far greater implications than either of them could have imagined. For most of us a discussion about the things that really matter—the fundamental questions of how we are to live our lives and, just as important, how we are to make sense of the lives we live—is a rare event. We do think about such matters, but our contemplation of them tends to be sporadic and darting. And when it comes to talking about them with friends, embarrassment often prevents us from anything but the most superficial discussion. Or life gets in the way: we are too busy, too preoccupied to ask each other what we think about these most essential and profound matters. For most of us, life is lived with the philosophical volume turned half down. Yes, the world may be beautiful and intense and moving; yes, the very fact of human existence poses the most extraordinarily profound dilemmas; yes, our every act may involve finely nuanced decisions that have to be made; but we have a bus to catch, but we have a bill to pay, but we have to collect the children from school, but . . .

Jonathan went home that evening in a frame of mind that was completely unfamiliar to him. It had not been a particularly long conversation that he and his friend had had, but it had given him a glimpse of the way in which he might think about his life—about life in general. And even if the advice that he had received at the end of it— the suggestion that he needed a change—might have sounded glib—the sort of nostrum that the dispensers of practical wisdom love to recommend—it predisposed him to action. And now, after that quite unexpected meeting with Bruce, his double, he had been able to engage in a wild and ridiculous escapade that offered the most significant change imaginable: that of becoming, for a brief period, somebody else. The temptation was too great to resist, and he did not resist it.

Of course Jonathan had Bruce's measure even before they gave each other their keys. He had observed certain similarities in their tastes and in the externals of their lives, but beyond that it was clear to him that they were very different people. Jonathan had encountered narcissists before, and he could see that Bruce was a classic example of the type. That said, he rather liked him. There was a certain cheery confidence to Bruce—a rather jaunty, optimistic attitude that he found curiously appealing. There was no question of Bruce's being haunted by doubts as to what his life meant; that would be the challenge, really. If he were to pass as Bruce, then he would have to stop thinking for a couple of days. He would have to stop thinking and start doing.

On the morning that they each went into the other's office—the morning when Bruce made such a thoroughly bad start and had his uncomfortable encounter with Freddie's boil—Jonathan had actually rather enjoyed himself. The deception worked perfectly. His in-tray had several requests for properties to be given a general evaluation, and he had been able to do that easily enough. Indeed there was a standard form that the firm used that merely required the ticking of boxes and the appending of the occasional additional comment.

He had managed that without any difficulty, and, on returning from the second of these assignments—a flat in Northumberland Street that was just about to come onto the market—he had noticed a small coffee bar in a basement in Dundas Street. He must have walked past it before, he thought, but had never given it a try. Well, he was in no hurry to get back to the office and he could detect the delicious smell of freshly ground coffee wafting up the steps. He went in.

Jonathan entered Big Lou's coffee bar at a busy and rather interesting time. Matthew and Bo, the Danish filmmaker, were there. From behind her vigorously polished coffee bar, Big Lou was talking to Bo, who had a video camera on his shoulder, the lens pointed directly at her. Matthew, who had just been served with coffee by Big Lou, was seated at a table, looking rather glum.

"Aye," said Big Lou to Bo as Jonathan pushed open the door, "I remember how it was with the lambing. Some of the lambs didn't do too well and we used to bring them on in the kitchen. We had one of those big ranges, great for keeping porridge warm, and we'd put cardboard boxes in front of this for the heat and put the lambs in them. Pair wee things, with their spindly legs and their bleating for their mothers. And my Uncle Davey would come in from the fields and bring another one in for us to look after till the whole place was a bit of a nursery.

"My mother was a very good cook. She also made marmalade and jams and things like that, and there was a whole line of preserving jars on a kitchen shelf. She read the *People's Friend*, which an aunt of mine used to send on from Dundee when she'd finished with it. We used to line the boxes for those lambs with old issues.

"The local policeman was a friend of my father's. He was called PC Murdoch as I recall . . ." She stopped and glanced at Jonathan. "Well, well, it's himself."

Jonathan hesitated. It was immediately apparent to him what had happened—this coffee bar must have been a haunt of Bruce's, and these people, not only the owner but also the couple sitting at a table, were staring at him. They knew him—or rather, they knew Bruce.

It was too late to withdraw. "Good morning," he said to Big Lou, and then nodded briefly to Bo. "Don't let me interrupt anything."

Bo switched off his camera. He was looking at Bruce with interest.

"Your usual, Bruce?" asked Lou.

That was easy enough. "Yes please . . ." He faltered. He did not know Lou's name but had noticed something embroidered onto the rather curious housecoat that she was wearing. "Yes please, Big Lou."

The salutation passed without comment.

"This is Bo," said Lou. "He's making a film for . . ."

"For Danish television," said Bo, extending his hand. "How do you do? Please tell me your name—you have a very interesting face, you see."

## 63. *Economic Statistics, and Other Creative Activities*

"You know," said Stuart, looking out of the kitchen window, "I've had a very demanding day—a very demanding day."

The evening sunlight had caught the tops of the trees at the end of Scotland Street, had painted them with gold. The air was still—heavy with the weight of a long summer's day behind it—and the branches of the trees were motionless in their torpor.

"Working hard on a warm day like this is so much more difficult than in winter," Stuart went on. "I don't feel it in winter, but in this heat . . ."

"I've been busy too," said Irene, tipping strong bread flour into the top of her bread-making machine. "I had a meeting of the Melanie Klein Reading Group and an essay for my Open University course. 'A Durkheimian Analysis of Post-Industrial Society.' Not simple."

"No," mused Stuart. "Are we post-industrial in Scotland, by the way?"

Irene gave her husband a withering look. "Everybody's post-industrial, Stuart."

Stuart frowned. "Everybody? But somebody must make something—unless we don't need things any more. Do we need things, do you think?"

"Of course we need things," said Irene. "Things are made . . ." She waved a hand in the air, in a vaguely eastern direction. "Things are made in China."

"So I believe," said Stuart. "So what's there left for us to do?"

"Service industries," said Irene. "Intellectual industries. We can earn our living through thinking, Stuart."

"Inventing things?" asked Stuart.

"Yes, if one has to put it simply."

Stuart thought about this. "But of course that presupposes that other people won't invent them first."

"They might," said Irene. "But there'll be some things we invent first, and then protect the intellectual property."

Stuart looked doubtful. "But there are lots of places that won't respect intellectual property," he said. "China for one. They just ignore it—or many of them do."

Irene sighed. "International capitalism will find a way of dealing with that," she said.

"I thought you disapproved of international capitalism," said Stuart mildly.

"Of course I disapprove of it," snapped Irene. "Who doesn't?"

Stuart could think of one or two names. But he did not want to get into a discussion with Irene about international capitalism, and so he returned to the subject of his own day.

"I had a very trying meeting," he said. "The minister is about to make a speech to some gathering of influential businessmen at Gleneagles and . . ."

"Typical," interrupted Irene. "People like that love Gleneagles."

Stuart shrugged. "It's rather nice, yes . . ."

"If you can afford it," said Irene forcefully. "What about all those other people who can't afford to go to Gleneagles? What about them?"

"Oh, I imagine they'll find somewhere else to go," said Stuart. "They could go to the pub, for example."

"As Marie Antoinette might say," retorted Irene.

Stuart bit his lip. "I didn't mean it in that way. There are lots of people who would actually prefer to go to the pub than to go to Gleneagles. They'd feel more comfortable in the pub." He paused. None of this was going down well with Irene, and so he returned—again—to the subject of his trying day. "Well, be that as it may, the minister was jumping up and down about getting some figures on North Sea oil. She needed them in order to prove that Scotland would be the sixth richest nation in the world if our economy were to be looked at on its own."

"In your dreams!" said Irene.

"Well, as you know," Stuart continued, "you can do all sorts of things with statistics—which is where we as statisticians came in. And because John is off at some meeting or other in Amsterdam, it fell to me to deal with the ministerial request. I got out my calculator and did a few sums on the back of an envelope and showed them to the minister. As far as I could work out, we'd actually be the sixty-second richest country in the world."

"Ah!" said Irene. "I bet she didn't like that."

"Not very much," said Stuart. "She's doing her best, though. So she asked me to look at the figures again and see whether I could present them in a different light. They all do that—all the parties. I asked her what she had in mind, and she said that I could perhaps base my calculations on the assumption that a whole lot more oil will be found, and perhaps quite a bit of gold and other precious metals too. If those possibilities were taken into account, perhaps it would be possible to portray us as the sixth richest country in the world, or even the richest, if they found lots of these things."

"I see," said Irene, shaking the contents of a small packet into the breadmaker's nut dispenser. "Nuts."

"That's what I thought," said Stuart. "And so I explained that this was not an accepted technique in economic forecasting or in statistics. So she looked very disappointed and then said that surely we could do the calculations again on the basis that the fifty-six or so countries above us could all become poorer, in which case we would then be the sixth on the list. She seemed quite pleased with this suggestion, but I'm afraid I had to pour cold water on it."

"On politicians," said Irene.

"Anyway, I told her I couldn't do any of that and so she told me to come up with some figures for North Sea production that she could use. What she wanted was how much oil would be produced next year. Unfortunately, I didn't have the data, and so I had no idea what to do."

"Olive oil," said Irene, pouring a small quantity into her bread-maker.

"No, crude," said Stuart. "So you know what came to the rescue? *The Scotsman*'s Sudoku. One of the interns in the office had completed the Sudoku, filling in all the numbers, and then left it lying on a desk. So I decided to put it to good use. I wrote down all the Sudoku numbers and passed them on to the minister, and she was very pleased. She seemed to think that they looked good. She asked me whether they could be interpreted as suggesting that Scotland would be the sixth richest country in the world after all, but I said that the statistics were still tentative and that it would be best to wait, and she reluctantly accepted that."

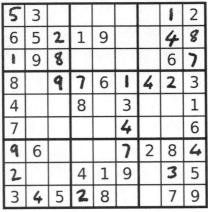

*North Sea Oil production figures.*

Irene had stopped listening. The following day was a Saturday and she had remembered something that she had planned to do. "I mustn't forget the Yoga Fest," she said. "I'm planning to take Bertie."

"Yoga Fest?" asked Stuart. "I was actually hoping to take him fishing. Remember how I took him fishing last year? He loved it so much. I thought we might go again. We could invite that wee friend of his, Andy—the one we met last year. The one with the Swiss Army penknives."

Irene turned and stared at her husband. "I'm sorry, Stuart," she said. "It's the Yoga Fest. And I'm not having Bertie playing with that heavily armed child."

318

# 64. One Out of Three

Stuart bit his lip.

"I'm not sure," he ventured, "that I'd say that the possession of a few Swiss Army penknives merits the description heavily armed. I had a penknife when I was a boy."

Irene looked down her nose. "Oh yes?"

"Yes, I did. It had four blades, as I remember, and a hook for taking the stones out of horses' hooves."

"Very useful," said Irene scornfully.

He ignored the jibe. "I loved it."

There was a silence. He looked at his wife. Why had he married her? It was difficult to remember how he had felt, but he must have thought it a good idea at some point. But now, with Bertie and Ulysses and the mortgage and the insurance policies all to think of, it seemed to be altogether too late to ask that question. Life just leaks away—he had read that somewhere and had thought at the time how true it was and yes, it was true, so very true. What did he do? He went to the office in the morning and played around with figures for the government. Then he came home and he had his evening meal. Then he went to bed so that he would be able to get up in time to set off for the office next morning. And in between all of this, he had to listen to Irene going on about Melanie Klein and psychotherapy and yoga and such things.

He loved Bertie—he loved him to distraction, but he had so little time to spend with him because Irene seemed to dominate their son's life so completely. So it seemed that whenever he suggested doing anything with Bertie—a fishing trip or something of that nature—he had to endure her ideological opposition. Fishing was cruel; penknives were dangerous; rugby was barbaric; cub scouts were paramilitary; dogs were dirty; and so on. He sighed.

And as for Ulysses, Stuart hardly dared even to think about him. To begin with, he was sure that he had never intended Ulysses. He thought that he and Irene had decided not to have another child and he thought that she was in charge of ensuring that the family did not get any bigger, and yet . . . Then there had been the remark that Bertie had passed about how Ulysses looked remarkably like his psychotherapist, Dr. Fairbairn, and Stuart had at first laughed and said that lots of people looked a bit like other people, and then Bertie had said, "But his ears, Daddy—have you looked at his ears? Dr. Fairbairn has these really unusual ears— here, let me draw you a picture . . . You see that bit there? Both Ulysses and Dr. Fairbairn have that bit over there, you see, that bit."

That had worried him. He had said nothing to

Irene, but he had examined Ulysses' ears more closely and had seen what Bertie was talking about. Nobody in his family had ears like that, he was sure, and as for Irene, he had not known her mother, who had died before he and Irene had got together, but he had known her father and his ears were perfectly normal, as far as he could recall.

Of course it was a simple matter to do a DNA paternity test. He had investigated the matter online one evening by typing paternity testing into a search engine and following the results. One site had promised a result in three days if one sent a few hairs from the child and a few hairs from the putative father. That's me, he thought. I'm a putative father.

It was a strange description, but it could have its uses. Perhaps he might one day say to Irene—quite casually—"as Ulysses' putative father." And then wait to see how she reacted. A guilty person might in such circumstances be expected to gasp, or at least blush, but he was not sure that Irene would do even that. Irene was not an easy woman, and he had never been able to show quite the resolve that he might have wished to show when she locked one of her stares onto him.

He had sat at his computer screen, riveted by one of the frequently-asked-questions on the testing service's website. Q: What proportion of test results show that the putative father is not the real father? You'd be surprised! In our experience about one in three tests reveal that the man who is acting as father is not the real father. Stuart had been astounded. One in three! What did that say about people's behaviour? Did it mean that one in three women were misleading their husbands or partners and having clandestine affairs with . . . psychotherapists and the like? Stuart thought the figure really rather high and wondered whether that statistic needed geographical refinement. Whatever was happening elsewhere in the country, it was highly unlikely that one in three women in Edinburgh were behaving in that loose way. Of course, as a statistician, he could tell the flaw in that figure. All that this showed was that among those who have reason to suspect the fidelity of their partner, one out of three will find that he is not the father of the child. That was because the sample was a selective one. It was really a case of no smoke without a fire: only those who had some reason to doubt paternity would have it tested. So that meant that the sample was already biased towards including unfaithful women.

His eye ran further down the column of frequently-asked-questions. What should I do if the result shows that I'm not the father? You need to talk to your wife or partner. Sound advice, thought Stuart, but what if . . . he hesitated, and then articulated his own supplementary question: What if you're frightened of your spouse or partner? He wondered what the answer to that would be, and then it came to him. The answer would be this: See a psychotherapist. He smiled. Yes indeed. See a psychotherapist and say to him: see this child's ears . . .

He had not heard Irene push the door open. He had not heard her walk quietly across the room and lean forward, not quite over his shoulder but not far behind it, in order to see what he was reading with such interest. How many husbands have experienced that disturbing sensation? How many husbands have been enjoying some piece of research on the internet and have suddenly been aware of their wife standing behind them and saying, "And what are you doing?" Two rather than one out of three, thought Stuart.

Irene cleared her throat. "Stuart . . ."

Stuart's hand darted forward; he was swift with the cursor. "Nothing," he said quickly.

"Nothing what?" she said. "I didn't ask you what you were doing."

"It was nothing anyway," he said.

Her eyes narrowed. Stuart had rapidly navigated from the paternity testing site to an altogether more innocent site advertising holidays in Sri Lanka. "There," he said, pointing to the screen. "I've always wanted to go to Colombo."

Irene said nothing. For his part, Stuart thought, Why should I feel guilty when she is the one who should feel guilty? And why should one not want to go to Colombo?

# 65. Consultation Over

Irene remained icily quiet. But then she said, "It's not Colombo."

Stuart affected surprise. "Not Colombo? Oh well, I suppose not everyone's interested in Colombo. One can't expect Colombo to appeal absolutely universally. There are bound to be those who . . ."

"Stuart," interrupted Irene. "I am not in any way referring to Colombo. Colombo is irrelevant."

"Not if you're Colomban," muttered Stuart.

Irene moved closer. "I was referring to the site you were visiting earlier on—that paternity site. Why were you there?"

Stuart shrugged. "Accident," he said. "The Web's like that. You click by mistake when the cursor's travelling innocently along and there you are . . . looking at something unexpected. Twenty-four-hour plumbers, for example. There's no telling."

Irene moved closer. "You wouldn't be thinking of carrying out a paternity test, would you?"

Stuart gasped. "Paternity test! Whatever gave you that idea? And why would I want to carry out a paternity test?"

"Why indeed?" said Irene coldly. "It would be very unwise, I'd say."

Stuart thought about this. Why would it be unwise? Why should men be frightened to establish that they are not the father? Why should he be frightened?

"Sometimes it's best to know the truth," he ventured.

Irene moved closer still. "Oh yes?"

Stuart rose to his feet. He had had enough—at least for the time being—and the matter was shelved. There will come a time, he thought, even if that time is not yet.

Now, on that Saturday morning, he was not thinking of Ulysses but of Bertie, and of his promise to take Bertie fishing.

"Sorry," he said to Irene. "Sorry about the Yoga Fest. I'm sure there'll be another one some time. They're always holding Yoga Fests." He met her gaze. She was watching him. Medusa, he thought. One has to be careful about looking directly at Medusa—without a mirrored shield, of course, which Stuart did not possess.

"So it's fishing," he concluded, looking away. "I've told Bertie already. So that's it finished."

"What do you mean—that's it finished?" Irene snapped.

"Exactly that," said Stuart. "Consultation over." He had picked up that phrase at work, from a minister who used it to announce his decisions. Consultation over meant that there would be no further debate on a particular item of policy, but the phrase could also be used in advance of any announcement, even before any consultation was carried out. Stuart, like all his colleagues, had long understood the purpose of most government consultations: this was to get public support for decisions that had already been taken. Everybody knew this, except perhaps those members of the public who submitted their views in the hope that these might be taken into account.

Stuart looked at his watch. This was another trick he had learned at work. If one looked at one's watch it unnerved any potential opponents and certainly cut short any further consultation. Rather to his surprise, it seemed to work, and with an indecipherable mutter about yoga fests, Irene busied herself with some other task. Heady with victory, Stuart helped Bertie prepare for their fishing trip and made a telephone call to Andy's mother to ask whether her son would care to join them. "Of course he would," she replied. "Andy loves going fishing."

Bertie grinned with pleasure. The thought of seeing his friend, who would almost certainly have a Swiss Army penknife on him, was exciting enough, but when compounded with the thought of actually going fishing in one of the Pentland lochs, and possibly, just possibly catching that large trout that had so narrowly escaped on their last fishing trip, the effect was to swell his heart with an almost uncontrollable joy.

"Now," said Stuart when everything was ready, "it looks as if we can go and get into the car, Bertie."

Bertie nodded enthusiastically. "I can carry all my stuff, Daddy. You just get your things and the key."

Stuart nodded. "I have the key in my pocket, Bertie. So it's off we go! Off to . . ." He hesitated. He was the last one to use the car. He had used it about three weeks ago and had parked it . . . He scratched the side of his head. He had driven to Perth for a meeting of the Statistical Society of Scotland, of which he was secretary. Then he had come back—he was sure of that—and had parked . . . It was Nelson Street, he thought, or possibly Northumberland Street. Somewhere up there. They would find it easily enough, he decided. There would not be many red Volvos in Northumberland Street and it would be spotted easily. It was becoming quite distinguished, their car, now that modern cars all looked the same. Their car, which was sixteen years old, stood out from the crowd in a rather distinguished way. And that was useful when one had to locate it.

Stuart and Bertie walked up Scotland Street and into Drummond Place. It was barely nine o'clock and the streets were quiet, with only one or two residents out enjoying the warmth of the morning sun.

"That's Mr. Irvine Welsh over there, Daddy,"

said Bertie, pointing to a tall man striding down the opposite side of the street.

"Indeed it is, Bertie," said Stuart.

"He wrote a book about trains," said Bertie.

"Yes he did, Bertie. That's quite correct."

And round the corner, completing an energetic circuit of Drummond Place, Magnus Linklater waved a cheerful greeting. "That's Mr. Linklater," said Bertie. "He writes newspapers."

"I believe he does, Bertie."

They continued up Nelson Street to the point where it becomes Northumberland Street. Somewhere here, thought Stuart. Somewhere along here—I'm sure of it. He glanced down the street, hoping to see the familiar red roof of their ancient Volvo. There were several red cars, but none of them was a Volvo.

"We'll just walk along the street, Bertie," said Stuart. "Sometimes cars are rather tucked away and you don't see them until you're right up against them."

Bertie nodded. This had happened before, and the outcome had usually not been a good one. And if they did not find their car, then what? No fishing?

Suddenly Stuart remembered. Just along the street was the premises of an art dealer. It was not a gallery like Matthew's—more of an office really—a business called Art International that represented a number of artists, including a number of rising stars. Stuart knew the proprietor, George MacGregor, and he had remembered that he had parked the car outside his office that day because he had spotted the proprietor standing in the window, his back to the street.

"I've remembered where the car is, Bertie," he announced. "Panic over."

Bertie said nothing. In his experience, panic over did not necessarily mean panic over.

## 66. The Turner Prize!

It soon became clear to Stuart that there was no red Volvo parked outside the office of Art International although there was a smaller, non-Swedish red car not far away, now sporting a collection of parking tickets.

"I'm sure I put it here," he said to Bertie. "I drove back from Perth that afternoon and I parked right here in front of George MacGregor's office. I remember it, you see, because I looked up and saw him standing in the window."

Bertie thought for a moment. "Maybe you were drunk, Daddy," he said politely. "Maybe you were drunk and put it in another street."

Stuart laughed. "I'd never be drunk in charge of a car, Bertie. That's a very bad thing."

Bertie nodded. "I just wondered, Daddy. I didn't say you were definitely drunk. I just wondered."

"Well, I can assure you I was stone cold sober, Bertie."

Bertie looked down the street. "Perhaps you didn't put the brake on properly, Daddy. Perhaps our car just rolled down the hill. Maybe we should look down at Canonmills."

Stuart suppressed a smile. "I don't think so, Bertie. No, it's very strange."

Bertie had an idea. "Maybe it's been stolen, Daddy. Maybe somebody came over from Glasgow and stole it. Tofu says that happens all the time. Glaswegians come over to Edinburgh and steal all our cars and take them back to Glasgow and drive round in them. He says that Glasgow's full of Edinburgh cars being driven round in by people from Glasgow who've pinched them."

Stuart shook his head. "That's nonsense, Bertie. Tofu really does talk a lot of nonsense."

Bertie had another suggestion to make. "What about your friend, Daddy? If that's his window up there maybe he saw our car. Maybe he saw what happened to it."

Stuart was about to reject this possibility too when it occurred to him that it was really a rather good idea. "Good thinking, Bertie," he said. "Let's give his bell a ring."

George MacGregor gave a warm welcome to his old school friend. He and Stuart had been exact contemporaries at James Gillespie's High School in Edinburgh. Stuart had been particularly good at

330

mathematics and George had excelled at art. Their later careers had reflected those talents, Stuart graduating with a first in statistics from Heriot-Watt University and George carrying off a distinguished degree in art history from St. Andrews. George had worked for some years for Bonhams, where he developed his expertise in Scottish art, before branching out as an agent for painters and sculptors, representing them in their dealings with galleries and dealers in London and further afield.

Stuart introduced George to Bertie, who shook hands gravely with his father's friend.

"I wondered if you've seen our car?" Stuart asked. "I parked it right outside your place a few weeks ago."

George looked puzzled. "There are a lot of cars in the street," he began. "I don't really notice them very much."

Bertie decided to help. "It's red," he said. "A red Volvo."

George looked down at Bertie. "A red Volvo? Right outside?"

"Yes," said Stuart. "You must have noticed it."

George MacGregor put his hand to his mouth. "Oh . . ."

"Something happened?" asked Stuart quickly. "Was it towed?"

George had now turned distinctly pale. "It was put on the back of a large lorry."

"But I've got a parking permit for this area," protested Stuart. "They've no right . . ."

George was shaking his head. "Oh no," he said. "It's beginning to make sense."

Stuart was now beginning to show his irritation. "Listen, George, you're being a bit obscure. What exactly happened to my car?"

They had been standing in the doorway, and now George invited them in. "I need to explain something," he said. "And it might be better if we were all sitting down."

"Me too?" asked Bertie.

George nodded. "Yes, all of us. Come in."

They went into George's office, a large room decorated with the posters of exhibitions and with shelves laden with books on art. George indicated two seats while he sat behind his desk.

"It's a very odd story," he began. "You see, I have an artist by the name of Geoffrey Airdrie. He's been doing rather well recently. He's a conceptual artist—cutting-edge stuff." He waited for a reaction, but Stuart remained silent.

"Geoffrey's work is pretty challenging," George continued. "The essential idea is that things either go forwards or backwards, but not in two directions at the same time. It's a fascinating concept and he's devoted much of his practice as an artist to exploring it. He had a big show down in London last year.

"One of his best-known works is called *Time's*

*Chariot*. He based it on an old tractor he found up near Dunblane. He painted it yellow and attached it to a plough. It caused a big sensation in London and there was talk of it going on to New York. A bit reminiscent of Koons, really, but maybe more radical. Important stuff.

"Then there was his *Razor Blades of Memory* which wowed them big time at the Venice Biennale. That was a large collection of used razor blades arranged in a very impressive fan-shape. That went for two hundred grand at Christie's in South Ken. A very encouraging price. Hirst would have really loved that piece, I think."

"My car," muttered Stuart.

George looked down at the top of his desk. He was clearly embarrassed. "Yes, your car. Well, the truth of the matter is this: Geoffrey was nominated for the Turner Prize and was thinking about a work to be called *Machinery IV*. He told me that it would be a red car that would be given artistic preparation down in London, at the Tate. He said that it should be collected from Northumberland Street, outside my office . . ."

Stuart had worked out where this was going. He sat wide-eyed as the story continued to unfold.

"Well, I'm afraid I assumed that the red Volvo outside was it. So I arranged for it to be carted down to London. And now . . ." He paused. "And now comes the bad news. And the good news too. It went down to London where it was cut in half and then mounted on a large board. Not perhaps the best of news for you, but then . . . then, well I'm really happy to tell you: it won the Turner Prize!"

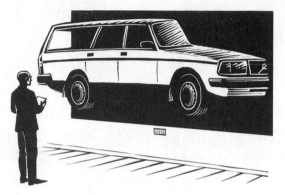

The effect of this news was to render Stuart speechless. Bertie, however, reacted in a more lively way. "You mean our car won the Turner Prize, Mr. MacGregor?"

"Yes," said George. "That's about it. Good news, isn't it? Of course it's now an art work rather than a car, but that's the price of art, Bertie."

"But it's cut in two, Mr. MacGregor," wailed Bertie. He had loved that car, had been so proud of it.

"True, Bertie. But just think: that's what great art does. It obliges us to re-examine our relationship with the material world. And sometimes that means bifurcation."

# 67. News for Bruce

Bruce returned from the office in a state of extreme discomfort. This state of mind was very unusual for him, as his normal mood was one of optimistic breeziness. After all, if one was a narcissist—as Bruce undoubtedly was—what was there to feel unhappy about? The person one really cared for—the object of one's desires—was always there to hand, ready to agree with whatever was proposed and very rarely inclined to complain.

Now, however, Bruce felt both physically and emotionally uncomfortable. The cause of his physical distress was self-evident—anybody encountering him walking home that day would have immediately realised that there had been some difficulty with a yellowish substance—probably custard—that was spattered prominently across the front of his shirt and the lapels of his jacket. Such an observer, noting Bruce's scowl, would perhaps have wondered why custard should provoke such an intense reaction; but of course it was not custard but a florescence of a very different, and more objectionable nature: pus from Freddie's boil—and that, understandably enough, would have dismayed anybody in Bruce's position, even those not afflicted with his vanity.

Bruce's emotional discomfort stemmed from his awareness of having made a bad mistake. He had agreed to the ridiculous exchange of identities, but now, after only a few hours as Jonathan, he had had enough and was impatient to bring the whole episode to a close. That could be done, he decided, that evening. He would return to the flat, spend the day mindlessly watching some of the films he had noticed on Jonathan's shelves, and then resume his real identity when his partner in deception returned from work.

After a long hot shower and change of clothing, Bruce felt distinctly better. Jonathan's taste in films was not exactly the same as his, but once Bruce had settled into watching *Surfing Boys IV*, a film that had some exceptional shots of impressive waves, he decided that he could now enjoy the last few hours of being somebody else. And it was not too bad being Jonathan, he concluded: the flat was extremely comfortable, the clothes were pretty good, and there was something to be said for the stock of wines and gourmet snacks that he had unearthed in the kitchen. And as for *Surfing Boys IV*, the dialogue might not have been all that exciting but there was certainly plenty of action. *Surfing Boys V* and *VI* were also on the shelves and they would pass a few hours as well, although there were aspects of these films, he felt, that could become a bit tedious. Was it really necessary to flex one's muscles quite so much before launching a surfboard? Bruce doubted it, but then he knew very little about surfing and perhaps this was some sort of ritual followed in the surfing world.

At four thirty the doorbell rang. Bruce had now reached *Surfing Boys VI* and the young men involved were about to investigate a beach on the Western Australian coast. Careful, thought Bruce: if you want to make *Surfing Boys VII* you had better be aware of great whites . . .

He paused the film and made his way to the front door. Opening it, he saw Freddie standing before him, a wide grin on his face. Remembering who he was—or who he was still meant to be—Bruce invited his workmate into the flat.

Freddie reached out to grasp Bruce's upper arm. "Guess!" he said. "Just guess!"

Bruce was at a loss. Was this something to do with the recently lanced boil?

"You're fully recovered. The boil's disappeared altogether."

Freddie shook his head. "Nothing to do with that," he said. "Listen to this, Jono. You're going to freak out, really freak out."

Bruce raised an eyebrow.

"The syndicate," said Freddie, the words tumbling out of his mouth almost uncontrollably. "The lottery . . . the Euro Millions lottery."

Bruce remained calm. "So? What of it?"

"We won!" shouted Freddie. "We did it! I checked and spoke to them early this afternoon. Everything's confirmed. They sent their rep round to see me and he examined the ticket and confirmed. We won! We won!"

Bruce fixed Freddie with an intense stare. Was this a practical joke? But Freddie met Bruce's eyes with utter equanimity.

"Nine point nine million euros," Freddie shouted. "Almost ten million euros between the four of us!"

Bruce did a quick mental calculation. Then he sat down. Just short of two and a half million euros each. Was that right? He repeated the calculation. Yes. "When do they pay?" he asked.

"They said they'll come and talk to each of us," Freddie explained. "They'll come round with one of their investment adviser people. They are very concerned about people going crazy and doing stupid things."

"Will they pay in cash?" asked Bruce.

Freddie nodded. "I asked them that and they said that it was unusual, but they would. Yes. Not that I want it in cash—a cheque's fine for me."

Bruce smiled. "And when will they come to see us?" he asked.

"Tomorrow," said Freddie. "I gave them your address and phone number. They'll get in touch."

Bruce looked out of the window. He would have to remain in character for slightly longer now, but in view of this development it would hardly be a chore.

"What are you going to do with yours?" Freddie asked eagerly. "I've resigned already. I'm going to open a restaurant and bar in the West End. I've already seen a suitable place."

"I'm not sure," said Bruce. "I might go away somewhere." He would have to go away, he decided. He really would have no choice. Barcelona, perhaps? Rio?

He returned to the subject of payment. "So they'll pay up quickly?" he asked. "There won't be any hassle?"

"None at all," said Freddie. "Just think, Jono: a couple of million quid each. In our hands within three days."

Bruce allowed himself a laugh. "Amazing!" he said.

Freddie looked at his watch. "I'm meeting some friends for a celebratory drink," he said. "Are you interested in coming?"

Bruce shook his head. "No thanks." He paused. "Actually, Freddie, I'd like to keep this pretty quiet. Would you mind? I'd prefer if nobody knew about it."

"Absolutely right," said Freddie. "I haven't told anybody yet and I won't let on to my friends this evening. I'll just tell them I've had a stroke of good luck."

"Very wise," said Bruce. "Discretion is the

best policy when something like this happens."

"In case somebody tries to take it away from you?" suggested Freddie.

"Exactly," said Bruce, raising a finger to his lips in a gesture of conspiratorial silence. "In case somebody tries to take it away."

## 68. Millions of Pounds

"It's very unusual," said the lottery official.

"Maybe," said Bruce. "But then one size doesn't fit all, you know."

The official, a small man with a carefully combed middle parting, looked down at the file he had extracted from his briefcase. "We do try to accommodate our winners," he said. "We are prepared to be extremely flexible in appropriate cases, but . . ."

Bruce frowned. "I don't see what possible difference it makes to you. It's exactly the same amount of money, whether it's cash or a cheque. What's the problem?"

"It's not us," said the official, now sounding slightly peevish. "It's not our welfare that concerns us—it's yours. Just over two million pounds is a lot of money. How are you going to keep two million pounds safe? Where will you put it?"

"I'll be careful," said Bruce. "I won't keep it in

cash for all that long. I just want to have the cash to begin with."

"But why?"

Bruce smiled expansively. "I want to look at it," he said. "I want to come to terms with the fact that it's real. Can't you understand that?"

The official looked at Bruce reproachfully. "I don't think you should imply a lack of understanding on my part," he said. "I'm doing my best to help you."

"Well then," said Bruce. "That's what I want."

The official sighed. "All right. I've been in touch with our bankers," he said. "They've agreed to make the money available this afternoon. It will be delivered by a firm of high security couriers. They'll come here at three thirty and I shall attend as well to ensure that all is properly counted and signed for."

Bruce reached out to shake the official's hand. "Good man!" he said.

"I do this reluctantly," said the official. "I have the very gravest misgivings about it. And for that reason we'll require you to sign a form stating that you are acting against our advice."

"Fine," said Bruce. "I'm happy to sign that. No problems."

There were further forms to sign that morning. There was an elaborate document that all four members of the syndicate had to sign, confirming that they were paid-up members of a syndicate and had agreed amongst themselves to share the proceeds of any win. That had already been signed by the other three when it was presented to Bruce, and his signature finalised it. Then there was a form about investment advice—Bruce had to sign this to confirm that he had received advice but that he had opted not to take it. Finally there was a form that stated that no form of fraud or deception was being practised in the claiming of the prize. Bruce read this and hesitated briefly.

"Everything clear?" asked the official.

Bruce closed his eyes. He thought of his parents. He thought of his father, who was an elder of his church in Crieff. He thought of his old head-master at Morrison's who had been a good man and much loved by the pupils. He thought of the day the Moderator of the Church of Scotland had visited Morrison's and had spoken to the assembled school about the choices that life presented.

But then he thought of two million pounds. He thought of a low-slung powerful sports car with a large and effective spoiler; he thought of dinner at some expensive Michelin-starred place with an adoring woman on the other side of the table and the wine list in his hands; he thought of a new Hugo Boss suit he had seen in a shop window in George Street and a Patek Philippe watch he had spotted in Hamilton & Inches, and of how he had thought that this watch would look so good on his wrist, even if he was merely keeping it for the next generation.

"Something wrong?" asked the official.

Bruce shook his head. "I was remembering something I need to do," he said. "Where do I sign?"

"Here," said the official, pointing to a line at the bottom of the page. "And date it too please. We like to have everything legal."

"Yes," said Bruce. "Legal."

The official departed, to return again that afternoon ten minutes before an ugly security van, all sharp corners and riveted steel, arrived outside Jonathan's flat.

"That's them," said the official. "You stay here—I'll go and let them in. Have you got an alarm by the way?"

Bruce looked down at the floor. Did Jonathan have an alarm? He had no idea. He had not seen one, but that did not mean that there was not one. And what if he said that there was no alarm and the official then saw one? Would he guess that something was wrong?

He shook his head. "No alarm."

The official left the room. Bruce remained where he was, his heart beating loudly within him. Adrenalin, he thought. Two million pounds' worth of adrenalin. When he returned, the official was accompanied by two burly men in uniform, each carrying a large metal case attached to his wrist with a form of handcuff.

The official called Bruce aside. "You said there was no alarm," he whispered. "And yet I see there's an alarm box outside and a control panel in the hall. Why did you say you had no alarm?"

Bruce thought quickly. "Oh that," he said, trying to sound as casual as possible. "I meant no working alarm. That's kaput—has been for months."

The answer seemed to satisfy the official. "You should get it fixed," he said. "Once you've got two million pounds hanging about the place you should get it working. You'll be able to afford it now."

Bruce laughed. "Of course. Thanks to you."

The official produced a form and placed it on a table. "Please sign at the bottom there," he said. "This is a receipt for the money."

Bruce sat down at the table, with the official standing over his shoulder. Picking up the pen given to him by the official, he removed the cap and signed carefully along the line indicated to him. His hand shook slightly, but not noticeably. He could hear the blood rushing through his veins. He felt his pulse hammer at his temples. This was the most significant, important moment in his life so far. Two million pounds, and all he had to do now was to sign his name.

He moved the pen over the paper. Two words. It was so easy. *Bruce Anderson,* he signed.

# 69. Big Lou Goes Viral

After the filming in Big Lou's cafe, Matthew returned unaccompanied to his gallery across the road. He had imagined that Bo would stay with him all day—that was certainly the impression that the Danish filmmaker had given him—and it was a bit of a let-down to discover that the rest of his day would go unrecorded for the viewers of Danish television. Nothing had been spelled out to Matthew, but Bo's attitude was clear enough: he found Matthew's existence every bit as uneventful as Matthew found it, and that meant it would not make the documentary that Bo wanted.

"I'll catch up with you later," Bo said to Matthew. "Perhaps I shall do a little bit more filming in this place and then I think I'll go and get some street shots."

Matthew did his best to appear unconcerned. "Of course," he said. "And perhaps if I have some meetings this afternoon that you'd like to attend I can call you and let you know."

Bo nodded politely. "Perhaps," he said.

Matthew knew, of course, what was going on. Not only had Bo decided that he, Matthew, led too dull a life, but he had also decided that Big Lou was somehow more authentically Scottish than he was. The injustice of that cut deep in Matthew's mind. Why should people treat one sector of Scottish society as being more Scottish than another? Not everybody could be Rob Roy—there were plenty of people who did not sound particularly Scottish but were every bit as Scottish as Big Lou. It was a delicate issue, something to do with accents, that nobody liked to talk about. Matthew could not help the way he talked, which was in the accent of South Edinburgh, refined perhaps here and there as a result of his education at Watson's. If he did not sound as Scottish as Big Lou's braid Scots, then that showed that you should never judge a book by its cover, nor a person by his voice. What counted was what was said, not how it was said. If, Matthew thought, one said I have gone rather than I have went; if one never pluralised the word you; if one said goodbye rather than a jaunty see you later; if one never prefaced a remark with see, one could still be authentically Scottish. Not that Bo could be expected to understand that, of course.

And as for Bruce suddenly turning up and hogging the camera, that was equally galling. Of course it was perfectly obvious why that should have happened—Bruce was immensely photogenic and the people in Denmark whom Bo kept mentioning would presumably love just to gaze at his features on their screens. It did not matter that everything that Bruce had ever said, or was likely to say, was completely superficial: the people in

Denmark would not be looking for pearls of wisdom from him.

Matthew's assessment of the situation, carried out as he sat in the gallery and fumed, was broadly correct. Bruce was of much greater interest to Bo because the Dane understood the appeal of a well-sculpted face. Bruce would make good television whatever he did, and as for Big Lou, she was an out-and-out gift. They would love her in rural Denmark in particular, and it was possible that her appeal could be even wider than that.

That morning Bo got at least two hours of Big Lou on film, and a good three-quarter-hour of Bruce as well. Going back to the flat in which he was staying, he downloaded and edited each film before placing them on his website. But he did something more with Big Lou's clip; this he placed on the Web, in a prominent site used by filmmakers of every description. *A Scottish Lady Remembers* was the way in which the brief film was described. Join Big Lou in her coffee bar in Edinburgh to hear her views on just about everything!

The reaction to this posting was extraordinary, even by the standards that offer instant stardom to those of mediocre talent or no talent at all. Just as talking cats and accident-prone toddlers could suddenly entertain hundreds of thousands, even millions, of people throughout the world; just as a brave and confident songstress could appeal across the globe because of her lack of cynical guile; so too could a direct-speaking woman from a farm outside Arbroath speak to receptive multitudes. It was not something that could have been engineered. Had Big Lou set out to communicate with a large audience, had she said what she thought people might wish to hear or had she been speaking to a script written by somebody else, then the effect would have been quite different and the film would have been comparatively little watched. But speaking as she did, in complete sincerity and with no regard to artifice, her fame spread with astonishing alacrity. The film went up at four that afternoon. By six o'clock, eighty thousand had watched Big Lou and voiced their satisfaction over what they saw. By midnight, by which time the populations of the vast conurbations of the eastern United States were sitting down to their computer screens, Big Lou had been watched by four hundred and twenty thousand people. And by the following morning, when Bo turned on his computer to check the results of his labours, Big Lou had gone viral.

Bo had added information about his website to the film and already there were several hundred messages for Big Lou. Many of these came from Denmark, and from the rural areas of that country. Most were from single farmers—men whose wives had died or left them, or who had yet to find wives who might leave them or die in the future. They responded particularly warmly to Big Lou, many of them suggesting a meeting either in Edinburgh or in Copenhagen, and at the first opportunity. One dairy farmer went so far as to announce that he had booked a flight to Edinburgh and looked forward to meeting Big Lou the following day. What were her favourite flowers? he asked.

Bo lost no time in going into the cafe to tell Big Lou of her success.

"I think you've become famous," he said. "Everybody liked your film."

"Did they now?" asked Big Lou, in apparent unconcern.

"Yes. You've gone viral, Mrs. Lou."

Big Lou shook her head. "I cannae see any difference," she said.

## 70. The Wisdom of Solomon

It took only a second or two for it to dawn on Bruce that he had made a potentially fatal mistake. When the lottery official had given him the document to sign—a receipt for slightly over two million pounds—Bruce had calmly put pen to paper and signed along the indicated line. But he signed his own name, rather than Jonathan's, and it was, of course, Jonathan to whom the money was to be paid.

He brought the pen to a stop and left its point on the paper, so shocked was he. "Oh," he muttered, and then, "Oh . . ." again.

The official craned his neck to see what Bruce had written. "Some problem? Something not quite clear?"

Bruce thought rapidly, but before he could say anything the official, frowning, had pointed to the signature. "Bruce Anderson? Why have you signed Bruce Anderson?"

Bruce sighed. "Oh no, have I done the wrong thing?"

"Who's Bruce Anderson?" asked the official. His tone was suspicious now, and he glanced over at the two security guards still encumbered with their cases of money.

"He's my . . . my partner," blurted out Bruce. "We have a joint account. I was going to give him half and I thought I should sign for him too. I was going to put my own name afterwards . . ." It sounded extremely lame, he thought, but it was all he could think of saying.

The official hesitated. "Your partner . . ."

Bruce, emboldened, smiled at him. "Yes. Have you got a problem with that?"

It was a brilliant move. By challenging the official, Bruce had caught him on the wrong foot. He, rather than Bruce, was on the defensive now.

"Of course not," said the official hurriedly. Lottery wins were available to everyone irrespective of their social or psycho-sexual profile. "It's just that I wondered why you'd signed for him."

"Equality," snapped Bruce, challenging the other man to contradict him.

The official looked away. "Fine. Fine. But you don't have to put his name in. Just sign yours."

Bruce obliged. He was sweating profusely—he could feel the beads of moisture run down the small of his back, but he said to himself: I've done it! Two million! In the bag! Silently he watched the official cross the room to where the two security guards were standing. He watched as the cases were opened and the money taken out and placed in stacks on the tables. It was not as large a pile as Bruce had expected, for the notes were all fifty pound notes and unused, and therefore did not have great bulk.

Once the official had checked that everything was in order, he took his leave. "May I repeat what I said earlier on?" he said, fixing Bruce with a cautionary stare. "Please don't leave this lying about."

Bruce nodded. "I'll be careful." And then he added, "I don't think I said thank you. So thank you!"

The official smiled wanly. "It's only my job," he said. "But I do hope that all goes well with you. Be careful."

"I shall," said Bruce, and showed him to the door . . . just as Jonathan was arriving. The official looked at Jonathan and then at Bruce. He hesitated for a moment, but then nodded and left.

Bruce had no alternative but to admit Jonathan. "Well," he said cheerily. "How's it going?"

Jonathan pushed past him and made his way into the living room. He stopped when he saw the pile of money, and turned to Bruce. "So they've already paid," he said.

Standing behind him, Bruce looked at the back of Jonathan's neck. It reminded him, curiously, of Freddie's neck and the boil, and he was staring at it when Jonathan spun round and confronted him. "I see that I'm just in time."

Bruce affected to be casual. "You've obviously heard of my win."

Jonathan's nostrils flared in anger. "Your win? My win, if you don't mind. I'm in that syndicate, not you."

Bruce shook his head. "No. I gave Freddie my money. I became a member when I did that. You were out of it when I joined."

Jonathan reached forward to grab Bruce's shirt but Bruce intercepted the lunge and held the other's wrists in a firm grip.

"No, you just listen to me, Jonathan. I became a member of the syndicate and I get my share of the winnings. But . . ." He hesitated. An idea had occurred to him. "But there's a lot of money there. If we don't fight about it, it's a million each. If we fight, it's . . . well, it'll be a major fight—

352

lawyers et cetera—and neither of us can be sure of winning. So why don't we act in a civilised fashion and split the proceeds?"

Bruce felt the tension go from the wrists he was holding, and he knew immediately that Jonathan was going to be satisfied with his proposal.

"A million each?" asked Jonathan.

Bruce let go of Jonathan. "Yes, a cool million. Think of what that means. One million."

Jonathan began to smile. "All right. Shake on it?"

They shook hands.

"I feel very odd," said Jonathan. "I feel that I'm in a dream."

"You're wide awake," said Bruce. "This is real. We're rich."

"Did you enjoy being me?" asked Jonathan.

Bruce nodded. "You're cool," he said. "And what about you? Was it easy to be me?"

Jonathan laughed. "You're cool too. It was easy. I felt that I was being myself really. I don't think you're all that different from me."

"Maybe not," said Bruce. "I like your clothes, by the way. Although your jacket's going to have to go to the drycleaners."

"I can afford that now," said Jonathan. "In fact I can afford a new jacket. Would you like to keep that one?"

"Thanks," said Bruce. "I'll get the cleaners to get the pus off it."

Jonathan frowned.

"It's a long story," said Bruce. "Freddie had this boil, you see . . ."

"I don't want to go there," said Jonathan. "He had a boil before. But, as I say, I'm not going there, if you don't mind."

"Very wise," said Bruce.

They sat down and drank a cup of coffee together. "I see you've been watching my DVDs," said Jonathan, looking about the room. "Did you like them?"

Bruce nodded. "Yes. Not bad."

"I'm glad you enjoyed them," said Jonathan. He paused. "What about dinner later on?" He glanced at the money on the table. "Let's go somewhere expensive. Prestonfield House?"

"Yes," said Bruce. He looked at Jonathan and smiled. Then he winked.


## 71. Matthew's Decision

Matthew tried not to feel discouraged by his failure to provide Bo with anything worth filming, but he could not help himself from feeling despondent. He had always been susceptible to swings of mood, and although he had never suffered from full-blown depression, he knew the warning signs for what might be a day or two of the minor blues, a period during which he believed the serotonin levels in his brain dipped. Or so a medical friend had told him, although the same friend had pointed out that nobody knew whether serotonin levels diminished because we felt low, or we felt low because there was not enough serotonin in our system. Whatever the reason, there were moments when Matthew suddenly felt empty and sad.

It could happen without warning, and often did so, just as a cloud may suddenly dull a bright day. He knew these moments of sudden, inexplicable gloom, and he knew that they would pass quite quickly; rather slower to dispel were those changes in mood that came about reactively, as when somebody made a cutting remark, or when he heard or witnessed something disturbing or discouraging. Reading the newspaper could do this to Matthew: stories of woe had a profound effect on him, and could appal and distract him even if those of us who are more thick-skinned can read them, shake our heads, and then get on with what we were doing before we opened the newspaper. Matthew, for all his good qualities, was not robust.

He returned to the gallery and took down the sign that said *Back in Twenty Minutes*. He gazed out of the window for a few minutes and then looked back at his empty desk. There was no point staying, he thought. It was highly unlikely that anybody would come in and buy anything, because nobody had done so the day before, and the day before that. He sighed. Bo's right, he thought: my life is completely uneventful; the audience of any documentary, had it ever been made, would have been lulled into sleep, or switched channels.

He stood up. He would close the gallery. He would walk away from it. He could do something else, something more exciting, something that involved high-adrenalin decisions, travel, intense meetings lasting late into the night through cups of strong coffee and hard bargaining . . . There were so many other jobs that would be more fulfilling, that would be more documentary-worthy than this. He could even make documentary films—that was a thought. He had the money. He could go to Napier University's Film School. He would make important films about . . . about . . . well, the subjects would no doubt suggest themselves once he started. He had seen a documentary made by one of the students from Napier. It had been about a family of Bulgarian wrestlers—not the most obvious choice of subject, but it had certainly been interesting.

Reaching for a piece of paper he scribbled a sign. *Closed Until Further Notice.* Then, sticking the sign onto the glass front door, he locked the gallery behind him and began to walk back to India Street. The decision made, the low mood seemed to lift almost immediately, and by the time he reached the flat, he felt perfectly normal.

Elspeth was surprised to see him. She and Anna were preparing the triplets for an outing to Inverleith Park—a walk that they both enjoyed. There was nothing much to see in Inverleith Park—for all its numerous merits—apart from grass and trees, but it was about the right distance away and there were often dogs there. The boys, although still very small, were old enough now to appreciate the sight of dogs cavorting on the grass, and would shriek with delight at the canine spectacle.

"Let's go somewhere else," suggested Matthew. "How about . . ." He thought of the possibilities. Tantallon Castle, where the breeze came off the sea and there was the shriek of gulls? St. Andrews, where they might stroll about and imagine that they were once again students— admittedly students with triplets? Gullane beach, where you could walk on the sand and look over the cold firth to Fife? Anna could look after the boys while he and Elspeth went off together and talked and he could tell her about his decision to change his life.

Or the Pentlands? They could park in the Flotterstone car park and then walk up the glen to the place where there was a little bridge across the burn. Behind that was a hillock that gave commanding views without requiring too much of a climb; they could have a picnic up there and look at the sky and he could think about all the things that he could do now that he had his freedom from the millstone that was the gallery.

"A picnic in the Pentlands," he said. "You, me, Anna and the boys."

Elspeth looked doubtful. "But won't you have to be back for work this afternoon?"

Matthew shook his head. "No," he said. "A change of plans. Big time. I'll tell you. Let's just make some sandwiches."

It was not a long drive out to the hills—twenty minutes or so, Edinburgh being blessed with such an accessible hinterland. They parked the car and each then placed one of the boys in a sling, Matthew carrying Tobermory, Elspeth looking after Rognvald, and Fergus strapped to Anna. The picnic things, contained in a copious straw basket, were borne by Matthew.

They walked along the reservoir road to the

point where it branched off towards the burn. Now they were on rough ground, although the path was firm underfoot, the mud being dried by the fine weather into a tiny landscape of crusts and crenellations. They negotiated the bridge and ascended the hillock beyond, to find a natural picnic place where they sat and placed the boys on a tartan rug that had been tucked into the basket.

"Perfection," said Elspeth, as she extracted from the basket a package of sandwiches and a vacuum flask into which cold lemonade had been decanted.

"Denmark is so flat," remarked Anna, looking down towards the distant Lammermuirs. "We would love to have hills like this, but we do not have them."

"I'm so sorry," said Matthew.

He wondered whether that was the right thing to say. He wondered too how many there were who lived in flat landscapes and dreamed of hills; and how many who lived with hills and yearned for plains. Our world, he thought, our geography, our lives, are not always as we wish them to be.

## 72. On the Importance of the Local

They ate their picnic slowly, relishing the sandwiches that Elspeth and Anna had prepared; sipping, rather than gulping, the still-cold lemonade. The boys, Tobermory, Rognvald, and

Fergus, behaved impeccably; if it occurred to any of them to cry, then the thought must have been a fleeting one, as they sat contentedly, propped up against one of the adults, trying to focus on what must have been to them a landscape of impossible vastness.

"The Pentlands must seem like the Himalayas to them," mused Matthew. "Look at Rognvald: he's transfixed."

"Yes," said Elspeth. "The thrill that any child feels on seeing the world . . . Do you know, that's why young children, toddlers and above, run around all the time. It's as if they're intoxicated. The world is so exciting they're quite over-come."

"The world can continue to be exciting," said Anna. "How sad it would be if it became predictable. Dull and predictable."

"For some, it is," said Elspeth.

Matthew thought: me. They're talking about my life in the gallery.

"Of course not everyone . . ." began Elspeth, but stopped. A figure, a walker in stout country breeches and a tweed jacket, appeared over the brow of the hillock, coming upon their picnic spot with a suddenness that surprised both him and the picnic party.

"My goodness," he said. "I didn't expect to find a party going on."

Matthew knew immediately who it was. He rose

to his feet, brushing crumbs from his lap. "Hallo. I think we've met."

The stranger looked at Matthew and seemed for a moment to search his memory. "I think so too. Now, don't tell me . . . Yes, you're called Matthew, aren't you? You came to my place not all that long ago—my place just down there. Some evening. A party, I think."

Matthew nodded. "Yes, and you're the Duke of Johannesburg, aren't you?"

The Duke nodded. "Just call me Johannesburg," he said. "We don't need to be formal."

Matthew introduced the Duke to Elspeth and Anna.

"And these fine boys?" asked the Duke, sitting down on an unoccupied corner of the rug.

"Rognvald, Tobermory, and Fergus," said Matthew, pointing to each in turn.

"No," said Elspeth. "That one's Rognvald and that one's Tobermory."

The Duke laughed. "Triplets? I have three boys myself: Midlothian, West Lothian, and East Lothian. I used to get them mixed up when they were very small."

"I met them," said Matthew. "Great boys."

"Thank you," said the Duke.

There was a silence, and Matthew wondered how he might keep the conversation going. The Duke was an easygoing person, but they could hardly sit there in complete silence. "What are you up to?" he asked, and then added, "These days." It was, he thought, a question that although trite could be asked of anybody, of the humblest, who had nothing to do, and who could reply "Nothing much," or of the great and the busy, of a prime minister or a president perhaps, who could reply "Still governing" or something of that sort.

"Very busy," said the Duke. "I'm a member of the Clan Maclean Association, as I think I may have told you. I'm a Maclean really, and I try to do my bit for clan affairs. I've got hold of a very interesting Maclean portrait that I'm trying to find out something about so that I can write it up for *Maclean Notes*. It's a very fine painting, actually. We know that the subject's a Maclean because he's wearing Maclean tartan and he's got that Maclean look to him."

"Is there such a look?" asked Matthew.

The Duke seemed surprised by the question. "Of course. Just as there's a Campbell look." He paused before continuing, "I ran the picture past James Holloway. He thought it could be by a painter called Macbeth, who was reasonably well known, but he could not be sure. I'd hoped that it was a Raeburn, but James said no. Pity. I also asked Dochgarroch whether he could identify him, but he couldn't come up with any suggestions. It's a bit of a mystery."

Matthew agreed. He liked Raeburn too. "But tell

me," he said. "Why is it so important to know who this Maclean was?"

The Duke looked thoughtful. When he answered, he spoke deliberately. "We need to know about these things. It's because we need to be anchored—we need to have some sense of where we've come from and who we are. That's what being Scottish is all about, don't you think? Same as being anyone else. We need to know who went before us. We need to know how we're linked with them."

Yes, thought Matthew, we do. Yes.

"Because," the Duke went on, "without that sense of being linked with each other, we have every temptation to be selfish and unmoved by others and by their plight. Our towns, our cities, our places become no more than hotels, with all that lack of intimacy that is a feature of hotels—strangers under one roof, no more. Well, we should not be strangers to one another. We should feel for one another what a brother feels for a brother. We should be able to share a sense of being together—what people today call community. I don't much like that word, but the sentiment behind it is commendable enough. It means the same thing as what I'm talking about."

Anna was frowning. "But today we think far beyond these old boundaries. We don't just think of being Scottish or Danish or whatever. Those are old-fashioned things. We think of being human."

The Duke smiled at her. "Of course, we think of our shared humanity; of course we do. But I must disagree with you about the rest. We have to have some meaningful sense of the local in order to understand what our shared humanity is. If you take that away from people—as is happening—then they don't know who they are and that means they won't care very much about others. You'll get a crude materialism, because the material is all that we will have in common. You'll get vast, anonymous societies where we are all strangers to one another. We get much of our humanity from the local, the immediate, the small-scale. We do, you know."

Matthew said nothing; neither did Elspeth, nor Anna. There was nothing that could be said. And even Tobermory, Rognvald and Fergus, who had no words anyway but could give loud vent to feelings if the need arose, seemed moved by the moment, and were silent too.

## 73. A Reunion and a Vision

On receiving the message that Angus and Domenica had returned from their honeymoon in Jamaica, Roger Collins gathered Cyril's possessions together and prepared to take the dog home to his owner. Cyril did not have much: an old blanket, torn but much loved, a bowl with CYRIL painted on one side and DOG on the other, and his leash. Rather like Lear's sad dweller on the Coast of Coromandel, his worldly goods were few, and they easily fitted into a large Jenners bag that Roger kept on a hook behind the kitchen door.

They travelled by taxi. Cyril sensed that something important was happening, as he was aware, through smell, that the Jenners bag contained his blanket. But he was unable to work out why this should be packed; from his point of view the arrival of the taxi meant an outing, a walk along the shore at Cramond, perhaps, or possibly along the slopes below the Salisbury Crags, both attractive destinations for a dog but not places in which a blanket would be necessary.

"You're on your way home," said Roger, as the taxi made its way over the Dean Bridge. "Back to Scotland Street."

Cyril, seated on the floor of the taxi, looked up politely, opened his mouth and allowed a large pink tongue to protrude. In the sharp light of morning his solitary gold tooth—the only such tooth ever to have been placed in a dog's mouth in Scotland—caught the sun and glinted.

The traffic was light and within a few minutes they were making the turn from Great King Street into Drummond Place. Cyril stirred, cocking his head and sniffing at the air rushing in through the open window.

"Familiar?" asked Roger.

Cyril was standing, struggling to keep his balance as the taxi negotiated the final turn of its journey. When the vehicle finally came to a halt, he whimpered, and scratched tentatively at the taxi door. Roger paid, and clutching the bag in one hand and Cyril's leash in the other, he led the excited dog towards the door of No. 44.

Cyril was now tugging at his leash. He had lowered his nose to the ground and had picked up on the pavement a scent that was both more familiar to him than any other and more highly prized. He had discovered that Angus, his owner, his god, his reason for existence, had walked this way and moreover had done so very recently, so fresh was the scent.

Together they climbed the stairs, Cyril pulling increasingly impatiently and Roger trying to prevent his charge from strangling himself in his enthusiasm to reach the top landing.

"Don't get too excited," said Roger. *"Festina*

*lente.*" Roger had discovered that Latin had a calming effect on Cyril, but not now, it seemed; with reunion so imminent, even those admonitory vocables could not slow him down.

Angus answered the door. For a moment both man and dog stood quite still, but then, with a sound halfway between a howl and a yelp, Cyril launched himself into his owner's arms. Roger let go of the leash; had he not done so he would have been pulled into the general fankle of wriggling, ecstatic canine. This melee continued for several minutes before it slowly subsided, and the three of them made their way into the kitchen, where Domenica sat bemused at the display of emotion she had witnessed.

Over coffee, Angus and Domenica listened to Roger's account of Cyril's sojourn with him and Judith.

"He behaved impeccably," he reported. "We had no bad behaviour at all—he couldn't have been an easier guest."

"He's a good dog," said Angus. There was a note of pride in his voice, and he glanced at Domenica as he spoke, feeling that she perhaps needed further convincing.

"Yes, a very good dog," agreed Roger. He had often noticed how important was the phrase good dog in human interaction with dogs. People commonly used it when meeting a dog for the first time—they would bend down, pat the dog on the head, and say "Good dog." Why they should do this was not altogether clear: we do not give moral compliments to other people or creatures we meet—who says "Good cat" when introduced to somebody's cat? That was strange. Perhaps it was because so few cats were good, one view indeed being that cats were inherently psychopathic. They were prepared to engage with humans but only in so far as it suited them to do so; beyond that, such affection as they showed for humans was a calculating cupboard love or, at most, a passing, almost pitying scrap of recognition, withdrawn at the blink of an eyelid.

After they had finished their coffee, Domenica saw Roger to the door while Angus remained in the kitchen with Cyril. The dog, calmer now, sat at his feet, gazing up at him with adoration. That look, the look of adoration, was one that Angus, as an artist, knew about from the old masters, it being something they captured well. Contemporary art, he thought, had no time for the adoring look; it was uncomfortable with the human face, and reluctant to see glory in it. Now, looking at Cyril, he was reminded of what it was that had been caught in those paintings—that look of trust, of satisfaction, of utter contentment at being in a place where one might gaze upon that with which one is completely satisfied. The thought made him wonder: have we lost the capacity for adoration because we have persuaded ourselves that we can never be satisfied with anything; not again, now that we have lost the innocence that once allowed it?

Domenica reappeared in the doorway. Cyril looked at her, and then looked back at Angus. The dog's eyes conveyed the thought that he could never articulate but was there nonetheless: have things changed?

Angus understood; he understood perfectly. He reached down and placed his hand on Cyril's head, fondling the ears in the way that the dog so appreciated. "Yes," he whispered. "Things have changed round here, Cyril. Your bachelor days are over."

It still felt odd. But it was better, far better. And he thought: what happens to men after they marry? The answer came quickly. They put on weight. And then he thought: and their dogs? Do they put on weight too? He closed his eyes and allowed a brief vision of the future to come to him—of a portly artist walking down Scotland Street with his portly dog. He smiled: if that was indeed the future, there were surely worse things than that to be envisioned.

# 74. The Good Fortune of Others

Bertie did not become aware of the return of Angus and Domenica, and therefore of Cyril, until a day later, when he heard barking emanating from the flat above.

"It sounds as if that awful dog is back," said Irene, looking up from her crossword. "Polish off with a Cockney greeting; it roams the plains. Odd clue."

"Buffalo," said Bertie.

Irene looked at him in astonishment.

"Buff is polish," said Bertie. "And don't people in London drop their aitches?"

"Of course," said Irene, scribbling in the clue. "Mummy would have worked all that out." She added: "In time."

Bertie did not contradict her. "Do you think I could go up and say hallo to Cyril?" he asked. "Just for a few minutes?"

Irene hesitated. She did not have a great deal of time for Domenica, and now that she had married that dreadful Lordie man she supposed that they would have to get used to their presence as a couple. But she would definitely not be making the first move, nor the second one either if she could help it.

"I suppose that's all right, Bertie. But don't let that dog lick your face. *Capisci?*"

Bertie nodded. "*Ho capito*," he muttered. He did not like talking Italian. It was all very well for Italian boys to talk Italian, but he had never seen why Scottish boys should have to do the same. When he was eighteen, he would never talk another word of Italian, he had decided; and if anybody spoke Italian to him he would pretend not to understand. By then, of course, he would have mastered Glaswegian, as he was planning to move to Glasgow the day he turned eighteen and could leave home, and thought that he should soon start having language lessons, in order to be prepared. Ranald Braveheart Macpherson had told him that he had seen a book that purported to teach you Glaswegian, and Bertie had decided that he would try to find that and begin his studies.

He went upstairs and stood for several minutes outside Domenica's front door, plucking up the courage to ring the bell. From within the flat he heard the mumbling of voices and the strains of a radio playing music. He listened for sounds of Cyril, but the barking that had alerted him to the dog's presence was not repeated. Perhaps Cyril was sleeping, he thought; dogs needed a lot of sleep, he believed, in order to build up energy to run round in circles later on.

When Bertie eventually rang the bell, Angus answered the door.

"Well, well," he said. "It's my new neighbour!

Come away in, Bertie—Cyril will be very pleased to see you."

Bertie looked down at the floor. "I'm really sorry I couldn't look after him, Mr. Lordie. I tried, you know."

Angus put a reassuring hand on Bertie's shoulder. It was so small. "Heavens, Bertie, don't think about that for a moment. I heard that it wasn't you, it was . . ." He stopped himself in time; he could hardly go on, "it was that dreadful mother of yours." But that was what he would have liked to say. So he continued, "These things happen. And Cyril had a very good time with Roger and Judith. He was company for them while they were writing in their study. We may even see Cyril thanked in the preface to Roger's next book. Who knows?"

Bertie smiled. He was relieved that there were no recriminations about his having handed Cyril over to others. He had tried his best; he really had.

"Why don't you come into the kitchen," Angus said. "You can say hallo to Cyril and talk to me while I make cheese straws. Domenica's teaching me, you see. We're having a homecoming party tonight and I'm making cheese straws for that." He paused. "Would you like to be a waiter for us? Do you think your parents would allow that?"

"I could ask," said Bertie. And he thought: one day I won't have to ask. One day I won't have to ask anybody about doing anything. That will be in twelve years' time, when I'm no longer six. But time seemed to move slowly; so slowly. I've been six for ages and ages—it's really not fair.

In the kitchen, Cyril gave Bertie an effusive welcome, licking him thoroughly, especially around the mouth and nose. Bertie grinned at the sensation of the dog's tongue against his skin, and briefly licked Cyril's brow in return. Then he sat down at the table and watched as Angus started to roll out the cheese straw pastry under Domenica's instructions.

"You could make cheese straws too, Bertie," said Domenica. "If you watch Angus, you'll see how it's done."

They talked as Angus worked. Bertie was allowed to sample a bit of the raw mixture, which he pronounced very tasty. Then he was encouraged to dip the tip of a finger into the cayenne pepper so that he could experience the fiery taste. "Jamaican cookery is very hot," said Angus. "On this honeymoon of ours we ate a lot of very spicy food. It was lovely. Lots of spicy chicken and a tremendous vegetable called ackee. They pick it off trees and boil it up. It tastes a bit like scrambled egg. It's a great delicacy out there." He paused, cutting out a further line of cheese straws. "Then there's something called a Scotch Bonnet pepper. You have to be careful with those, Bertie. You put those in the stew but you don't eat them. You'd burn your mouth if you did—they're that hot."

"Jamaica sounds very nice," said Bertie. He looked out over Angus's shoulder to the window, and beyond that to the afternoon sky. Was Jamaica in that direction, he wondered—somewhere far away, in a place where there was blue sea and dark green jungle and music?

"It is," said Angus. "It's a very colourful place."

Bertie nodded. He looked thoughtful. "Do they have psychotherapy there?" he asked.

Angus glanced at Domenica, who looked briefly at Bertie before turning away sympathetically. "Do they have psychotherapy in Jamaica?" he said. "Well, I suppose some people do, Bertie . . ."

"But do boys have to have it?" asked Bertie.

Angus lifted a whole, uncooked cheese straw and handed it to Bertie. "No, I don't think they do, Bertie." Angus thought of the boys he had seen in Jamaica. There had been boys riding about on bicycles, shouting out to each other. There had been boys fishing off the beach—and catching fish. There had been boys clowning about outside a church, joined by a pack of scruffy-looking dogs who were clearly enjoying the fun. There had been no boys having psychotherapy.

Bertie laid the cheese straw down on the table and began to pick at it. "They're lucky," he said, almost to himself—but Angus heard him.

# 75. Of Cheese Straws and Charity

The guests arrived—all of them old friends of either Angus or Domenica or, in some cases, both. These friends were used to Domenica's parties, at which Angus had always played a central role, but this was the first time that he had joined Domenica as the official host, receiving people in what was now his home. And Cyril, too, was in that position, being the resident dog rather than merely a dog attached to a guest.

Two well-liked and well-known people can have a lengthy list of friends and the party could have been a large one. But that was the style of neither; they both preferred smallish parties at which there could be proper conversation rather than small and inconsequential chat. "Three is the ideal number for a party," Angus had once observed. "One to do the cooking, one to do the clearing up, and one to do the talking." In that view he was not entirely serious, but he was certainly in favour of smaller rather than large gatherings.

From his side of Domenica's drawing room, Angus turned to James Holloway and remarked on the motley nature of the company. "Our friends," he observed, "come in rather a bewildering variety of shapes and sizes, James."

James Holloway agreed. "If it were otherwise, it

would suggest that we had gone out and chosen them," he said. "Which we don't, you know."

Angus looked thoughtful. "No? You don't think we choose our friends?"

"No," said James. "There are some people who choose friends, as one might choose a sweater or a pair of shoes. They choose friends because they think that the friend will bring something to them; will enhance them, perhaps. But most of us, you know, don't do it that way. At least not in the first instance."

Angus looked thoughtful. "Well, I suppose . . ." Had he chosen his friends, he wondered, or had they simply turned up?

"We encounter our friends by accident, so to speak," James continued. "Life brings us into contact with them in an unplanned way. You find yourself working with somebody or sharing a journey or meeting somebody at a dinner party; you find yourself turning a corner and bumping into somebody. Chance allocates us many of our friends—no more than that, just chance."

Angus thought that was probably true. He had never thought about it in those terms, but when he looked at the friends present that evening, he realised that neither he nor Domenica had acquired them in exactly that accidental way. There, for example, standing by the window deep in conversation with the sculptor Sandy Stoddart, were Dilly and Derek Emslie. Dilly had served on a committee with Domenica years earlier and had become a friend through that shared membership. And Derek had played football with Tim Clifford and with Alistair Moffat too, who was standing near the kitchen door with Hugh Andrew, Professor Higgs, and David Robinson, who had come with his wife, Joyce, who had once acted in an amateur production of *The Tempest* with Domenica and Richard Godden, both of whom were chuckling over a shared joke on the other side of the room. And so it continued, round the room; with links between people that went in all sorts of directions and had made for friendships that would otherwise not have come into existence. The forges of friendship, thought Angus, may be busy ones, but their doors are always open.

He looked at Bertie, who had been given permission—by his father—to act as waiter and was moving about the room with a tray of cheese straws, bursting with pride, Angus observed, at the important adult role he had been given. Dear wee boy, thought Angus. May life be kind to you . . . some day. May you get what you want: a friend, a fishing rod, a Swiss Army penknife—such little things to us, but to you so very much. He looked at Domenica across the room, who at that moment looked back at him and smiled. Bless you, my darling, he said beneath his breath. Bless you.

And at that moment, in Angus's eyes, the room was transformed. This small crowd, brought together to mark the return of their hosts from a short absence, became not just a collection of people conversing with one another at a party, but an infinitely precious band of souls. Souls, thought Angus; that is just the right word. And he remembered reading something that had made a deep impression on him—a small thing, in one view of it, but a very major thing in another. He had read that in the language used for radio communication at sea, the number of people on board was always expressed in terms of souls. "We have ten souls on board," a sailor might say when asking for assistance from a passing ship. Ten souls. Not ten people. Not ten passengers. Not ten customers. Ten souls.

And this realisation that he had was not specifically religious—although it could easily and appropriately be that. It was, rather, a spiritual notion—the idea that each of us, even the least of us, has a rich hinterland of value behind us: the lives we have led, the thoughts we have had, the love we have given and received—the little things of our lives that may not mean much to others unless and until they are granted the insight that Angus was suddenly vouchsafed; that insight that brings love into the heart, sudden, singing, exalting love. To see another as a soul was to acknowledge the magnificent, epic course that life is for each of us, and to experience sympathy for the other in his or her negotiation of that course. It was quite different from seeing others simply as people. The word soul had a big job to do, and it was the only word that could do it.

James was saying something to Angus that he did not catch. "What?" he asked. "What did you say?"

"I said they're expecting a poem," James repeated. "As they always do."

Angus put down his glass, and the hubbub of conversation in the room died away. He looked out of the window. He had not prepared anything because he had been so busy with the cheese straws, and sometimes in this life one must choose between making cheese straws and writing poetry. But that did not mean that the words were not there; they were, and now, in the silence of that room, in the presence of his friends, Angus cleared his throat and spoke the words that came to him so easily, and expressed, so fully and unerringly, what was in his heart.

> Dear friends, *he began,* some questions occur
> At quite the wrong moment; as do those
>     nagging doubts
> As to whether we've done everything we
>     needed to do—
> Rich territory, I believe, for obsessive-
>     compulsive disorder.

A party like this, composed of friends, may
  not be the place
For the question that comes to my mind;
I ask it, though, because it seems to me
That although nobody likes a moralist,
Especially at a party, this question
Is not just the moralist's preserve:
How, dear friends, are we to lead our lives?
Of the Decalogue I learned as a boy
Few commandments remain;
Fidelity, we're told, is neither here nor there
(Especially when you're having a good time)
It is quite de trop in fashionable circles—
A meretricious view, I know;
While coveting the goods of others
Is positively encouraged by those slick
Practitioners of the advertiser's art
Who want us to have those things
We do not need but which they are so keen
For us to buy; the Buddhists are right:
You'll never satisfy a material appetite.
Honouring one's father and mother
Is hard when Dad is a donor, perhaps,
Or otherwise somewhere else, and
Mother has her career to consider.
But although the rules are vague
And widely disregarded now
Some precepts remain: live with love—
That is a rule we all can understand;
Forgive those who need forgiveness,

Which I think is everybody, more or less;
Be kind—that, perhaps, is first and foremost
In any postmodern, new-fangled
Code we devise for ourselves;
Yes, be kind: love one another,
And most of all tend with gentleness
The small patch of terra firma
That is allocated to each of us,
In our case, Scotland.
Wish that for Scotland there may burn,
As in all other places too,
A flame of Agape, that disinterested love,
Translated by Jamie Saxt as charity,
That illuminates our world,
That is our beacon, and in the darkness
Is our singular comfort, our sole night-light.

Alexander McCall Smith

Alexander McCall Smith is the author of the No. 1 Ladies' Detective Agency series, the Isabel Dalhousie series, the Portuguese Irregular Verbs series, the 44 Scotland Street series, and the Corduroy Mansions series. He is professor emeritus of medical law at the University of Edinburgh in Scotland and has served with many national and international organizations concerned with bioethics.

www.alexandermccallsmith.com

**Center Point Large Print**
600 Brooks Road / PO Box 1
Thorndike, ME 04986-0001 USA

(207) 568-3717

**US & Canada:**
**1 800 929-9108**
www.centerpointlargeprint.com